THE DRAGONCLAW PLOT

Also by G.D. Matheson:
   The Naples Prediction

Coming soon:
   The Garibaldi File

THE DRAGONCLAW PLOT

G. D. MATHESON

D'ÉLAN PUBLISHING

This is a work of fiction. While many of the places and historical events are real, some have been fictionalized. The characters and their circum-stances are pure invention. Any resemblance to persons living or dead is entirely coincidental.

ISBN 978-0-9938786-1-9
Also available as an ebook.

Published in Canada by d'Élan Publishing
delanpublishing.ca

This novel is dedicated to my grandchildren and to my great-grandchildren, whose generations must deal with a warming planet and other high-impact events like those depicted herein. A special thanks to my children, who encouraged me, and to Dawn Renaud, who helped me re-set and present this story.

PROLOGUE

Emily Munson looked out across the bleak landscape with a sickening feeling of dread. "It's getting much worse, Oaaqutsiak," she said, glancing at the Inuit man who was setting the pace. "I'm just back from the west coast of Greenland, and I saw the same thing there. I thought it perhaps it was from the radiation, but that wouldn't account for it here on Ellesmere Island. What's going on?"

"This red sky is from southerners," said Oaaqutsiak. "Dark stuff falls from the air in small pieces, makes our snow black. Makes it melt fast. Southerners burn a hole in the sky, let the sun come in too hot."

Emily turned to her twin, who was trudging across the ice beside her. "Curtis, what is that black stuff?"

"What you're looking at is the black cryoconite powder that drifts up from the south," said Munson. "It's residue from coal plants, diesel engines and forest fires. But in my view, while they may have a part in climate change, those are not the key factors. Climate change has been going on for millions of years."

Emily turned back to Munson's guide. "How are your people adapting, Oaaqutsiak?"

"Not good," he said. "Life in the north is always is difficult, but we survive. Now, the ice is going. Everything is going with it." Oaaqutsiak glanced at his young son, who was amusing himself by kicking a lump of snow across the ice ahead of them. "When Kim begins his family, the ice will be gone. The polar bears, the walrus, the seal, our way of life—all will be gone."

1

Emily frowned. "There must be something we can do."

Oaaqutsiak peered at her from under the hood of his parka. "What is this radiation in Greenland?"

Emily and Munson exchanged a glance. Kim circled around them, kicking the snow lump, and she waited until the boy had trotted a little further behind.

"A B-52 crashed near the military base there in 1968," she said quietly. "It was carrying nuclear weapons. One was lost at sea and never recovered."

"Nuclear, like Hiroshima?" Oaaqutsiak made a dramatic mushroom gesture with his mittened hands.

Emily nodded, and Oaaqutsiak looked to Munson for confirmation.

"Why did we not hear of this?"

"The bombs didn't detonate," explained Munson. "They were built with a very sophisticated series of detonations that triggered the final nuclear detonation. When the plane crashed, the bombs burned up instead of exploding."

Oaaqutsiak frowned, then smiled. "Like gas? It can burn, or explode?"

Munson nodded. "Kind of. When the plane crashed, it scattered radioactive waste across the ice."

Oaaqutsiak stopped in his tracks. "This will kill—everything!"

"The military had to keep it a secret. So they had a bunch of people quickly clear the debris from the area and transport it away."

"Yes," said Emily angrily, "without proper protective gear. They were so busy protecting all their precious top-secret weaponry that they completely ignored the—"

Munson put his arm across his twin's shoulder. "Emily, it was different times," he reminded her.

"I know, but still…"

Oaaqutsiak held an arm across their path. "Wait," he said. "Ice here is not good." He pondered a moment. "Let me lead," he said, edging forward. "Kim you will wait with—"

A crack louder than a rifle shot split the air as a slab of ice tilted upward from Oaaqutsiak's feet. He vanished, and the slab slammed back into place.

"No!" Kim darted forward, and Emily grabbed for his arm, holding him back as he struggled to run to his father.

Munson was already down on his stomach, pulling himself along the ice surface to where Oaaqutsiak had disappeared. He clawed at the ice with his hands, then pulled the small rock pick from his belt and began wielding it awkwardly from his prone position.

As the tiny shards of ice flew, Emily pulled the sobbing Kim down alongside her, and they watched helplessly as the minutes stretched by.

Finally, Kim began to quiet.

Emily stood carefully. Munson was still hammering away pointlessly at the edge of the slab.

"Curtis," she called, holding the sobbing boy. "Please, Curtis, it's too late. Come back before you go through, too."

———————+———————

At the Galaxy-21 base camp, Emily helped young Kim Sorqaq pack up the room he'd shared with his father. Oaaqutsiak's meager possessions fit in a single small carton. She watched Kim take a shiny nugget from the bedside table, cradling it reverently in his hands. "What's that, Kim?"

The boy held it out. "This is my father's rock," he said shyly. "You will keep it to remember him."

"Oh, no," said Emily. "I think he'd want you—"

Kim shook his head. "I have much to remember him. This rock he liked so much, he always keeps it. Now you will keep it."

"Okay." Emily swallowed her tears and studied the boy, amazed at his composure. "Is there a story behind it?"

Kim shrugged. "I do not know."

They looked up. Munson stood in the doorway. "Your aunt is here, Kim."

He nodded. Turning to Emily, he held out his hand. "Goodbye, Miss Emily," he said.

She shook his hand gravely. "Goodbye for now, Kim. I will come back and try to help. I promise."

He sighed and settled his backpack over his shoulders.

"Let me help you," said Munson as he picked up the carton of Oaaqutsiak's clothing and followed Kim.

Emily sat on the edge of the bed, wiping her eyes.

Munson returned, and handed her his handkerchief. "Thanks," she said.

"What's that?"

She glanced down at the nugget, then passed it to him. "One of Oaaqutsiak's prize possessions. Kim insisted I keep it."

Munson examined it. "This rock must have held special significance to Oaaqutsiak." He looked closer. "Good lord. Did you ask Kim where his father found it?"

She nodded. "He didn't know."

"Too bad."

"Let me look at that." She studied the nugget. "Oh, my god. Curtis, do you know what this is?"

He smiled. "When Kim's grown, we'll have to retrace his father's steps. This could hold the key to his future."

"Meanwhile, I'd like to set up a trust for him."

"I suggested to Bolavar that maybe Galaxy-21 should kick something in," said Munson. "He seemed okay with the idea, but he might not follow through."

She frowned. "Why not?"

"I think I'm through with the company." Munson leaned on the doorframe. "He wants me to grab another guide and head out again. I told him it's not safe, but he seems to think the Inuit are expendable."

"Anything for the oil."

"I asked him how he values human lives, and he got all virtuous on me; said he can't keep funding your project over in Palestine unless his business is turning a profit." Munson scowled. "He seems to think it's okay to risk lives up here as long as he's saving them somewhere else. I'm fed up, Emily. Time to throw in the towel."

"You've worked hard to become director of Arctic operations, Curtis," she said quietly. "Are you sure you're ready to do something different?"

"Yeah," he said. "Do you realize we've grown to become the fourth largest oil company in the world? I think we've gotten too big for our britches. Time to start again with someone smaller."

She stood and took his arm, and they headed for the kitchen. "You could form your own consulting firm," she said. "It would free you from corporate expectations. Besides, you haven't been happy with big oil since returning from your military tours in Afghanistan."

"True," Munson agreed. "And the oil industry is in for a rough ride for a while. The Middle East uprisings are creating enormous uncertainty around oil production and delivery. It may be a wise time to get out." He poured her a cup of coffee and got one for himself.

Emily tried to suppress her excitement. "Are you sure?"

He nodded. "I'll contact Irish Harrigan to see if he'll join me as a senior partner. To work the Arctic we would have to be close to the federal government as they are the key to connecting with the Inuit regional administrators. If we set up operations in Ottawa, we can more effectively lobby and influence government on Arctic policy."

"Ottawa." She thought a moment. "I could apply for a government post there. I'm sure they need metallurgists in federal mining—"

"I'm sure we do. And Emily, what do you say we enroll young Kim Sorqaq in college when he finishes school. He'll need benefactors."

She grinned. "Maybe save him a spot in your save-the-world company."

"My save-the-world company," said Munson, laughing. "I rather like the sound of that."

"Curtis, are you sure?"

"I'm not sure about forming my own company, but I am sure I need to call it quits with Galaxy-21." Munson wrapped his hands around his coffee mug. "I'll call Bolavar and let him know. But sis, what if he pulls the plug on your work in Palestine?"

Emily shrugged. "I'll cross that bridge when I come to it," she said. "In the light of what happened here, I think he'll be trying to maintain whatever charitable image he has. If not, I'll find someone else to help."

"I just don't want to get in the way of you saving the world."

"You won't." She grinned at her brother. "Start your own company, and step away from the dark side."

He laughed. "That's a big step."

"But you could help make such a change," said Emily. "Maybe even reverse what's going on up here, before it's too late."

Munson's smile vanished. "It's already too late for some," he said.

"But not for Kim." Emily reached for his hand. "We do what we can, when we can. Better late than never."

CHAPTER 1

"Ladies and gentlemen, the first annual climate congress welcomes Dr. Caroline Fraser." Applauding along with the rest of the audience, Dr. Curtis Munson watched a silver-haired woman take the podium.

"Fellow scientists," she said, "remember this date. For today I unveil a seismic shift in energy technology—a breakthrough of such significance that it will end—yes my colleagues—it will *end* the era of oil!"

Dr. Fraser sipped from a glass of water as a murmur of disbelief ran through the audience. Munson smiled, wondering if this tiny woman with a British accent was truly onto something new. Unlikely, he thought; probably just another unremarkable energy solution that would cause more problems than it solved.

"An era of ultra clean power has dawned," Dr. Fraser continued, "of natural power, available in unlimited quantity." She paused, sipped again and then picked up the top page of her speech. The sheet quivered in her hand and she spent a long moment adjusting her glasses. "As you know, hydrogen is the world's simplest atom: a single electron orbiting a single proton. One of chemistry's wonders is how hydrogen bonds with oxygen to form water. To undo that bond and capture the hydrogen as an energy source has always needed an expensive process requiring extreme heat, one where we either burn natural gas or use electricity." Her voice wavered and she cleared her throat. "However, burning natural gas forms carbon dioxide, as does generating electrical power from fossil fuels. So here's our problem: using our dirty energy to create a cleaner energy." She paused and rubbed her throat.

"My mission has been to create an economical, clean power system, a method of generating hydrogen without using either natural gas or electricity." Her face grew pale, and Munson glanced sideways along the front row of the audience. From his position just to the right of the podium, it seemed clear Dr. Fraser was unwell, but no one else in the audience seemed to share his concern.

"The advanced research began at Penn State University in 2008. It was about reclaiming hydrogen molecules from saltwater by weakening the bonds that hold sodium chloride, oxygen and hydrogen together, thereby creating a flame of intense heat as the hydrogen released." Dr. Fraser paused again, took another sip from the glass and swallowed with increasing difficulty. Surely someone else could see she was in distress. Munson glanced at the monitor; Dr. Fraser's face was not in focus. To the side of the stage, the conference chair and emcee was busy, scanning her phone.

"My adaptation if this discovery will shift us from the *era of oil* into the *era of sea water*..." Dr. Fraser reached a shaky hand back toward the water glass, lifted it to her lips and then froze. Eyes widening, she dropped the glass and swayed unsteadily.

Munson vaulted to the stage, barely catching the scientist as she fell. "We need a doctor!" he shouted. Shedding his jacket, he placed it under her head. "Stay with me, Dr. Fraser."

Her eyes focused on him. "They want seafire...they've killed me for it... the woffa..." She reached toward him, clutching his hand in both of hers, pressing something into his palm, wrapping his hand around it. "Please," she whispered, and he lowered his head. "They'll come for you. Promise me... give this to Whitey... Whitey." Her eyes widened.

"I promise," he said.

Her eyes rolled back, and she released his hand.

Turning, Munson called out again. "We need—!"

"Easy there." A man crouched beside him. "I'm a doctor. Keep everyone back."

The crowd hushed as the physician worked. Munson unclenched his hand to look at the coil wristband Dr. Fraser had given him. Attached were a small key and a USB drive. He slipped the coil into his pocket. *They've killed me... the woffa*—maybe he'd misunderstood, *water* with a British accent? Unlikely, but...

Turning to retrieve the overturned water glass, he realized Dr. Fraser's notes were no longer on the podium. A trail of drops lead across the stage, where a man in a tweed jacket was pushing past the paramedics, papers in hand.

Pursuing him, Munson found himself in a vacant hallway. To the left was a dead end. Retracing his steps he found a maze of storage rooms and a half open exit door to the street. The short alleyway was empty.

As Munson returned to the group on the stage, one of the men standing near the medical team flashed a badge at him. "Can I have a moment, sir?"

Munson nodded, and the man reached into his jacket for a notebook and pen. "Your name?"

"Curtis Munson," said Munson. Fumbling in his pocket for a business card, he realized he was still carrying the water glass. "Here, you'll need this, I think. Dr. Fraser seemed to be saying someone was trying to kill her, with the water."

The officer took a plastic bag from his pocket and held it open while Munson dropped in the glass. "What exactly did she say?"

"*They've killed me... water.* I think. Actually it sounded like *woffa*, but..." Water? Now that he was repeating it out loud, it sounded rather silly.

One of the paramedics working over the gurney stepped back as the other covered Dr. Fraser with a blanket. The physician turned to Munson, returning his jacket. "We lost her. Cardiac arrest," he said. "But your quick response was laudable."

The officer stepped forward. "Any possibility she was poisoned?"

"Unlikely." The doctor frowned, then shrugged. "Although yes, it's possible. An autopsy will confirm."

As Munson donned his jacket, he saw his image on a television monitor. Under brilliant television lights, the tragedy had been shared with an audience around the world. Dr. Fraser's lapel microphone could have picked up her last words.

Had the camera also shown the world that Dr. Fraser had given him her wristband?

Munson resisted the urge to check for it in his trouser pocket until he had eased out of range of the camera. Retrieving it along with his cell phone in one smooth motion, he plugged the USB into the phone's port. A message flashed on his phone screen: *Restricted Access — Password*.

He glanced up at the conference room's large monitor screen to make sure the camera hadn't somehow followed him. The conference chair was standing at the podium. Unplugging the USB, Munson turned to listen.

"Delegates, I have sad news" she said, "Dr. Fraser has suffered a fatal heart attack." She waited as the crowd reacted. "I share your shock and sadness. As this is the final session of our conference, we will take a short recess and wrap up early. Please return at 2:30 p.m. for the panel's closing comments."

Munson pushed his way through the crowd toward the exits and out into the long hallway leading to the hotel, dialing his sister's cell number. "Emily, where are you?"

"I'm in our suite," she said. "My flight from Palestine was delayed, so I got in about twenty minutes ago, and I've been watching the conference on the television. How shocking, Curtis! Why did Dr. Fraser give you a USB drive?"

Munson winced, then clenched his jaw. "Emily, have you unpacked?"

"No, I—"

"Good. Don't. You must travel on to Canada without me. Dr. Fraser thought someone was trying to kill her. If she was, and if her murder is related to whatever is on the USB drive—then I'm probably being watched."

"Oh, Curtis!"

"We must not give them any reason to think I could have transferred the USB drive to you, so if you see me on your way through the lobby, don't come near me."

"But—"

"Go directly to the taxi stand, and then head for the airport. Hurry, Sis."

"But Curtis, do you really think—?"

"I don't know, Em. I just don't know. And a sightseeing trip in London is hardly worth the risk."

"Well, if you—"

"Yes, Emily. Yes. Please, just do it!"

—————————

Munson watched from just outside the hotel entrance as his tall, golden-haired twin carried her bags past the checkout desk and toward the main street exit, her cell phone pressed up against her cheek. He jumped as his own cell phone buzzed.

"Curtis, you're scaring the hell out of me," said Emily. "Even if we can't stay in London, surely we can fly home together."

"Sorry Sis, but you must take a different flight." He edged further away, back against the building, pleased when a valet parked a loaded luggage rack between himself and Emily.

"But Curtis, even if someone is trying to hurt one of us, they couldn't get a weapon on a plane."

"Look, if I am being watched, I have to make sure they don't think I've given you anything. I love you. I don't want you in danger. And there's another thing, Emily. If something happens to me, the world will learn too late about the Saudi oil shortfall. I'm going public today."

"But you wanted to tell the North American governments first. This bombshell, right after getting elected prime minister—Joe's going to be—"

"Joe will just have to understand." He watched her join the taxi queue. "I can't risk this knowledge dying with me."

"But your team, Pavel and Akira, they could tell everyone—"

"Once I realized what the data meant, I pulled them off the project. I'm the only one with the whole picture."

"It can't wait?"

"Not if Fraser was murdered."

"But you don't know she was."

"I can only go on my instincts, Em, and right now they're screaming that she was assassinated and now I'm a target."

"Your instincts could be wrong."

"I can't take that risk, and neither should you. Go straight to Heathrow. Call my office and have Addy Hangren get you on a flight to Toronto."

"Curtis, who the hell is after you?"

"I'm not sure. If Dr. Fraser's discovery has any merit, probably big oil."

The valet placed Emily's suitcase in the trunk of a cab, and she handed him a tip.

"Em, don't go home to Ottawa yet—they may target our house. Get Addy to book you a room at the Four Seasons in Toronto. Stay there and keep a low profile. I'll meet you there. Don't call me again; I'll call you."

"But I need to talk to you. Curtis," her voice dropped to almost a whisper as she climbed into the cab, "does the name Dragonclaw mean anything to you?"

"Dragonclaw? No. Why?"

Emily raised her head and glanced at the cab driver,

then she lowered it again. "I got a strange email a while back," she said, her tone still hushed. "I can't talk now. Call me as soon as you get into Toronto."

"Of course, Em."

"Be careful. I love you."

"I will. Love you, too Sis." His jaw tensed as he watched the cab vanish into traffic.

CHAPTER 2

Munson turned back toward the hotel lobby and found himself face-to-face with a stranger. "Doctor Munson? Hank Watson."

"Sorry, no time." Munson stepped around the seedy looking character, but Watson cut him off.

"Your firm has been be training the Saudis in new ways of ramping up oil production." He reached into the pocket of his stained tweed jacket and produced a tattered business card.

Munson ignored the card. The man had that look—that attitude. "Let me guess—CIA."

"Oooh. Give the man a teddy bear." Watson grinned. "Now, about those Saudi oil reserves. You are going to keep your findings secret."

Munson scowled. "Forget it. The public needs to know."

Watson spoke softly. "Here's the deal. Two hundred and fifty thousand, offshore bank, tax-free."

"Take your bribe and go back to your rat-hole."

"That's a good offer, Munson." Watson's tone changed. "If I were here for the other side, I'd be whisking you back to their desert kingdom. I'm afraid your dual Canadian-U.S. citizenship certainly won't help you over there. The jails in those places are unpleasant, and they are unsentimental about executions."

"Executions?" Munson forced his voice to stay calm. "I still haven't forgotten Afghanistan."

"Ah, yes, the eight Afghan trainees you lost."

"Plus two of my platoon," Munson snarled. *"Lost.* Faulty CIA intelligence led us straight into a Taliban trap."

"Perhaps." Watson shrugged. "If so, mistakes happen."

"People with integrity *own* their mistakes. Unlike the CIA. Liars, cowardly liars."

Watson stuffed his card into Munson's coat pocket. "Work with us or face the consequences."

"Screw your bribe and your threats."

Watson's eyes went icy. "Suit yourself." He skulked off.

Great, thought Munson. This situation was already complicated enough without the bumbling ineptitude of the CIA contributing to the confusion.

In the lobby, he spent a moment trying to gauge if he'd been followed. The elderly couple at check-out looked harmless. From the elevator, he watched a portly man cross from the stairwell, turn to cast an appreciative eye at the attractive auburn-haired woman who was approaching the front the desk, and then exit toward the street. The elevator doors drew closed, and Munson tried to relax.

Emerging into the hallway, he saw that the door to Emily's room was not properly closed. He cautiously entered his own room, adjacent to hers. No one was there, but while packing his bags, he had the distinct impression someone had rummaged through his things. That would have been very unlike Emily. Someone else had been here in his room. Or was it just his imagination?

Munson collected his bag and took the elevator down, casting a wary eye over the lobby before walking back down the long hallway to the conference chamber. Picking his way past small groups of delegates waiting for the meeting to reconvene, he climbed the steps to the stage and approached the podium. The conference chair glanced up at him.

"Dr. Munson? Thank you for trying to assist Dr. Fraser."

"Of course," said Munson. "Would it be possible for me to take a few moments to address the audience? I'd like to share a game-changing development."

She looked puzzled. "Game-changing?"

"It's a major one." Munson lowered his voice and leaned close. "The Saudi reserves are failing."

"Yes, but—"

"Much more rapidly than anyone realized," he assured her, speaking slowly. "Like I said, this really is a major game-changer."

The chair's eyes widened, and she glanced at her watch. "How much time would you need?"

"Ten minutes at most."

"I'll put you on in about two minutes, if you're ready?"

"Works for me," said Munson. The sooner the better.

"How shall I introduce you?"

Munson pulled out a business card and handed it to her. "I can introduce myself if you like."

The chair nodded and began tapping the microphone, and Munson stepped back a few paces.

"Delegates," the chair began, and the crowd hushed. "We thank you for contributing to our conference. Your presence here gives me great hope for the future—" she glanced at Munson, and swallowed. "And we truly hope that by televising these last three days, we can help the world realize that we are like the proverbial frog in the pot of water, oblivious to the fact that it is gradually being brought to a boil.

"Since the 1970s our planet's temperatures have risen zero point one six degrees Celsius per decade. In the past three years, however, we have experienced an increase of zero point eight zero degrees Celsius—an alarming rate of acceleration, with most of that increase occurring in the past year alone.

"We are all aware of the controversy surrounding climate change related to human activity. In the past, some of us have argued that CO_2 had little impact on climate change, others insisted that it did. Regardless, now that the graph line is veering upward, those arguments are of less significance. Most here agree that the cause of the acceleration is *not only* CO_2. Growing evidence suggests it is also from a change in the intensity of heat from the sun.

"We have also discussed how this acceleration has unleashed massive political pressures. Governments are now struggling to respond to drought and famine as population drifts toward cooler northern latitudes. Hard-hit countries have begun coveting each other's territory, seeking food and water for their starving masses. Answers are needed, and needed fast.

"Now it seems we have another global crisis. I have yielded ten minutes to Dr. Curtis Munson," she glanced down at the card, "senior partner in Munson-Harrigan Associates of Ottawa, Canada. Dr. Munson also is a marine geologist. As I recollect, their firm is world renowned for their unique extraction processes for failing oil wells?" She looked to Munson for confirmation, and Munson nodded, stepping forward.

"Thank you, Madame Chair." He surveyed the crowd. "Colleagues, for the past months, a branch of my organization has worked in Saudi Arabia. One of our teams has been assisting the Saudis in training their petroleum engineers in our new, less environmentally destructive oil extraction methods. We now have accurate technical data on thousands of the Saudi's wells. From that data, we can extrapolate the life-span of Saudi oil. The news is not good." He paused as a murmur ran through the crowd.

"Their wells have been in operation for over eighty years. As many of you know, the Saudis inflated their stated oil reserves back in the 1980s. Knowledgeable observers gave that data little credence, although back in 2010, Saudi officials assured us that Saudi reserves were 260 million barrels which would last for eighty years. This is just not so. Their wells are operated by a state-owned oil company which has kept their records secret for decades.

"As their oil is pumped out, underground pressures reduce, requiring them to pump billions of gallons of seawater underground to force the oil upward. Years ago they re-drilled their Ghawar field, the largest oilfield in the world, with horizontal holes to improve water injection and oil recovery. However, when that seawater reaches those horizontal recovery wells, the game is over. Within four years, by our careful calculations, over two thirds of Saudi's producing wells will fail." The audience sucked in their breath.

"You already know about Saudi Arabia's eastern desert. While that shortfall was quickly refuted by the Saudis, it is also true. The Saudis have talked their customers into selling them jet fighters and armaments to bolster their military, presumably to protect their oil. But there is a problem. The oil is no longer there." He braced himself against the podium.

"Since the catastrophes in the Gulf of Mexico and the deep well accidents that followed, most countries have drilling moratoriums along their coast lines. With burgeoning global demand, the world's oil fields are already operating at full capacity. Now that Egypt, Yemen, Algeria, Tunisia, Libya, Syria and Iran have joined Islamic states that are hostile to the West, they have shut down strategic shipping points for much of the world's oil.

"With Russia's recent break with the West, petroleum shortages have become even more problematic in Europe. Oil supply is a very dangerous problem globally, and most particularly for Canada; it's second only to the acceleration of climate change."

He turned to the conference chair with a nod. "Thank you for allowing me to speak."

The crowd erupted. "Question, Dr. Munson. What about the Arctic?"

Munson turned back to the microphone. "We believe the Russian high Arctic is now largely devoid of untapped oil and gas," he said. "Only the Alaskan and Canadian Arctic have undeveloped reserves. And as you know, Russia is still disputing Canadian sovereignty over some areas of the Arctic." He turned to leave.

Several delegates rose. "Question," shouted one. "You say this is a particular problem for Canada. Why is this?"

"The largest recoverable oil reserves are in Canada," said Munson. "There are several powerful nations on this planet, each desperate to secure Canada's oil."

"But surely you are being melodramatic, Dr. Munson. No one is going to invade Canada for its oil."

Munson raised his eyebrows as the crowed murmured disagreement. Surely the delegate was not so naive.

"Question," called another. "What's your view on shifting to alternate fuels?"

"I can tell you this," said Munson. "Such a shift will not be possible until we find a fuel that is *readily available and cheaper than oil*. It's the only way we will beat the powerful oil lobby and break our unquenchable world petroleum addiction." The chair stepped forward, glancing pointedly at her watch, and Munson nodded. "Thank you for your time."

———†———————

At Heathrow, Emily was nowhere in sight. Munson scanned the departures board. Several trans-Atlantic flights had recently left. Thank god for Addy; she must have found Emily a seat on one of them.

Over a beer and a sandwich, he turned on his phone. Three missed calls from Joe Telford; no messages. No messages needed, he thought, dialing Joe's number. He wasn't surprised when it went straight to voicemail. "Joe, it's Munson. I know you're pissed, and you have every right to be, but please understand I couldn't sit on it. I'll be there tomorrow and we'll talk in person."

He hung up and scanned the news headlines. *China backs North Korea; Russia Loses Arctic Sovereignty Challenge; China Masses Troops for Taiwan Invasion; Russia – U.S. rift widens.*

God, poor Joe. His childhood friend had chosen one hell of a time to get elected prime minister of Canada. A decent man but never the brightest, he would have his hands full with all the climate-change-induced saber-rattling. Maybe with Dr. Fraser's research, he'd be the PM who could help the world switch from fossil fuels to cleaner energy — perhaps relieve some of the growing global tensions.

Munson wondered if there was anything to Dr. Fraser's discovery. Well, there probably was, if in fact that's what had gotten her killed. Frowning, he took the wristband from his pocket and inserted the USB drive in the phone's port. The same message flashed on his phone screen: *Restricted Access — Password.* What had Dr. Fraser said they were after? Seafire. Shrugging, he started to type in the word.

Wait, he thought: what if it's spelled C-fire, or if it's some other word entirely? How many tries before his fumbling attempts tripped some kind of security override and got the whole file scrambled? Unplugging the USB, he slipped the wristband into the inner pocket of his suit jacket as his flight was announced.

Near the boarding area he recognized several of the conference delegates, and remembered they were going on to another international brainstorming session in Vancouver. He'd opted out, planning to spend some time in London with Emily. Now it looked like the whole lot of them were headed for his plane.

Great. He didn't feel much like talking.

Boarding, he was relieved to find they seemed to be travelling together in another section. He slipped into his aisle seat, hoping for the best.

Seconds later, a man stopped alongside him. "That's me," he said, nodding to the empty seat next to Munson.

Munson stood to let him in, and the man settled beside him. "Aaron Anderson," he said, extending a hand.

"Curtis Munson." They shook briefly. To head off conversation, Munson made a bit of a show of checking his phone for headlines again.

There it was, on BBC World Report: *Saudi Oil to End!*

Someone had supplied a photo of him. Great. He hadn't been able to relay all the data to anyone yet. Maybe he should have sent his passwords along to Emily, just in case—

"That's you." Aaron Anderson was peering at his screen.

Munson sighed, scrolling for more headlines. "That's me."

"Can't be good," said Anderson.

"As if the world's not dangerous enough," said Munson. "China and the U.S. are squaring off over the escalating Korean conflict; the Chinese are amassing troops on their south coast near Taiwan. Russia's an oil exporter and they want to add capacity; they've already been trying to invoke international law to seize much of Canada's Arctic, and the situation in the Ukraine is either a temporary distraction or a trigger. Sorry—you probably know all this. What's your line of work?"

Anderson grinned. "Not one I chat about on airlines." He handed Munson a card.

Homeland Security Weapons Specialist. Munson whistled.

"But today I'm just a businessman on vacation, hoping to get some shut-eye on my way home to Chicago."

Is that all, thought Munson. Just a coincidence someone from Homeland Security's sitting next to me?

A soft ping drew their attention to the flight attendants, who welcomed them aboard and waxed enthusiastic about the new AC-990 Centwenti's many luxuries, then droned on through the emergency features.

After the plane took off, Munson leaned back, loosened his seatbelt and listened to the weather report. A hurricane was approaching the North Atlantic. Emily's flight should be well ahead of it. He wondered if he was perhaps overly protective of his twin. After weeks in Saudi, it would be good to catch up with her at home, where she lived in the other half of his duplex in Ottawa.

Home. Stretching his long legs awkwardly under the forward seat, he glanced about.

In the seat ahead of him, the air marshal was trying to be inconspicuous, her underarm bulging; across the aisle from her, the auburn-haired woman in a leather jacket, poring over her laptop, seemed familiar. One of those women who turned men's heads, he thought idly, and realized where he had seen her. She was the woman who had been in the lobby, after his run-in with Watson.

He tensed, wondering if she was a journalist or an oil operative tracking him to destroy the discovery.

The sense of being hunted was new and disconcerting; unsure who to trust, he would have to avoid paranoia. Rational fear was one thing, but—

Fear. That's exactly what he'd heard in Emily's voice when she asked him about the name Dragonclaw. What was that, a brand of some kind, maybe a new oil company? Dragonclaw couldn't really be the name of a person—well, he grinned, it would be a fitting name for a Chinese spy.

Spies, conspiracies... maybe he was getting paranoid. Still, he felt in his pocket for the wristband and transferred it to his security belt. While he was at it, he transferred his wallet, tucking in the business card from Aaron Anderson, wondering again if he was just a vacationing businessman on his way home to Chicago.

Munson grinned at himself; he was already paranoid.

He glanced at the flight monitor. Toronto was hours away. He'd deplane there to ensure that Emily was safe instead of flying on to Ottawa as previously planned.

CHAPTER 3

Realizing she had nodded off, Ellen Niiqway repositioned her laptop. The reflection in the monitor showed Dr. Curtis Munson in the same position she'd last seen him, presumably napping. She glanced at her watch. Had there been time for him to go to the washroom? Unlikely. The wristband he'd taken from Dr. Fraser was probably still in his money belt.

Niiqway loosened her leather jacket, raised her shoulders and rolled her neck, scanning her surroundings. The air marshal across the aisle had fallen asleep, too; Niiqway cleared her throat and the marshal's head jerked up. Niiqway kept her gaze firmly on her laptop.

Soothed by the hum of jet engines, she realized her eyelids were drooping again. The reflection in her monitor shifted; Munson sat up and raised his seat-back.

A blinding flash and deafening explosion thrust Niiqway violently against her loosened seat belt, and her laptop was ripped from her hands. The shrill scream of escaping air signaled cabin decompression, and she was enveloped in frigid cold. Reefing her seat belt tighter, she gasped as the plane shuddered, nosing over like a diving whale. Lungs collapsing she grabbed for an oxygen mask, grabbing another and passing it to the woman on her right. Unbelted passengers swept past, clutching, screaming, sucked out through a gaping hole just ahead in the aircraft's side. Cabin attendants tumbled and overhead racks emptied as the plane rolled and tipped toward the sea.

Those belted in gripped their seats in terror. Seconds ticked by with G-forces pulling harder, then beginning to diminish as the aircraft came out of its dive and gradually leveled out.

Niiqway pulled her mask back to inhale the thin air, testing it. They were on borrowed time. The illuminated flight screen monitor showed them nearing the Canadian coast well north of their normal flight path, probably to stay north of the storm.

Even if they did make it to Toronto's Pearson International airport, landing the huge new AC-990 in this condition would be nearly impossible. Only a miracle would keep the big jet flying. She hunkered down, teeth chattering. Was this sabotage, or storm?

Buffeted by heavy winds, the aircraft vibrated harder the lower they flew. The hole in the fuselage was breaking away and getting larger. Mind-numbing cold dulled her thoughts.

"This is your Captain" the intercom crackled. "We've—*static*—if we cannot maintain—*static*—be prepared—"

"God almighty," said Munson from behind her. She glanced back. His eyes were fixed on the flight monitor, and as she glanced forward she realized they weren't far above sea level. Their flight path had changed drastically and she suspected the pilots were trying to find the safest way to ditch.

The woman to Niiqway's right had begun to cry, and Niiqway took her hand. "We're going to land in the ocean," she said, raising her voice to be heard as the howl grew louder. "With the flight attendants gone, we're going to have to help people. You with me?" The woman nodded. Niiqway looked for the exits.

Across the aisle, the air marshal was slumped in her seat, eyes staring vacantly, a crimson stream running from her temple.

Niiqway turned back to Munson. "I'll need help with that exit," she yelled, pointing.

Munson nodded, taking charge. "Flotation on!" he yelled. "Back rests up! Belt tight! Shoes off! Assume crash positions. Relax your body. Get ready to lean forward, head down."

Niiqway followed his orders. This would not be like the miracle on the Hudson. The river had been calm, the ocean was not. Only seconds now. Smoke! Black acrid smoke was billowing from the front; fire in the forward cabin. Niiqway's eyes, like those of the rest of the still-conscious passengers, were fixed on the forward flight monitor.

"Down! Down! Down!" Munson yelled from behind her. Niiqway felt the jet shudder as the engines thrust into reverse. Would it hold together?

Impact! A kaleidoscope of brilliant color, searing pain, another impact, unbearable screeching of tearing metal — slewing sideways — crashing down — water — liquid blackness —

Niiqway regained her senses immersed in frigid churning water. Find the belt release! Sharp pain. Focus. They were in one piece, floating; less smoke now, but seawater was pouring through the hole in the cabin wall. People were struggling in their seats. The exit was above water. Munson scrambled to it and found the raft release. The door burst open and the raft inflated on the waves.

Niiqway and her seatmate eased dazed people out of their seats, over the body of the air marshal. They were clearly sinking now. "To the doorway," she urged. "To the raft!" So few survivors. "Go," she told her seatmate, taking a last hurried look around. Munson had returned to where he'd been seated; in the seat next to his, a man was thrashing about, his head barely above the water.

"Anderson!" Munson shouted. "Release your belt!"

"Arm's broken," the man answered, choking as water lapped his chin.

Munson turned to Niiqway. "Go," he yelled before sucking in a breath and disappearing under the water.

With only a small opening still above water, Niiqway

dove through and into the raft. Someone had found a couple of flashlights, and on each side of the raft a passenger was already gripping the carabineers that still shackled the raft to the sinking jet. "Release them!" Niiqway yelled. "Release them or we'll all be dragged down!"

Crashing on the waves, the raft bobbed violently as the plane tilted forward, tail rising briefly before disappearing, taking Munson and his struggling seatmate with it into the depths.

———+———————————

"Over here!" A woman's voice. Senses dulled, Munson was unable to judge direction. He struggled to keep a grip on Anderson's sagging body.

"Here! Grab the rope!" It splashed alongside him in a bobbing beam of light. Grasping for the rope with one hand, he fought to loop it under his own shoulders, then turned his back to the light and clutched Anderson's body as the rope tugged them backward against the waves. The rope groaned, and he glanced behind him to see the raft rise high, above his head. He braced himself as it smashed back down, and then they were pulled against it.

Hands reached for Anderson. "Gotcha," the woman said. "Now let's finish reeling you in."

On board the raft, Munson pulled the rope loop over his head and collapsed in exhaustion. One of the survivors had already started CPR on Anderson, and within moments he sputtered. Munson sighed, closing his eyes.

"You're bleeding." It was the auburn-haired woman, crouching next to him. "You okay?"

Realizing he was covered in blood, Munson took inventory. The blood gushed from a head wound, and from his nose. His ears hurt unmercifully. The third and fourth fingers of his right hand were bent backwards, dislocated. "Yeah," he managed. "I'm okay."

She examined his hand. "I can fix that, but first we'll stop this bleeding." She tore off a piece of her shirt and wrapped his head. "Hold still." Deftly grasping his dislocated third finger, she looked him in the eye. "Ready?" Ignoring the pain of his knuckle being jerked back into position, he studied her. This woman was extraordinary while under stress. "Once more." She pulled the second finger into its socket.

Munson scanned his surroundings. The plane was gone. They were riding large swells in a heavy wind. He counted the soaked survivors—four more women, two of whom had bandages on their hands; three small children, all clinging to one of the uninjured women; Anderson; a man sporting a head bandage not unlike his own; another man whose leg seemed to be badly broken. Eleven all told. He watched the water, but only a single light bobbed a few hundred feet away; beneath it, between waves, he could make out the dim outline of another raft.

Only one.

The aircraft must have gone under with almost all still on board.

Amazed to be alive, he floated silently on the pitching raft until his pounding pulse slowed. Gradually the stark hopelessness of it struck home. They were a mere speck on a huge ocean, under a threatening charcoal sky.

"I thought we'd lost you." He struggled to focus in the dim light. The auburn-haired woman smiled, perfect white teeth pale in her soot-stained face. She was tall and slim, soaking wet, her breasts plastered against her wet shirt, her long hair whipped by the wind. "You saved ten of our platoon," he said, staring at her in awe.

She looked at him oddly, "Platoon?"

"Yeah," he faltered, pulling himself together. "Sorry. I mean we saved ten passengers. Munson," he extended his hand. "Curtis Munson."

"Niiqway," she said, gripping his hand firmly but somehow not crushing his injured fingers. "Ellen Niiqway."

"You a nurse?" He waved his fingers.

"No. Common basketball injury."

"An unusual name. How do you—"

"N-i-i-q-w-a-y."

"Ah. Inuit?"

"Yup. I was born in Arctic Bay, Baffin Island," she said proudly.

"You were pure gold back there, Niiqway. You got all of these people onto the raft and even got me and Anderson aboard. Thank you."

She nodded. "Teamwork."

He grinned. "Common basketball trait."

Niiqway grinned back, handing him a small packet. "We found some of these thermal blankets in the emergency supply canisters. Cover your head. Keep body heat in to prevent hypothermia."

"You activate the locator beacon?"

Niiqway nodded. "The pilots would have had time to call in a mayday," she said, her voice calm and reassuring. "They'll find us."

Munson wasn't so sure.

＋————————————————

A thud brought him awake. It was darker now, and if anything the waves were more intense. The other raft had drifted alongside, and Niiqway and a couple of the other passengers had grappled on.

"Just the two of you?" Niiqway asked as the passengers hauled first a woman aboard, and then an obese man who flopped heavily into the raft and clumsily settled next to Munson, cursing and wringing his hands.

Munson noted the man's expensive suit and jewelry. "Are you okay?"

"I'm half blind," the man whined. "And my hand is busted up. Is there a doctor on this raft?"

"You'll be okay," said Munson, wishing he hadn't asked. "Hunker down and stay warm."

As Niiqway brought the other raft's emergency supplies,

aboard, he turned his attention to the woman. Her face was blackened with soot. "Are you injured?"

"No, just a bit shaken up," she said, extending her hand. "I'm Martha Ambrose."

"Curtis Munson." The woman's hand was icy, and she was shaking with cold. Munson pulled back his blanket and drew her in. "Just the two of you made it?"

"I was in the forward section with a friend. The masks failed. Smoke filled the cabin. We lost my friend before we hit water, but there were others." Teeth chattering, she glared at her companion. "I dropped into the raft so I could help people board, but this pompous hippo was already on and he pushed the raft away before anyone else could get on board."

Munson turned to look at the man, but he was still moaning over his injured hand.

One of the survivors passed along some more blankets, and Munson opened one for Martha Ambrose. "Cover your head and try to stay warm," he said, pulling her alongside him. "They'll find us."

They drifted in silence for a while, and Munson realized she had fallen asleep.

Anderson crawled across the raft. "Thank you," he said quietly. "I owe you big time. If we get out of this, and you are ever in Chicago, look me up." He winced each time the raft thumped in the waves.

"We'll get out of this," Munson assured him. "How's the broken wing?"

"Hurts like hell," he said. "It's wrapped. There's nothing to splint it with, or Nurse Niiqway would have seen to that."

Munson grinned. "You'll be glad to get back to work—something less dangerous."

Anderson nodded, settling next to the sleeping Martha Ambrose. "I'll be glad to get back to work where things only blow up when you expect them to."

"Any idea what blew?"

Anderson shook his head. "Your guess is as good as mine."

Munson looked at the rest of the survivors. None of the conference delegates were on board. What a huge loss for the scientific community. Was that intentional?

"Could it have been a bomb?"

Anderson shrugged. "Could have been. Could have been a missile. All those headlines you were reading on board would make you think so. But it could just as easily have been lightning. Storm was heating up pretty good when it happened."

Munson watched the roiling ocean. "I suppose."

Anderson had fallen silent, his face pale in a brief shaft of moonlight; Martha Ambrose's shuddering gradually grew less violent.

Munson closed his eyes. Was the explosion an act of sabotage, aimed at the conference scientists? He thought of Dr. Fraser's death. Cardiac arrest, or had she been murdered? If so, who was behind it? Rogue energy moguls, out to quash her discovery?

Maybe. Munson knew something about those big tigers who padded around corporate board rooms. He frowned, realizing had been one himself, during his own career with big oil. But he knew of no one in the industry who would stoop to terrorism. His ethically challenged former boss had done some unscrupulous things, but even Max Bolavar was no terrorist.

Or was he? The increasingly unethical demands of his boss had made it easier to resign from Galaxy-21, follow Emily on her mission to resolve climate change issues and alleviate the devastation their quest for oil had caused people like the Inuit. And since then, Bolavar had gone on to become one of the most influential oilmen on the planet. At what cost?

Munson had done the right thing. In all the years since, he had no regrets over leaving Galaxy-21.

Regrets. He certainly had some. He had failed his father.

The old man would probably go to his grave tormented at what the World War II accident could cost the world.

And he regretted Kristin.

Kristin. Munson winced at the memory. Why hadn't he looked for her, gone to Iceland, as Emily had urged him to a hundred times? Perhaps if he had swallowed his pride, she wouldn't have gone to Africa. Perhaps he would have gone with her. Everything could have been so different. Life was too—

He opened his eyes and found Niiqway watching him.

"It's a miracle we're alive," she said, her tone hushed.

"Perhaps," he said. The bandage was itching and he pulled it off, hoping his scalp wouldn't start bleeding again.

Niiqway tilted her head, aiming the beam of her flashlight at his injury. "Looks like it's stopped," she said. "Thank God." She lowered the flashlight. "Do you believe in God, Munson?"

"God?" He gave a slight shrug. "Our pilot achieved the impossible."

"Remember the miracle on the Hudson?"

He nodded. "We were lucky. The wings didn't come off and the aircraft stayed in one piece after we pancaked."

"A miracle," she said. "And then we had time to get out before it went down."

Munson shrugged again. "Jet fuel in the wing tanks is lighter than water. It kept us afloat for few moments before the seawater filled the cabin through the rupture in the wall."

"Yes, but there's a reason we've been spared."

"You're religious, Niiqway?"

She tilted her head. "I believe in God. I said a prayer while we were going down. But it's more than that. I've just have this feeling. It is going to be very, very difficult for you and me." She smiled and added lightly, "I sense such things."

He nodded, thinking back to his own rather irrational

insistence that Emily leave London immediately. "Your gift is no mystery," he said. "Your Inuit genes go back eleven thousand years."

She looked at him closely. "No, you're not being scornful; you're serious, aren't you?" She pulled a blanket around her. "There *is* the genes thing I guess. But there is a reason we were spared, a reason you saved Anderson from certain death. "

He frowned, but was saved from responding by an announcement from Anderson himself. "Helicopter!"

The whump-whump-whump grew louder, and a search light swept back and forth, finally focusing on their raft. Munson grinned at Niiqway. "Perhaps your prayer was heard."

A dark figure jumped from the helicopter, hit the water and swam to the raft. They helped him climb aboard. "Hendrickson, Coast Guard Rescue," he yelled above the roar of the helicopter, surveying the wretched group. "The injured, children and women go first. Just the thirteen of you? Any other rafts?"

"Just us."

"Is there a second chopper?" Munson shouted.

"No. We had several on their way behind us, but the rest have been forced back by the storm."

Munson glanced up at the helicopter. Given its load capacity, it would only be able take ten survivors—eleven, since three of them were small. At least two of the adults would be left behind.

The chopper moved overhead and as the retrieval basket swung close, Hendrickson directed the rescue. In the wind, the waves and the darkness, each basket lift up to the chopper took time. The first of the children, a small boy, rode up with Martha Ambrose and as the basket neared the chopper he began screaming, which set off the others; their mother reassured them but her voice, too, was breaking with fear.One of the uninjured women insisted on waiting for her husband, the man with the shattered leg;

the big man with the injured hand took the opportunity to jump queue. While they waited for the basket's return, Hendrickson explained that he'd need to ride up with her husband, to help lift him out. Sobbing, she relented and rode up with Anderson, gazing down at her husband until hands reached from the chopper to haul her inside.

The basket came back down. Munson and Niiqway helped Hendrickson lift the injured man, who groaned, went white and then fell silent. Looking at the blood where the man had been sitting, Munson hoped he'd simply passed out.

A gust of wind set him off balance, and Niiqway, who was watching the basket's progress, caught his arm and pointed. He looked up. The winch had stalled, and the basket swung wildly ten feet below the chopper. "Wind caught it," said Niiqway.

Hendrickson called something up, and with a jerk the basket started moving again, only to stall a couple of feet short of its destination. Niiqway shook her head. "My god, Munson." They watched helplessly while Hendrickson struggled to lift the unconscious man, finally heaving him high enough that the crew in the chopper was able to reach him. Hendrickson fumbled with the winch and the basket dropped a couple of feet, then stalled again.

"If they can fix the winch, Hendrickson will bring it back down," Munson yelled above the chopper's noise. "He'll stay with me and send you up. That chopper is already overloaded."

"Really?" Niiqway looked at him, then back up at the chopper. "Then we need to wave him off."

The basket lurched upward. Hendrickson climbed into the chopper and reached out to jiggle the basket. Clearly the winch was stuck. He looked down at them, and Niiqway began waving furiously. "Go," she called up. "Get them to safety. I will stay on the raft." She sat down, still waving. "Go!"

After another long look, Hendrickson dropped a couple

of packages into the raft, then the door of the helicopter slid closed. It hovered a moment longer, then sped away into the storm.

Munson opened one of the packages. Dry-bags, with some kind of thermal flotation suit inside, bright orange with built-in boots.

"Nice," said Niiqway, inspecting hers. "Wool lining, thank god. These wet jeans are freezing my legs. Crap. This is a men's large and tall; what have you got?"

"Ladies' medium," grinned Munson. "Trade you."

Squatting with their backs to each other, they stripped down to their underwear and donned the suits, pulling up their hoods and fastening the flaps made to keep their hands warm. Munson was particularly relieved to get out of his cotton dress shirt, which like Niiqway's jeans only seemed to amplify the cold when wet.

Opening their raft's emergency canister, they transferred what was left in it to the canister from Ambrose's raft, then stowed the dry-bags and their sodden clothing inside the empty one. "Maybe toss in a few of these blankets, too," suggested Niiqway. "Leave the bailing buckets out; we'll need them."

The sky was opening up again. Munson secured the canisters to the raft, while Niiqway hunkered down under the blankets, beckoning him to join her.

CHAPTER 4

When Niiqway woke, it was still dark. The raft continued to pitch wildly, and the rain beat a thunderous tattoo on the aluminum blankets overhead. Wondering how long she had slept, she switched on the flashlight, peeled the suit flap from her wrist and peered at her watch. It had obviously stopped working. She trained the flashlight beam over the inside of the raft. They'd need to bail soon.

Munson stirred beside her. "It's getting worse," he said.

She nodded. "I didn't figure it would end this way—in a hurricane."

He shrugged. "We're likely to survive it. They'll send another chopper as soon as they can."

"I'm an oceanographer," said Niiqway. "I've studied hurricane winds on the water's surface. Our chances are slim."

"An oceanographer?" Munson snorted. "Since when did a career in oceanography require military training?"

Niiqway weighed her options, considering which parts of the truth to tell, what to hold back.

Munson's eyes had narrowed. "What brought you aboard my flight, Niiqway? You tailing me? I saw you at my hotel."

"Yes, I was at the hotel. Terrible what happened to poor Dr. Fraser," she said. "You spoke with her. Did she have—"

"Were you tailing me?"

"Yes."

"Why?"

"Saudi Arabia."

Munson cocked his head. "What about it?" Then his face hardened. "You CIA?"

Considering the intel on Munson's distrust of the CIA, Niiqway chose her words carefully. "I am a CSIS agent, Munson. My goal is national security."

"So you are an oceanographer working for the Canadian Security Intelligence Service, tailing me. Tell me, what makes CSIS think I'm a matter of national security?"

"We've followed your firm's Saudi project."

"And?"

No reason not to tell him what he already knew. "The Saudis still supply almost a third of America's energy. If their oil was ending, Canada risks being in the middle of a resource war for the planet's remaining reserves. CSIS needed your knowledge about Saudi oil. We'd hoped to get the inside track, prepare for what's ahead. Too late now. After your big disclosure yesterday, our worst fears are likely to become a reality."

"A resource war."

She nodded. "You probably know more about this than I do. Alberta's oil sands, our Hibernia field, our untapped Arctic and our newly proven Pacific Shelf will become the largest world reserves. But the deep sea drilling moratoriums have kept the oil in the sea beds." She shifted to a more comfortable position. "That leaves the oil sands. The Chinese will depend on much of our oil sands production, but now that Saudi oil is failing, the U.S will demand it all."

"So you think China will go to war to get what they want?"

"What they *need*," she said. "It wouldn't be the first time. Remember when China drove the U.S. out of North Korea? Tensions with China over the Korean peninsula are back at the boiling point."

"That's true."

"Like it or not, with your revelation about the Saudi oil fields, we're at risk of an oil war."

Munson wiped the spray from his face. "Okay so you wanted my Saudi data. Why didn't you just ask?"

"We considered it. We knew you despised the CIA but you were born to American parents in the Canadian Arctic and that you hold dual citizenship. It followed that you might help Canada's intelligence agency. My role was to find out if you would have."

Munson frowned. "You speak in past tense like we're already dead."

"No, I speak like you've already spilled the beans. Not very patriotic of you."

"Hey, Niiqway, I am a proud, patriotic, flag waving citizen of both countries. I had planned to give the U.S and Canada a heads-up about the Saudi oil."

"Then why didn't you?"

"I was concerned I may be assassinated, so I decided to announce in London."

"Assassinated?" Niiqway waited for him to explain, but Munson had clammed up. "Well, if you were, wouldn't your team have been able to get the word out, anyway?"

"They weren't completely in the loop."

"Oh." Still no mention of Dr. Fraser and the wristband.

Munson picked up a bailing bucket and began to scoop water over the sides of the raft. "So, Ellen Niiqway, oceanographer and CSIS agent with connections to the Arctic. Tell me about your family background."

"My mother was a Swedish-born physician in Alaska, where she met my dad. He was half Inuit, a meteorologist." She grabbed the other bailing bucket. "We lived in several communities across the Canadian Arctic. I'm an only child. My parents moved to Seattle when I was a teenager. I spent a stint in the U.S. military and then went back to Canada. I took Ocean Sciences at UBC. I've been an intelligence agent since graduation, usually stationed in Toronto, but currently on assignment in Ottawa."

For a while, they concentrated on bailing as the ferocity of the storm grew. "Why did you elect to stay with the raft and help all the others up, Niiqway? You could have saved yourself."

"My task is to stay with you and seek your help."

"But the risk—"

"I'm used to risk." She dumped her bucket, then looked upward, grabbing his arm. "My god! That wave!"

A wall of water crashed down, slamming the raft upside-down into the churning blackness. Munson was torn from her grip and she was flung, headlong, into the water.

CHAPTER 5

The raft crashed upside-down onto the waves, pitching wildly as Munson clung to its ropes in the darkness. After a few moments, he realized there was firm footing beneath the foaming water.

"Munson! It's land! Munson, where are you?"

He tried to focus. "Here beside you. The safety gear. The beacon, before it blows away—" Thrashing about in the churning waves, they retrieved the canisters.

"Haul those farther inland while I wedge the ropes," called Niiqway.

Struggling on the slippery rock, Munson got the emergency canisters to safety and turned back, only to see another huge wave bearing down on Niiqway and the raft. "Let it go!" Munson yelled, reaching out for her.

Niiqway released the rope, and the ocean ripped the raft away and back out to sea.

"We have to find shelter," Munson yelled, as another thundering wave dashed them against the rocks. Pulling themselves up and out of the maelstrom, they huddled against the rocks while the storm roared past.

When dawn broke, they investigated. They were on a narrow belt of rocky beach under a cliff. Niiqway cocked her head. "I think we're somewhere along the Labrador coast."

"Makes sense to me," Munson agreed, rummaging through the canisters. "Here's the beacon from the other raft. I'll set it up. And here's a lighter. Let's get a fire going.

These suits were a godsend in the storm, but I'd rather be in my own clothes."

They camped on a rock ledge, backed by the cliff. Fresh water trickled from above, and they refilled the empty bottles and returned them to the canister. Niiqway passed Munson a couple of biscuits. A cheerful camp fire, started with drier brush gathered from beneath the rock crevasses, brightened their spirits while they waited for sunrise. Across the ocean to the east, the brilliant orange ball rose from below the horizon, sending shimmering beams toward them. "It will be a better day," said Munson, watching a gyrfalcon fly to its nest in the rocks.

"God, I hope so." Niiqway was braiding her auburn ponytail. She was about thirty, he guessed, with a determined jaw line and soft chiseled features. Her tall, slim build and blue eyes reflected the Swedish side of her unusual lineage. Not much Inuit in her looks; that side of her ancestry had probably endowed her with that remarkable strength and resilience.

Too bad she was a damned intelligence agent.

"Tell me, Agent Niiqway, what personal information has CSIS dug up about me?"

"Personal information?" She tied off her braid. "Well. Let's see. Forty-five, six-foot-one, one-eighty; bachelor; twin sister Emily, who partners in lobbying for government support of the Inuit and volunteers with a service organization in Palestine. You hold a graduate degree from the University of Toronto and a doctorate in marine geology from Dalhousie; you're a Canadian Army reservist and were once a platoon leader in Afghanistan; worked your way up to oil mogul with Galaxy-21; now a principal partner of an Ottawa consulting—"

"Enough!" He raised his hands in surrender. "Besides recruiting me, what's your current assignment?"

"Classified." She looked at him, then out to sea. "The sunrise is beautiful. Crazy calm after last night's storm. What drew you to the Arctic, Munson?"

"The pull of magnetic north began with my father." He looked northward. "He flew B-52 reconnaissance missions out of Thule, Greenland, during the Cold War."

Niiqway sighed. "Our generation has no memory of what it was like to live one hour from Armageddon. Now civilization's part in accelerating climate change may eventually become our demise."

"Something has changed, alright. But although CO_2 may have helped to trigger it, this climate acceleration appears to be only partly caused by CO_2."

"You really believe that?"

"Yes."

Niiqway frowned. "What leads you to that conclusion?"

"About ten years ago, an experience in the Arctic with Emily began my serious study of climate change. A young Inuit lad named Kim Sorqaq and his father were instrumental in my decision to leave big oil, to free myself of big industry and to learn more. Along with many climatologists, I've become certain that human-caused CO_2 is not our only current problem."

"Kim Sorqaq—he's one of your geologists with Munson-Harrigan, isn't he?"

Munson nodded. Damn, the woman was thorough. "Although I don't know how much longer I can keep him on. He has a giant chip on his shoulder against all southerners, blaming us for the Arctic melt down and, of course, his father's death. Now, tell me something about your work. An intelligence agent must have amazing experiences."

She grinned. "Classified." Her smile faded. ""You worked the Arctic. Is there much untapped oil under the Arctic oceans?"

Munson scowled. "Pretty rude to grill a guy and not give him the satisfaction of a single straight answer. Fine, then." He adopted a professorial tone. "About one third of Earth's undiscovered oil is likely under Canada's Arctic's oceans, but because of our environmental disasters we've not yet developed it. Resulting moratoriums have stopped deep sea drilling in the Arctic. Safe deep-well drilling technologies and blow-out prevention systems have been under development for the past hundred years, but they are not yet foolproof."

She made a grim face. "That leaves Alberta's oil sands. With China and South Asia, the Chinese have a population of *two and a half billion* against North America's three hundred million. Those are tough odds, considering America has for years been weakened by the recessions, political party gridlock and a multi-trillion dollar debt."

He nodded. "I suppose you're right."

"Canada could become the most unsafe place on earth. Visualize several million troops of the planet's most powerful armies at each other's throats in our wheat fields."

Munson grinned. "A bit depressed this morning, are we?"

"Starving, and I could really use a coffee," said Niiqway. "Let's see what else is in the biscuit tin."

Niiqway checked the clothing. Munson's trousers, her jeans and their shirts were dry enough to wear, but his suit jacket was still sodden. She expected her leather jacket was probably damaged beyond repair. Using a couple of the aluminum blankets as a makeshift change room, they took turns. She checked the revolver she'd removed from the dead air marshal's holster; it seemed to have come through the soaking unscathed.

Niiqway cursed the international flight complications that had meant her own, more familiar weapon had been stowed in security and gone down with the plane. This one was heavier, bulkier. With no jacket to conceal it under, she'd have to figure something out or leave it behind. Draping the thermal suit over her arm to cover the gun, she vacated the change area. "Your turn," she said.

Damn, he'd already changed. He reached for her thermal suit. "Let me hang that for you," he said.

"I've got it," she said quickly. "That fire needs tending."

He raised his eyebrows. "Ug. Munson do man work. Woman hang laundry."

She forced a laugh. Relieved when he turned away, she draped the thermal suit over a nearby rock. One of its inner pockets felt pretty dry, so she stowed the gun there.

She turned to Munson. "Where's the knife from the canister?"

He took it from his waistband. "Woman need stuff cut?"

"Woman make poncho," she said, taking the knife to one of the blankets. "Too cold for no jacket. Man want poncho, too?"

"Sure," he said. "I'll bet it's what all the cool cavemen are wearing."

Stripping the belt from her leather jacket, Niiqway used it to secure the loose poncho around her waist. She waited until Munson was distracted with the beacon, then tucked the gun into the top of her jeans. It would have to do. "Let's take a hike," she said. "We should get our bearings."

Climbing upward, they found that they had washed ashore on a small island that poked forlornly out of the sea. They stopped at the edge of a drop-off that looked northward; far in the distance was land.

"Think it's the mainland?" Munson asked.

"Hard to say," said Niiqway. "If we're that close, you'd think the helicopter would have been here by now. You sure that beacon's working?"

Munson shrugged. "Seems to be—wow, check that out."

Below, the cliffs fell off into an inlet. Trapped in the blue water of the shallow bay, the remnants of an iceberg leaned grotesquely, grounded on the seafloor like a huge white cathedral that had slipped from its foundation.

"Come on, let's go look," said Niiqway. He followed her down the steep slope.

At the shore, they stood in the hulk's shadow.

"At least we have a supply of fresh water," said Munson.

Niiqway shook her head in awe. "It's wonderful."

Munson was peering down at his feet. Squatting on the

43

beach, he reached down and picked up a couple of rocks. "Well, will you look at this," he said.

She peered at them. "What are they?"

"Fosterite dunite," he said. "Not native to this island."

"Scour marks." She pointed. "They're made as a glacier ice grinds slowly down its bed, picking up bits of rock in its ice."

"Recent in geological terms," he agreed. "Must have been deposited here by other trapped icebergs, calved off distant glaciers."

Niiqway turned one of the rocks over in his hand. "Like a primitive tracking device."

"Emily should see these. This one looks to have—good lord." He held it up to show her a shiny metallic bead imbedded in a vein. "Niiqway, this has high concentrations of platinum."

"Seriously?" Niiqway peered at the rock.

"My sister is a metallurgist. She would be interested in this."

"And I'd be especially interested in figuring out where it came from."

"I've seen—" He clamped his mouth shut.

Niiqway tilted her head, waiting.

"Let's return to our beacon, Niiqway," he said, turning away. "We may miss our rescuers."

She laughed. "I was hoping we would be marooned on our island. You would fare much better than Tom Hanks in *Castaway*. I'm much more capable of carrying my end of a conversation than Wilson the soccer ball."

"Okay Wilson," he grinned. "Let's get back to camp so I can paint your round little face with charcoal."

CHAPTER 6

Late in the evening, Munson heard the sound of a small plane flying low.

"They've picked up our beacon," said Niiqway, watching the small, pontoon equipped plane approach.

"He can't land in these swells. They'll have to send a helicopter for us in the morning." Munson squinted at the craft; it was painted a distinctive creamy white with an unusual reddish brown trim. "It's not coast guard or military."

"You're right," said Niiqway. "Oh my god, Munson. It's woffa."

"It's what?" Munson waved at the plane. With a quick tip of the wings, it cut an arc back toward the north.

Niiqway was ignoring the plane, watching him. "You didn't recognize those unique trim colors?"

"No."

"Looked like the World Fossil Fuels Association's colors to me."

"What's the World Fossil—" Oh. WFFA. Woffa.

"Tell me everything you know about them, Munson."

"I don't know anything about them," he protested. "This is the first I've heard of them."

Her eyes narrowed. "You know something." She reached under her poncho and pulled out a revolver.

"Holy shit!" Munson raised his hands. "What the hell, Niiqway!"

"Tell me what you know."

"Alright, just point that somewhere else!"

Niiqway's hands didn't move. "Now."

"Look, all I know is that when Dr. Fraser was dying, she said woffa. I didn't realize what she meant until now. She must have been warning me about the World Fossil Fuel Association, WFFA."

"That's all you know?" Niiqway kept the gun trained on him.

"That's all." What the hell did this woman want?

"I find it hard to believe that a man in your position has never heard of them."

"I've heard rumors about a highly secretive organization of powerful oil moguls who are working behind the scenes to manipulate public policy," Munson said. "Shit like that was exactly why I was happy to get out of Galaxy, and quite frankly it's why no one would have invited me to join their league of villains. Now please, could you put that thing down? My arms are getting tired."

Niiqway lowered the weapon.

Munson shook his head.

"So your mission was to find out if I'm one of *them*?" He laughed bitterly. "I'm more likely to be a target."

"For the data about the Saudi reserves? I find it hard to believe you haven't sent all that on ahead to your colleagues, and that's what WFFA will think, too. Why would they bother to go after you now?" She sat on a flat rock, motioning with the weapon for him to do the same. "I'm betting it has more to do with the USB drive Dr. Fraser gave you."

She knew?

Of course she did. Munson sighed, taking a seat.

Niiqway rested the revolver on her knee still aimed in his direction. "If WFFA's helicopter gets to us before the search teams, they'll try to kill us."

He searched her face. Why was she so calm? And what was there about this woman that caused him to not fully trust her?

One thing was certain, if a coast guard search team

didn't find them early the following morning, they were in big trouble. Maybe he was in big trouble anyway.

"Tell me about Fraser," she insisted.

Munson shrugged. "Not much to tell, other than what you would have seen if you were watching it unfold, which I'm sure you were. I thought she was telling me her water was poisoned. She told me she was in danger, and gave me the USB drive. I figured if she'd been killed for it, I'd be next. So I let the world know about the failing Saudi reserves, just in case. Next thing I know, we're blasted out of the sky."

"Did you send the data on?"

Who was she really working for? Would she kill him if she figured the data would die with him? "Of course," he said. "I've sent it to several people."

He wasn't surprised when she tucked the gun back into her waistband.

"How did you get that onto our flight?"

"Took it off the dead air marshal."

He shook his head. Stranded on the island with a very resourceful woman he couldn't trust. And she'd managed to arm herself, too. Great. Just bloody great.

The chopper came at dawn. Niiqway crouched behind the rocks, under an overhang, gun at the ready. Nearby, at the base of the cliff, Munson's prone body lay twisted and bent. The chopper hovered briefly, then moved a hundred yards away to the only level clearing on the island and set down, its rotors gradually whupping to a stop. Two men emerged, one carrying a rifle, the other a handgun.

"Careful," said the one with the handgun quietly as they approached. "He may be playing possum. Better put a few rounds in him." He raised his rifle, but the other man held out his arm.

"Looks pretty dead to me," he said, "and we gotta find that woman. She's with—"

Niiqway fired twice, first dropping the man who held the rifle, then the man with the handgun. Stepping to them, she kicked their weapons away and crouched to check for vitals.

"Clear," she called.

Munson rolled to his feet, groaning. "My back's never going to be the same."

She looked up at him. "No I.D., nothing," she said.

He picked up their weapons, checking the safeties. "They were going to kill us." Crouching alongside her, he whistled. "Headshots, both of them. You are a damned good shot with that revolver."

"Just doing my job," she said, standing. "Wait—there's another chopper."

They both stepped back under the overhang. The new bird circled the area a couple of times, then landed a little uphill from the first one. Crouching behind the rocky outcrop, Niiqway raised her gun while Munson trained the rifle on the newcomers.

Niiqway squinted at the chopper as couple of men in uniform emerged cautiously, followed by another, taller man. She reached over to push the muzzle of Munson's rifle away from the men. "It's okay. They're ours." She stood. "Blake!"

"Niiqway?"

"About bloody time you showed up!"

The tallest of the three men enveloped Niiqway in a bear hug. "Niiqway, you are a sight for sore eyes."

She laughed, pulling away from him. "Curtis Munson, meet my boss, Scott Blake."

"The infamous Dr. Munson," said Blake, extending his hand. His grip was firm. He was about sixty, Munson figured; trim, gray-haired and distinguished, if a bit pale.

"You've been all over the news, first for your bombshell

announcement, then for surviving the crash." He turned to the corpses. "What the hell have you two been up to here?"

"WFFA," said Niiqway quickly, eying Munson. "Trying to prevent Munson from proving his statement about the Saudi reserves."

"I see. Jones," he turned to one of his men. "Get the handheld sweeper out of our unit and check that WFFA chopper for bugs, trackers. You and McCarthy get photos, bag the evidence, and get this whole damn mess cleaned up. Bring everything back to base in the WFFA bird. If there's a GPS onboard, disable it as soon as you're ready to take off. Total radio silence on this, understood?"

Jones nodded. "Yes, sir."

Blake reached for the rifle. "I'll take the weapons, if you don't mind. Niiqway, you and Munson grab whatever gear you got and come with me."

Munson followed Niiqway down to the camp, where they collected their jackets. He was folding one of the blankets in preparation for returning it to its canister when Blake stuck his head out of the CSIS chopper. "Leave all that for Jones and McCarthy. Just your personal gear. Let's go, people!"

Niiqway grinned at Munson and scurried up the bank and into the chopper. "Take the front," she said, climbing into the back and pulling on a headset.

Once they were airborne, Blake turned to Niiqway. "You bring him over to our side?"

Niiqway sighed. "I was getting to it."

"What the hell have you been doing all this time?" said Blake, looking back at her. "He's not dead, so I'm assuming you've decided it's not him."

"I guess not." Niiqway leaned forward. "Munson, I didn't tell you the whole truth."

Why didn't *that* come as a surprise?

"We need your help," she continued. "Part of my mission is to find who the real players are behind the WFFA. My other mission is to identify Dragonclaw."

Munson swiveled in his seat. "Who in the hell is Dragonclaw?"

Blake grinned. "Now that, my friend, is exactly what Niiqway has to find out."

She put a hand on Munson's arm. "For several months, I've been one of several agents tasked with finding a spy working in or near the oil industry, codename Dragonclaw. He has somehow gotten his hooks into the new Canadian Prime Minister."

"And you thought—you thought *I* might be this—this Dragonclaw?"

Niiqway looked at him levelly. "A lot of threads led to you," she said.

He laughed. "Ridiculous! Me, a Chinese spy? Surely that's not why you were following me."

"You're linked somehow." She shrugged. "Dragonclaw is certainly heaping suspicion on you."

"And we wondered if you would do something for us," said Blake.

Munson snorted. "Like what?"

"One of the reasons we considered you is your relationship with the prime minister."

"Joe Telford? But I've known him since we were kids."

Niiqway nodded. "And did you ever think he'd be elected leader of Canada?"

"Not in a million years would I have pictured that."

Blake turned to look at him. "So how do you figure it happened?"

"The usual. Backroom deals, friends in high places—" Did they think he was one of those friends? "He's obviously a puppet for someone," he conceded.

"Dragonclaw is influencing him somehow," said Blake. "Since his election, Telford's anti-American and pro-China bias has become public—"

Munson cut in. "Should we be talking about this over the headsets?" He could picture this whole conversation turning up on some YouTube video.

Blake shook his head. "We're so thoroughly scrambled, you'd have to be an insider—" He and Niiqway exchanged a look. "Still, you must be exhausted. We'll discuss it later."

Half an hour of idle chat later, they set down in Goose Bay to refuel. Munson used the restroom, then borrowed Blake's cell phone and called Emily. When she didn't pick up, he left a quick voicemail to say he was alright, and he'd be in Toronto in a few hours.

On the tarmac, Niiqway and Blake were standing in silence. Munson returned the phone to Blake. "Thanks. Is there time for us to stretch our legs?"

Blake nodded. "Go ahead, Niiqway. I'll finish up here."

"You didn't tell Blake about Fraser," said Munson, once they were out of earshot. "Don't you trust him?"

"I trust him totally," said Niiqway, her voice cool.

"But something's not right," he said. "So I take it Joe Telford's not the only one being influenced."

Munson thought about the last time he'd lunched with Joe. The newbie prime minister had, rather annoyingly, insisted on bringing his executive assistant. Ying Kao was stunning and brilliant, and their relationship clearly went beyond business. Munson had assumed sex, but maybe— "Have you investigated Ying Kao?"

Niiqway nodded. "She's certainly got her claws in him. I'm not sure they're dragon claws, though. If you are a friend, you might want to suggest he dump her."

"I'm not sure—"

"That's what Blake was hoping you'd do." Niiqway's tone was still clipped.

Blake whistled from across the tarmac. "Let's go!"

Climbing into the chopper, Munson felt Niiqway's eyes on him. What was her problem?

"Welcome back aboard," said Blake. "Next stop Gander."

CHAPTER 7

Munson slept most of the way to the base at Gander. There, he was given a change of clothing and put aboard a CSIS jet for Toronto. A crew member handed him a note. *Munson: We'll be in touch. Blake.*

"Niiqway's not coming?"

"No, sir. Her debriefing will take a while. Our orders are to get you back to Toronto a.s.a.p."

Munson wanted nothing more.

As soon as they touched down in Toronto, the crew member escorted him to a waiting SUV and opened the door to the back passenger seat for Munson. Then he climbed into the front. The driver wheeled the SUV into traffic, a little fast for Munson's liking. "I can take airport transit to the Four Seasons," he said.

The driver activated the lights and siren.

The agent from the jet turned to Munson. "Sir, we've been instructed to take you directly to the hospital," he said. "I'm sorry to tell you your sister was involved in an accident this morning."

"Is she—"

"I'm sorry, sir, that's all we know."

The ride seemed to take forever. As the SUV pulled up outside the emergency entrance, Munson leapt out and ran for the reception area. "Emily Munson? Please—I'm her brother."

A nurse directed him to surgery; from there, he was directed to intensive care, where a green-coated physician

52

took him aside. "Sit down, Mr. Munson," he said, gently but firmly.

Munson sat.

"The car Miss Munson was driving exploded. I'm sorry to tell you your sister is critical. She will not survive."

Munson closed his eyes and struggled to breathe.

"I'll take you to her. Prepare yourself; she's had amputations and massive internal injuries. She is heavily sedated and has been hanging on, hoping to see you."

Rising unsteadily, he accompanied the doctor to Emily's bedside. "Oh, Emmy." He bent down and kissed her, tears running down his cheeks. "Oh, dear god."

There was no bulge under the blankets where her legs ought to have been. An arm was missing. Monitor wires, IV and oxygen tubes snarled the bed.

She opened her eyes. Her lips twitched, formed words. "Curtis. You're safe."

"Yes Emily. Oh, god, I'm so sorry. Fight Sis, fight to live. Don't give up. I love you."

"I just … wanted to … get you some … new clothing … before…."

"Sh, Emily, sh."

"You are … in danger."

"Emily. I should never have become involved."

She whispered, "That's what … we do."

He held her bandaged hand, his face near hers, trying to will her to live. "Fight to live, Emily," he whispered. "I love you, Sis."

"Take me … back to … the Arctic… help them. … And Curtis…"

"Yes?"

"Next time … you find love … don't wait. Kristin … she was … so in … love with … you…"

"I'll try. I will help the Inuit, Emily, I can promise that."

Her breath faltered. "You can … make a … difference. I'll be … with you…."

"I will, Sis, I will. But try to stay with me now. Stay."

Minutes passed. She squeezed his hand, opened her eyes again briefly, smiled at him and stopped breathing. "No, no, no," he breathed, laying his head against hers. "Oh, Emmy."

The nurses came, shut off the monitors and left him with her. He sat by her side for a long time, stroking her hand.

"You're right, Emily, we always get involved. But what I did in London caused your death. I'll never forgive myself." He put his head in his hands. He would track her killers down. They would pay for this with *their* lives.

Finally he arose, jaw clenched. He would not stay under cover. He would advertise his presence, lure the murderers to him. Then, one by one, he would kill them all.

Outside the hospital room, a police officer waited to speak with him. "Dr. Curtis Munson?" She swallowed. "I'm so sorry about your loss."

He nodded.

"I'm sure you have questions," she said, holding out her card. "When you're ready, call me and I'll do my best to answer them. But before you—"

"It was a car accident? What happened?" Oh, god, let it be something random, truly an accident.

"Explosives, sir. It wasn't random. And we must warn you, Dr. Munson, because the car was rented in your name, we believe you may have been the target. Do you have any idea—"

He shook his head. She should have been safe. WFFA *knew* he was with Niiqway on the raft. Hell, half the world probably knew it once the survivors talked—

"When did she rent the car?"

The officer consulted her notebook. "Yesterday morning, sir. With a Munson-Harrigan credit card."

What the hell? Were the bastards just hedging their bets in case he survived the hurricane and the assassination attempt on the island? If so, no one would be safe around him now.

"My parents … they live in Seattle," he said. "Have they been notified?"

"They're on their way, sir."

God, no. How could he keep them safe?

"Our security detail picked them up at the airport and they should be arriving at the hospital—" He held his earpiece and cocked his head. "They're here, sir. I'm sure you'll want to be the one to tell them she's gone. Let me take you to them."

Munson nodded. His parents would be devastated. He'd have to leave security in someone else's hands, and focus on helping them through this. There'd be arrangements to make, things to decide, family matters to attend to.

Emily was gone.

───────────┼───────────

Before leaving Toronto with his parents, Munson called his office and had Addy rent him a safe deposit box at a nearby bank. Stopping there on his way to the airport, he deposited Dr. Fraser's wristband and hoped like hell whoever was after him was watching him do it.

Back in Ottawa, he settled his parents into his guest room and spent the day with them, making arrangements for Emily's service to be held the next morning. With the hovering CSIS agents providing a constant reminder of the continued danger, it seemed prudent to hold the service in Munson-Harrigan's large meeting room.

Munson's mother, horrified at the idea of holding Emily's service anywhere but in a church, finally relented.

The following morning they boarded one of the intelligence agency's requisite smoke-windowed black SUVs and headed to the office, tailed by agents in another black SUV; a third was parked at the building's entrance. Two CSIS suits identified themselves to him at the sixth floor elevators that led to his firm's entry rotunda. Niiqway and Blake were clearly looking out for his welfare, although he'd heard the prime minister would be attending. Perhaps some of the extra detail was for his benefit. Still, it was more than welcome.

Addy Hangren entered from Munson's office. "Mr. and Mrs. Munson, I'm so terribly sorry," she said, hugging each of them in turn. "We have a few minutes before the service begins. You'll be more comfortable here in your son's office. This way, please. Munson, I think most people are already seated in our meeting room, but I know a few more will be arriving. Would you like to wait with your parents, and I'll man the door?"

Munson nodded, returning her hug. "Thanks, Addy. What would I do without you?" He suddenly realized how glad he was that his parents were here; being strong for them would keep him from dwelling on his own grief.

The service passed by in a blur. He and his parents followed the officiant to the rotunda, where they stood to receive the condolences of the attendees.

His mother was buoyed by the presence of Prime Minister Joe Telford. "Why Joe," she said. "It's so nice to see you, with all your new responsibilities."

"Mrs. Munson." Stepping away from the plain clothes officers who hovered around him, he bent down to hug her. "Emily was a lovely woman. It was a privilege to have grown up with her." He turned to the tall, striking woman beside him. "Mr. and Mrs. Munson, this is my executive assistant, Ying Kao."

"I am so sorry for your loss," said Kao, extending her hand. "I have heard many wonderful things about Emily over the past few days. Not just from Joe," she said, turning to Munson, "but from everyone. My sincere condolences."

Munson nodded, while his mother blew her nose again. His father had buttonholed Telford. "You and I need to talk," he said. "You could do something for Emily. Fund the search for the nuke she was trying to—"

"Dad, not now," said Munson.

"It's okay, Curtis. Joe here knows all about the lost nuke, how upset we are about it. He knows how hard Emily was trying to find it." His father turned back to Telford. "It would mean a lot to her to put that to rest."

"I'll look into it, Mr. Munson" said Telford, soothingly. "Munson, call me and we'll talk about it over lunch."

Munson nodded, turning to accept condolences from his team. They all had known Emily and had liked her. He glanced over the room. Fifty or sixty people, he estimated, even on such short notice.Emily had touched a lot of lives, and would be very much missed.

His parents looked very tired, and he was glad he'd booked them on an early flight. While riding with them to the airport he tried not to be paranoid about every vehicle around them, and was glad they'd be heading home and out of harm's way. He was relieved when they arrived at check-in, where airport security would help ensure their safety. They joined the queue.

"That's quite the executive assistant your friend Joe has," mused his mother. "She seems a right smart woman. I wondered how he got himself elected."

Mr. Munson grunted. "Good to see he hasn't got too high and mighty for us little people," he said. "Think he'll put up some money to help you find the nuke, save the family name?"

"Dad, that wasn't your fault."

"It's a complete and total disaster waiting to happen," he growled. "I wasn't able to fix it. Now it falls on you."

Munson shook his head. "I get it, Dad. But I think if there was going to be a problem from that accident, we'd know about it by now. It's the planet's current health we should be focused on."

"You don't understand, Curtis," his mother said. "He doesn't believe in God. If he would just—"

"Easy on us, Mom. It's been a terrible few days." Cutting into his mother's oft-repeated lecture on why the men in her life ought to join her faith, he leaned down and kissed her cheek, whispering, "Lay off the old guy. He deserves to spend his retirement in peace."

CHAPTER 8

On the drive back to the office, Munson thought about his father's story of the nuclear accident. Kept secret for many years, the accident had always weighed heavily on the old man because of its potential to cause long term damage to the environment and to the Inuit. Their father's concern had influenced Emily's steadfast and passionate commitment to helping the people of the north.

Although Munson had never shared their deep concern about the risks associated with the aging nuke, the family had always been affected by their father's torment over the possible risks. Perhaps he should make some effort to find it.But not right now. Half a century had already passed; a few more weeks wouldn't make much difference.

Addy had bought him a new phone and loaded it with his contacts. The mail was neatly sorted into stacks: "urgent important," "important but not urgent," and "information only." After dealing with the first stack he checked his email, which she had similarly sorted; once he'd gotten through that, he buzzed Addy and asked her to set up a meeting with his partner.

Munson and Irish Harrigan had attended Dalhousie together in their post graduate years. A graying African-Irishman who had been raised in Ireland, he had emigrated to Canada as a teenager. Today he was a brilliant geophysicist with enormous energy, and his reputation had been one of the reasons for the firm's success.

Now, distracted by the climate change controversy, Irish

was losing interest in the partnership and Munson was keenly aware that he may soon move on.

"Irish, I have something you might be interested in," said Munson, handing him one of the rocks he'd found on the island.

"Dunite?" Irish turned the rock over in his hand and whistled. "Quite the little vein of platinum."

"A major platinum find could pay for a lot of green initiatives, maybe help us kick our addiction to oil."

"So where's the rock from?"

"That's the thing," said Munson. "I found it a few days ago, on the shore of the island I was stranded on. But that's not where it originated. My theory is that it caught a ride on an iceberg that washed up on there, just like we did."

Irish frowned. "So the trick is to figure out where the iceberg came from."

"I'd like to get some of our team on it," said Munson. "Think we can spare the resources?"

"Maybe." Irish frowned. "I'm booked for the geo-engineering conference in Paris, and Akira was planning to come along. She's pretty hyped about it, so I doubt she'll want to go north instead. You want to take Pavel and Kim, head up to the Arctic for a little exploration?"

"Not me. I'm toxic right now. Emily's death was no accident; somebody wants me dead."

"Figured there was more to the heavy security detail than was warranted by a visit from our school chum," said Irish. "Is it because of the Saudi data?"

"That was already out in the open, so I'm not being targeted for that. My bet is someone wants what Dr. Fraser was giving me when she died." He briefly described the scientist's last moments. "If that is why these people are after me, it's likely she was on the right track. And it means that until I can get her data out to the public, I've got a big target painted on my back. So, rather than watch over my shoulder indefinitely, I'm going to flush them out and deal with them."

"Where is the USB drive Dr. Fraser gave you?" Irish frowned. "You bring it here?"

"It's safe," said Munson, shaking his head. "Not here. Best I'm the only one who knows where."

"You've had a look at what's on it?"

"Not yet. It's protected, and I'll need time to figure it out." He grimaced. "And I need to do that as quickly as possible. Can I depend on your support?"

"You've always had *my* back, and I'm glad to help. Just don't get yourself killed."

"Thanks."

Munson called Addy in. "Addy, please call the partnership group together in the meeting room."

With the junior partners assembled, Munson passed around the rock. "I have here a sample of coarse grained fosterite dunite that I believe contains platinum, found along the coast of Labrador, a great distance from its source. Undoubtedly they were deposited there by melting grounded icebergs."

Akira's eyes widened. "Wow," she said, passing it along to Pavel. He passed it along to Kim, who looked at it in surprise.

"It's very much like my father's rock," he said, looking at Munson. "The one you tried to trace. Too bad he never said where it came from."

Munson nodded. "This may well have come from the same place. Somewhere in the Arctic is an ore body," he said, rising to pace the room. "Irish and I feel there's a huge opportunity here. We'll assign a team will begin searching for it. Akira, you're already committed to the Paris conference?"

She nodded. "I've been looking forward to it, but if you need me to go north—"

"No, I know how strongly you and Irish feel about the climate change issues," he grinned. "Pavel, do you have commitments that will conflict with leading the team?"

Pavel shook his head. "Not that I can think of," he said,

"although it probably makes more sense for Kim to go. He knows the north and their customs, speaks the language."

Munson turned to Kim. "Kim, you've been pretty vocal about your opposition to any further resource development in the north," he said. "Do you think you can set that aside?"

Kim's face was expressionless. "How will this help my people?"

Irish sighed. "Kim, surely you know by now that not all development is destructive."

"It's not all good, either," he said. "And when it is bad, my people are the ones who are left on thin ice. Literally, and figuratively. So I want to know: how will it help my people?"

"Well," said Irish, "say we discover a multi-billion-dollar vein of platinum. What would you have us do with it?"

Kim was silent for a moment. "Money will not turn back the clock."

"No," said Akira, "but properly used it could make a big difference."

"Money greases a lot of wheels," said Pavel. "Use it to lobby the politicians, convince industry leaders."

Kim scowled. "More money in the wrong pockets won't fix anything."

"He's right," said Akira. "But we could use it to fund greener energies, reduce the reliance on fossil fuels."

Pavel turned to Munson. "Speaking of which, weren't you given the keys to a new technology that's supposed to change the world?"

Munson raised his eyebrows.

"Dr. Fraser's USB drive," said Pavel. "We saw her hand it to you, on the conference feed. Wasn't that what was on it?"

"Dr. Fraser's work will have to be vetted," said Munson. "So, Kim, what do you say?"

Kim raised his chin defiantly. "I'll lead the team if you'll agree to give me some say in what happens next."

Munson looked at Irish, who sighed. "We can give you

that, Kim," said Munson. "But unless you can come to see that we're all on the same side here, your future with Munson-Harrigan is limited."

———————————

Munson was catching up on mail when Addy Hangren came into his office. "Mr. Blake and Ms. Ellen Niiqway to see you Dr. Munson," she said, smoothing her hair and adjusting the tailored suit over her small frame. "They don't have an appointment, but said you'd understand."

"I'll come out," he said, following.

Niiqway looked younger in a business suit, her auburn hair swept up in a neatly braided bun. "Hello Munson." She took his hand. "I am so sorry about your sister."

"Thanks Niiqway," he said, holding her hand for a moment. "Hello, Blake." Eyes welling, he ushered them into his office.

"Yes, our sincere condolences," Blake said, extending his hand. "We'll help to get to the bottom of this and find out who is responsible." He settled into a chair. "Munson, what we have to say is confidential—" He got up and closed the door. "Niiqway?"

She nodded at Blake. "Munson, tell me everything you know about Dragonclaw."

"Dragonclaw?" He blinked. "I only know what you told me."

"Oh, come on," she said. "That wasn't the first time you'd heard of him."

"You're right," he admitted. "Emily had mentioned the name briefly, just before she left London."

"Emily?" Blake frowned. "What did she say?"

"Only that she'd received an odd email, and she wanted to talk to me about it in private, and has I ever heard of Dragonclaw."

"That's all?"

"That's all," said Munson. "I didn't even know if Dragonclaw was a person. That was the last thing we talked about as she was heading for the airport, and then we didn't speak again until I arrived at the hospital, and then... it never..." He swallowed.

"No, of course not," said Blake sympathetically.

Munson looked at him. "Could that email have had something to do with her...?"

"Perhaps," said Blake. "You are clearly in danger, which is why we have arranged for continued security at your home and here at your offices."

"Thank you." He frowned. "Niiqway told me you want me to convince Prime Minister Telford to dump his executive assistant, Ying Kao."

"Yes." Blake settled back in his chair.

"I'll agree to do that," said Munson. "Whether Telford will listen is another matter. Meanwhile, I'd appreciate some background on China's infiltration activity in Canada."

"There is a long history of CSIS warnings about Beijing's efforts at espionage," said Blake. "It includes the recruiting of Canadian officials. You were aware of our warning some time ago that we believed a few of our municipal and provincial politicians and officials had become agents of foreign governments?"

Munson nodded.

"The furor back then was loud and clear. Canadian officialdom reacted with expressions of outrage at such an idea." Blake shook his head thoughtfully. "I must emphasize that until now, the main targets for recruitment of spies have not been people from China who have settled here. A case in point is Dragonclaw. We are almost certain he is not of Chinese extraction."

"There was talk Chinese spies have infiltrated our universities," said Munson. "Have they?"

"To some degree; back in 2004, the Chinese government began the Confucius Institutes in academic institutions in an attempt to win friends during their rise to a world superpower. Several Confucius Institutes operate in Canada's universities. Some countries have been wary, believing that they are used to recruit agents. There is no proof of any of this, only speculation. But you see how it fits."

Munson nodded. China had large investments in Canada and knew the country well.

"Now a question for you," Blake said. "We understand your Saudi revelation. What about all of the *other* Middle East wells?"

Munson made a dour face. "There's a Saudi saying that goes like this: My father rode a camel, I drive a car, my son flies a plane and his son will ride a camel." He paused. "I believe it applies generally to the Middle East."

Blake leaned forward. "As mentioned, we need your help and I suspect that you need ours. I have a proposition." He reached into his brief case and pulled out a document. "We know your background in the military, your political views, and your history. We have seen your army sharpshooting records and your full psychological profile."

Munson glanced at Niiqway. Her face was expressionless.

"We have taken the liberty of vetting you for a role as a CSIS agent," continued Blake. "If you sign this document, it will authorize you to carry this." He reached into his briefcase and brought out a military issue Colt 1911 semi-automatic handgun encased in a shoulder holster. He put it on Munson's desk, then added a CSIS associate agent I.D. badge.

Munson stared at them, stone-faced.

Blake looked him in the eye. "I understand you dislike intelligence agencies, but given the circumstances and the people who are after you, you need these. This authorizes you, subject to transportation protocols, to take the weapon on board aircraft—in fact everywhere, with a few exceptions. We know that possession of Dr. Fraser's discovery makes you a target. The deal is simple. You help us with Telford, we help you. All you have to do is sign."

Munson thought about it. They were not the CIA. This gave him an edge. Was it worth it? God, he was tired. Too tired to be making a snap decision. He sighed. "You should know, I won't work with the CIA."

"We can't agree to that," said Blake. "There is no telling where all this will lead."

"Well, you know my feelings." Munson reached over, retrieved the document and read it. He picked up a pen, hesitated and then signed it and handed it back to Blake. Locking the firearm and I.D. in his desk he looked at the two of them. "Okay. Thank you. So long as I trust you have my best interests at heart I will work with you, but I will resign from CSIS as soon as this is resolved."

Blake nodded. "Let's talk about your security detail. We're under pressure to scale it back. Are you ready to do your own driving?"

"God, yes. It's annoying to be chauffeured everywhere. I don't need a team on my house, now that I'm alone; just here at the office. I don't want anyone else hurt."

The discussion moved from there to the failing oil supply and then drifted to the accelerating climate change. When Munson explained his view, Blake grew animated. "Stopping climate change is an impossible objective," he stated emphatically. "More carbon dioxide is produced by natural means than by human activity."

"Well," said Munson, "you can argue that volcanic emissions and carbon dioxide from natural sources, plants, trees, animals and decaying vegetation, far outweigh our own production, and I agree with that. What is happening is certainly not totally caused by carbon dioxide. You can argue that climate change is natural and will reverse itself. But something changed three years ago, Blake. Unless we find the cause and correct it, many scientists believe we may eventually face extinction."

Blake frowned. "Well, if we have many more Fukushima Daiichi earthquakes and tsunami-related nuclear disasters, perhaps we will."

"So you're not in favor of nuclear power?" Munson asked.

"We have enough of it already," insisted Blake. "It's too damned dangerous. We will eventually need a different alternative to oil."

Munson glanced at Niiqway, who had remained silent, her lips twitching. He turned back to Blake. "Tell me more about Ying Kao, the woman who seems to be behind Joe Telford's political fortunes."

Blake nodded. "Kao was recruited by WFFA for her unusual characteristics. She has an extremely high intellect. Our profiler tells us that her superficial charm, coupled with her extraordinary linguistic skills, enables her to be very convincing. She can appear charming while being covertly hostile. She loves humiliating people and lies very easily. We suspect Kao is involved in espionage with the Chinese spy Dragonclaw, whose terrorist leanings are our greatest concern."

"Sounds like bad news for Joe," said Munson. "Can't you just deal with her?"

"We have not been able to come up with firm evidence against Kao," said Niiqway. "We need all the assistance we can get to convince the prime minister that she is abusing his trust."

Blake stood. "I appreciate your help."

Munson nodded, extending his hand. "I'll do what I can. Do you need my help getting access to Emily's email?"

"Thanks," said Blake, "we already have that covered."

As they parted, Niiqway held his hand and stood close for an extra second, her eyes meeting his with sympathy. "I'm so very, very sorry about Emily."

He nodded and held her gaze. "I wish you could have known her. Emily would have liked and admired you. You are very much like her."

"In what way?"

"You risked your life to stay with me on the raft to remain steadfast to your mission; Emily would have done something like that. She was so intent on making a real difference in the world—up north, where they're being so badly affected by climate change, and over in Palestine where she's so sure they can find some middle ground. She just returned from there, another failed attempt, I'm afraid; but like a dog with a bone she wasn't ever going to give up."

Niiqway smiled wryly. "I'm a dog with a bone?"

"No, I meant—like her, you're dedicated and persistent."

"That is a great compliment," said Niiqway gently. "I've noted the same qualities in her twin."

She left with Blake, and Munson returned to his desk and sat for a moment. He meant what he'd said, but Emily was an open book compared to Niiqway. There was still something about the CSIS agent that he couldn't put his finger on. Something not quite right.

That night he dreamed of Emily. She was with him in the Rocky Mountains. Hiking with friends, they fished in the creek that ran past an old cabin and then back-packed up to the glacier that fed the creek. He woke suddenly. The dream had been in vivid color. It was as though she had just been with him.

Her last words as she died had been, *"I'll be with you."* He swung his legs out from under the covers and sat on the edge of the bed, re-living the memory of that summer long ago. He needed real solitude, time to grieve.

The next morning, he was in the office by 7:00 a.m. and Addy Hangren, a perpetual early bird, was already at her desk. He stopped for a moment, appreciative of her excellent work ethic and watched the pint-sized dynamo preparing a complex report at her computer. She had been with him for several years, first as a confidential secretary with Galaxy-21 Oil and then as an administrative assistant with his consulting firm. Addy was one of the most competent, energetic employees he had ever known. She was always neat and calm and although she'd always maintained a perpetual tan, she somehow managed to appear ageless. He wondered how on earth she kept so fit.

"Good Morning Dr. Munson," she said, turning away from her work.

"You've been fantastic through all of this, Addy." He dug into his case. "And to reward all your hard work, here is a little light reading, courtesy of the bookseller downstairs. He flagged me down last night as I was leaving, said surely we must be getting close to administrative assistant appreciation day, or some such occasion."

Addy scanned the hefty book he had placed on her desk and smiled. "Ah, another Mensa challenge. Thank you."

"No doubt you'll be through it by the end of the day, unless I eliminate your lunch break."

Addy laughed. "Your appointment with Joe Telford is in your diary. And I've booked your flight for Edmonton."

"Thanks Addy."

She'd already returned to her work.

CHAPTER 9

Niiqway waited for Blake to finish his call, watching the color rise in his neck. "But that isn't the case," he said. "The provinces of British Columbia and Alberta are hardly *conspiring* to sell mining, oil and gas leases to China."

She couldn't catch the words on the other end, but the voice got louder. Blake closed his eyes and shook his head. "With all due respect, it seems to me it's *Canada's* oil."

Another outburst on the other end, then silence.

Blake held the receiver away from his ear and peered at it. "He hung up on me," he said. "Ass." He stroked a non-existent mustache. "Yuh see, Blake," he mimicked, "we have no intention of lettin' Western Canada's oil and gas flow offshore. We're gonna keep that oil in North America, and it is *not* goin' *overseas*."

Niiqway grinned.

"We can *guarantee* you that not a *drop* of that oil is goin' to China. We are makin' preparations for seizure of the Canadian oil fields to *protect* them from foreign invasion. Canada better *hear* them drum beats, if you get my drift."

Niiqway shrugged. "Our intelligence suggests that if necessary, China *will* consider a military option. You can read the tea leaves. Canada does not have the military muscle to protect their oilfields, but the U.S. does."

Blake sighed. "So just to be neighborly, the Americans will occupy Western Canada to defend the oil sands and the oil and gas fields."

"They currently purchase twenty-six percent of our oil

from Canada," said Niiqway. "That will rise considerably over the current decade. From their point of view, they cannot risk losing any of it."

"What's the latest from points east?"

"The Chinese are serious," said Niiqway. "They've initiated a huge military build-up, ostensibly to attack Taiwan. They think that we are unaware, but we've been bitten by an Asian surprise attack once before. They have six armies of crack paratroops that can be deployed anywhere in the world within twenty-four hours. That's a half-million men. And they can follow up, by putting another one-and-a-half million troops on our doorstep in a matter of days."

"Think the U.S. is involved with them, playing both ends against the middle?"

"No," said Niiqway. "The U.S. and China are trading partners, but they are not allies. They are already head-to-head over North Korea and Iran."

"With Dragonclaw stirring the pot," said Blake.

"Not just stirring. He's actually behind a lot of it, pulling the strings, making it happen." Niiqway frowned. "We have to figure out who he is and deal with him. You sure we accessed all of Emily's email accounts?"

Blake nodded. "No mention of a Dragonclaw. Our people are still looking for signs of tampering, but nothing as yet. You still think Munson's holding out?"

"He *was* holding out, so why believe him now?"

"Well, you're holding out on him." Blake grinned. "What about Kao? I still think she could be Dragonclaw."

"No," said Niiqway. "She wasn't in the picture a decade ago, when some of the groundwork was laid. Our intel says that from the beginning, Dragonclaw's fingerprints are all over it."

"And this intel's been coming through proper channels?"

"It was." Niiqway shook her head grimly. "Best I can tell, the Americans are no longer sharing military intelligence with Canada. Keep this between—" Blake's cell phone cut her off.

"Blake." He glanced at Niiqway and hung up. "Munson's booked on a flight to Edmonton. Get someone on him."

———————————

Spending the morning in his office, Munson cleaned up a number of issues. Then he strapped on the shoulder holster, slipped the weapon in and donned his jacket. He was still at his desk when a woman burst in, tossed her flaming red hair, crossed quickly to his desk and planted a kiss on his cheek.

"I be thankin' you! I'm buying lunch. Mmmm, your cheek is fuzzy and kissable," she grinned. "And you are even better lookin' than I remembered!"

"Do I know you?" he asked, jumping to his feet. "Who *are* you?"

Addy Hangren appeared. "I'm sorry Dr. Munson. Somehow she got by security."

"It's okay Addy. The lady has me confused with someone else."

The woman raised her eyebrows, feigning indignation. "Confused am I? You pulled me onto your raft, you scalawag! You helped me board the bloody helicopter! I'm Martha Ambrose, and I am at your service."

"Oh," Munson managed, remembering the pitiful soul that they had rescued. "Ms. Ambrose. I wouldn't have recognized you. You look—terrific."

"Of course I do. And it's Martha. Now you cancel your appointments, 'cause you're comin' with me. I've got a car. We're goin' to lunch." She took his arm and propelled him toward the door.

"You're pretty damned aggressive," he told her. "Are you always like this?"

"I'm the federal minister of energy in the your new government," she announced happily. "I'm also an electrical engineer, and if I don't get my way, I make sparks!"

"If you want to buy me lunch, it will have to be at a

nearby café. I have a meeting on the Hill at one-thirty, and I'm on the four o'clock to Edmonton."

"A café then." She waved over two assistants, who were lurking outside, and winked at them. "I'm going for a quick lunch with a friend. Get lost for an hour, fellas!"

Munson's security detail followed along in their black SUV, but stayed discreetly outside the café.

Over lunch, Martha and Munson chatted about the air disaster. "Who was the big man with you on your raft who refused to identify himself?" Munson asked.

"Oh, you mean Walpender." Martha rolled her eyes. "He bragged that he's first vice president of some kinda fossil fuel association, and on the board of directors of Centwenti Aircraft Company. I must say, I disliked that man intensely."

Munson would chew on that later. The beautiful Martha Ambrose was vivacious and full of fun. She had knock-out looks, and Munson suspected that she wasn't above using the allure of her personal magnetism to get her way in the political world. The keen mind of an engineer would only add to those attributes.

Martha passed him a dessert menu. "You say you were on your way home, via London," she said. "How long were you away? And were you workin' the Ghawar oil-fields?"

"I was gone a few weeks, just long enough to wind up our team's work and send them home. And yes, we were in the Ghawar field."

"Global oil usage has continued to grow since China and India have emerged as superpowers," she said, signaling their server. "The coming shortage will be disastrous. I can recommend the apple pie," she said.

"I couldn't," Munson said, setting down his napkin.

"Apple pie, a la mode," she told the server. "Two forks. He'll be havin' some of mine."

Munson grinned. This woman was unstoppable. "What do you think of Telford's assistant, Ying Kao?"

"Kao?" Martha stirred cream into her coffee. "She's our secret weapon; her intellect and strategic thinkin' give us an incredible edge."

"I see," he frowned, surprised that Martha was under Kao's spell.

"But let's talk more about you," said Martha. "I understand that your parents were American, but you lived in the north."

"Yes, we lived in Alaska, the Northwest Territories—all over the Arctic, when my sister and I were young."

"Your sister, what does she do?"

Munson froze. "You—you don't know?"

Martha's eyes grew wide. "What?"

"She was killed in Toronto, in an explosion."

"That was …" Martha put her hands over her face. "Oh, Munson." She reached across the table for his hand. "I am every kind of a fool. I am so sorry."

He shook his head. "We kept it all out of the media as best we could."

"Do you want to talk about it?"

He shook his head again. "Not … not right now."

She squeezed his hand again before letting go. "Alright. Tell me about your involvement with big oil."

"I was with Galaxy-21 as VP, Arctic operations. I worked for a guy called Max Bolavar, until I became disenchanted with big oil in general."

"Was that when you started your consulting firm, with Irish Harrigan?"

"He's an old school chum, as is Joe Telford." The pie arrived. "Tell me, how will he do as Canada's PM?"

Martha tipped her head and looked at him quizzically. "I suspect you already have an opinion. We are all on a very fast learning curve."

He nodded. "I hope Joe Telford recognizes that."

"Of course. Now, try this." She loaded a forkful and held it across the table.

Munson was powerless to resist.

As she popped the last of the pie into his mouth, one of her assistants approached the table and leaned low to speak with her.

"I must let you go," she said, setting down her napkin. "Thanks for draggin' me onto your raft. Give me a call. I'm interested. Don't let them charge you a cent—" she winked at the server, who grinned at her—"and don't feel you need to leave money on the table. This handsome young man's been tipped quite handsomely, too." She rose and was off, but not without a toss of red locks and a swish of swaying hips.

Munson watched her leave. He liked the sexy Martha Ambrose. And her information about the overweight Walpender was interesting. He'd have to let Niiqway know about the big man's boast about being VP of a fossil fuel association—might be a lead on the WFFA. And his involvement with Centwenti Aircraft was either another piece of the puzzle, or a very strange coincidence; they were the company who had built the new AC-990 that had held together long enough to save their lives, before taking so many others to the bottom of the ocean.

CHAPTER 10

Climbing the steps to the Parliament Building, Munson wondered if he'd get a chance to talk to Telford without the infamous assistant, Ying Kao. After showing his CSIS I.D. and surrendering his weapon he walked down the great hallways to the prime minister's office, where although he was ten minutes early, he was announced.

"Munson," Telford greeted him warmly. "Sorry again about Emily." He gave Munson a bear hug. "Addy tells me you're off to the Rockies for a few days. Wish I could—" The phone rang. "Sorry, I have to take this."

As Telford took the call, Munson studied him. The man was immaculately turned out, as always, and his ruggedly handsome face still had the pampered look of a man obsessed with his appearance. His friend was an ordinary guy, not particularly good at anything that Munson could recall, or well-endowed with the grey stuff, but with a gift of the gab that would make a car salesman blush.

Telford's connections to their youth and their ongoing love for fishing that were the bonds between them. In the past, Telford had often contacted Munson to pick his brain, and Munson's suggestions were routinely celebrated as Telford's own ideas. Annoying though it was, Munson had tried to provide good guidance. But since Telford had become involved with the beautiful Ying Kao, Telford had come to rely on him less and while Munson had hoped Telford simply needed less input, he now doubted that was the case.

As he waited for Telford to get off the phone, he considered the man's weaknesses. He had a lack of assertiveness, an impulsiveness and blind loyalty to his friends that were troubling. More of a front-man than a leader, these were qualities ideal for exploitation by a master manipulator. Perhaps eventually Telford's quick temper would prove problematic for Kao.

Telford put the phone down. "Do they have any idea about who the bastard was who murdered Emily?"

"I've got my suspicions," said Munson. "The authorities are on it."

"What about the plane crash—anything yet about what caused that?"

Munson shook his head. "You'd probably know before I would."

Telford changed his tone. "This is awkward for me," he said. "I am disappointed in you, Munson. We deserved a heads-up before you announced the Saudi shortfall."

"Sorry. Circumstances."

"Circumstances? Overnight, your name has become a household word. Announcing the Saudi oil failure has made you famous. Are you aware of the furor that your revelation has caused? I can't understand why you couldn't have given us some time—warned us."

"Were you following the conference, Joe?"

"A little," said Telford. "Not really."

"But you were aware of Dr. Fraser's announcement, and her sudden death?"

Telford nodded. "They were replaying that on the news after the plane crash, while you were still missing and after the first round of survivors showed up. Press had a field day emphasizing your Saudi announcement along with your efforts to save Fraser's life. There was some speculation that she'd handed something to you while she was dying—a USB drive?"

"She told me she'd been murdered," said Munson. "It may be that someone wanted to shut her up, and to keep her discovery from seeing the light of day. I was pretty sure the USB drive held her discovery, Joe, which meant I had became the next target. I couldn't risk—"

"So you figure she was murdered—"

"Perhaps," Munson explained patiently. "If so, and if her data was on the USB, that meant I'd be next. I couldn't risk being taken out before I released the Saudi information."

The door opened, and Ying Kao entered.

"Dr. Munson," she said. "You're early."

"I've asked Ying to join us," said Telford.

Munson rose, steeling himself to mask his emotions. "Ms. Kao."

"Ying, please." Kao's grip was firm and her eyes were wide and friendly.

"I wouldn't be here if it weren't for Ying," Telford beamed, settling back into his chair.

Munson leaned forward. "So tell me Joe, how in the world did you do it?"

Telford smiled. "We started three years ago. Selected our candidates in each constituency and helped them dig up every piece of crap we could on the backgrounds of each sitting member of parliament. Amazing what secrets people have. We avoided the media's political debates. Then with our help, the expense account controversy blew up into an all-party scandal that swung hundreds of thousands of votes our way."

"You had positioned ourselves to come up the middle," said Munson.

Telford grinned. "Siphoned votes off both the left and the right. It was close, but when the votes were counted we were able to form a minority government."

Munson frowned. "It must be difficult, Joe, forming a new government while having no experience. I'm glad that I'm not in your shoes."

"Who needs experience?" Telford grinned. "It's time for change. To begin, we are going to cut the deficit."

Munson glanced at Kao. She was watching Telford, her face impassive. He turned back to the prime minister. "What changes are you considering?"

"Well," Telford said, leaning back and forming a steeple with his fingers, "I'll tell you what we are *not* going to do. First, we are no longer going to pander to the Americans. They've have been given way too damned much influence up here. Second, we are not going to renew NAFTA. The North American Free Trade Agreement is up for renewal and we'll kill it. Third, we will close off *all* immigration; too damned many people looking to get away from the messes they've made in their own countries. Fourth we'll cut the large deficit. We have already mothballed our Victoria Class subs, stopped military shipbuilding and dry docked all of the Navy's expensive Arctic and B.C. west coast patrols. We are only providing air and satellite surveillance, in the Arctic—"

"Damn it, Joe! You need the Canadian Navy in the Arctic and on our west coast."

"Yeah," he smirked. "I knew when I mentioned the Arctic it would get your goat—"

"Aren't you at all concerned about the Russians?"

Telford's lip curled. "You think we should worry about the Kremlin's rusty old Cold War military museum pieces?"

Munson was incredulous. Disdain for the Russian bear? The man was daft. "The Russians have completely upgraded all their military," he said. "But it's not only the Navy's protection of the Arctic; it's your unbelievable anti-American bias—"

"Now Munson," Telford interrupted, clearly warming to the subject, "I'll tell you what we *are* going to do."

"I'm not sure I want to know," Munson said, sighing. "Hopefully your priorities will be dealing with the climate acceleration and the oil shortage."

"Ah yes, the oil shortage," Telford nodded. "The Americans currently control sixty percent of our western oil under the expiring NAFTA agreements. Now, thanks to your disclosure Curtis, the Americans will want *all* of western Canada's oil. We have no say in where the western provinces sell their oil and gas. They control their natural resources."

Kao cut in. "Those premiers have formed a Western Canada partnership to promote increased trade with China and Asia. They have reciprocal arrangements where they buy steel, equipment and a myriad of goods from China. It's important trade. We're not going to mess with it."

Munson watched Kao's expression. "So you are very pro-China, Ms. Kao—"

"In the last century, the U.S. was the world's economic and military powerhouse." Kao perched a hip on the corner of Telford's desk and swung one shapely leg over the other. "As the world already knows, this century is China's."

"So you see, Munson," Telford said, "the premiers of B.C and Alberta can negotiate with China all they want. At least it is not an American monopoly."

Munson shook his head. "With the Saudi shortfall, the Americans won't allow North American oil to go offshore. And tensions with China are already high over the Korean crisis."

Telford shrugged. "Well then, we are heading for a United States-China confrontation and it will be interesting to see who wins."

"But Canada will be caught in the middle!" Munson leaned forward. "You should convince those provincial premiers to back off petroleum exports to China."

"There is little hope of that," said Telford, "even if we wanted to. Our party has little support in Alberta or B.C. They despise our central and eastern power base. To interfere would only drive western separatism. No, it is the Americans who will have to back off."

Seeing he was getting nowhere, Munson tackled the Arctic. "I'm keen to know your plans for the north. Now that the Northwest Passage is nearly ice-free, the waterway could soon be open to tankers. An oil tanker going aground would be devastating to the Inuit who depend on hunting seals and walrus along the route. That passage should be closed to tankers."

"The Northwest Passage will be an international water-way," said Kao evenly.

Telford nodded. "We'll open our northern seaways."

"Damn it," Munson objected, "there are forty thousand Inuit who depend on those waters. It's their food supply. Opening it as a seaway will cause them untold harm."

"The Northwest Passage route is seven thousand miles shorter from Europe to Asia than going through the Panama Canal," said Kao. "It's good transportation economics."

Munson shook his head. "One of your priorities should be this acceleration—"

"As for climate change," she continued, "one hundred and eighty six billion tons of carbon enter the atmosphere each year, but a mere six billion tons of it is from human activity." She smiled earnestly. "Mr. Telford won't get far by championing unreasonable climate change initiatives."

Munson leaned back. "You miss the point. I wasn't going to refer to CO_2. Hydrocarbons generated by humans are not our only concern. They may well have contributed to this current emergency but they are not the cause. The Americans studied the sun's growing intensity—"

Telford's cheeks flushed. "I won't listen to American environmental bullshit or any other crap from all your goddamned American activist lemmings searching for a high cliff to jump off of! And I'm certainly not going to bow down to the goddamned American administration!"

Oh, Canada, thought Munson. With an emotional intellectual light-weight like Telford at the helm, the country was on a slippery slope. "Anti-Americanism is a political liability, Joe. The Canadian-American relationship has been built on trust. One misstep can destroy what it has taken two-and-a-half centuries to develop."

"Well, they're not going to come up here and push *me* around like my predecessors."

Kao leaned forward. "What about your father's request, Dr. Munson. How can we help?"

Startled, Munson looked up at her.

"What request?" Telford asked.

She smiled at him. "He asked for our help recovering a lost nuclear device, did he not?"

"Oh, that," said Telford.

"What can you tell us about this, Dr. Munson?"

Munson was relieved when Telford jumped in again.

"Just an old man's war story, Ying. Not worth our time. Right, Munson?"

Munson nodded, rising. "That's right. Well, it was nice to see you again Ms. Kao. Mr. Prime Minister."

Telford grimaced at the sudden formality. He rose too, and extended his hand. "Listen, Munson, come by my office on the Hill anytime. I mean it. I'll make time. I want to keep in touch with what the old guard is thinking. You're a good barometer of that. I like to keep my friends close."

And your enemies closer, thought Munson as he gripped Telford's hand. He nodded to Kao.

"Let us know if there is something we can do to honor Emily's memory," she said.

"He's off to their favorite cabin in the Rockies to sprinkle her ashes," said Telford. Munson didn't bother to correct him about his intentions; close enough.

"A very solemn responsibility," said Kao sympathetically. "I wish you a peaceful journey, Dr. Munson."

Munson made his way from the building, pondering her sincerity. If Kao was involved in his nightmare, she was doing a pretty damned good job of hiding it. Why had Niiqway decided Kao was one of Dragonclaw's puppets, and not Dragonclaw? The woman's mind was like a steel trap, but she restrained herself, let Telford take credit for her cleverness. Who would believe that the beautiful Ying Kao was a criminal sociopath, a spy, or a budding terrorist?

Obviously over his head, Telford relied heavily on her expertise. Munson had previously noted her incredible ability to recall names, dates, and facts. She had obviously influenced Telford to cut the Arctic and west coast naval patrols. And she seemed unperturbed by his ridiculous anti-Americanism, even though it was obviously a recipe for disaster. How did that fit into her plans?

Hopefully, Telford's minority government would fall before disaster struck. He checked his watch. Time to get to the airport. The stopover in Toronto would be long enough to swing by the bank.

CHAPTER 11

Munson took the shuttle from his Edmonton hotel to the airport, and found the hangar where he'd rented a Cessna. The maintenance man was seated by the hangar door. "Hello Roger," he yelled.

Roger sucked hard on his cigarette. "Munson. They said you was dead at sea, but I knew they was wrong."

"You got my call?"

"Yeah I had a fall. Doc says I was lucky."

"How's Rose?"

"What's that?"

"Rose. How's Rose?"

"Lost her, boy. Pneumonia. Dead three months now."

"You'll miss her," Munson shouted.

Roger nodded. "Every day." Rising, he hobbled into the hangar, and Munson followed him to where the Cessna sat parked. Roger patted the plane's cowling, ashes dropping from his cigarette.

"Should you be smoking in here, Roger?"

"No there's nothin' broken on her. She's a powerful little piston job. Good bush plane." He took another drag. "Ya remember the take-off and landin' roll on these birds, boy? She'll take off in eight hundred feet. Landin' roll is a bit less. Say five hundred feet. She's got one hundred and eighty-five horses, cruisin' speed one hundred and eighty knots and she'll carry sixteen hundred pounds."

Munson nodded. "I remember."

Roger dropped his cigarette to the floor, stamping it out

with his boot. "Where ya headed this time, boy? Out to the family cabin?"

"Yeah."

"Figured so when you asked for the huntin' rifle. It's on board, with ammo."

"Roger, listen. I'm expecting company, but you have to pretend I don't know they're coming."

"They plannin' a s'prize party?"

"Something like that. Here is a map of my exact location, see here?" Munson hollered in Roger's ear. "It's in Little Berland country, right where I've marked it. When they come, you give them directions so they can find me. Got it?"

"Don't have to shout boy. I understand! I'll show the map to them. My eyesight's gone and so is my memory. Only thing I got left that works good is my hearin'."

Grinning, Munson watched Roger shuffle back toward his office, lighting up another cigarette as he went. Then he filed his flight plan, loaded the Cessna and rolled it out of the hangar to do a pre-flight check. On the runway he fired up the little plane with all the controls pushed forward, set the flaps to zero and pushed the power in. As the motor roared to life it gathered speed—twenty knots, thirty-five, forty-five. He reached down and yanked the flap lever up. The little kite leapt off the runway, its nose to the sky.

As he gained altitude, Munson's sorrow over Emily's death deepened. Being at the controls of a small aircraft was usually exhilarating. Today he felt only sadness, guilt and anger. Trying to lift his thoughts, he recalled his youth. He was fortunate to have had a bush pilot father who had taught him to fly. Later, working the hot summer university breaks as a pilot extinguishing forest fires, he had learned to fly helicopters and water bombers; useful skills he'd enjoyed relying on in civilian life and occasionally during his military days.

When he reached 8,000 feet, he followed the ribbon of cars far below on the Yellowhead Route toward the Rocky

Mountains. An hour later, he turned north and followed the east slope of the Rockies until he was over the Little Berland River. There, he banked left, thinking of Emily and the friends who had accompanied them on a hike here, years before.

The area below was still pristine. Along the north boundary of Jasper National Park, the narrow valley shot off at right-angles to the ramparts. Losing altitude, he dropped down between jagged peaks into what had once been a lush river valley divided by the rushing melt waters of the Stern Glacier. Midway up the valley the stream bed widened to form the sand bars on which he would land.

He could not see it, but he knew where it should be, just off to his right wing at the edge of a clearing. He nosed over and brought the Cessna in, bouncing to a stop on a hard packed sand bar.

His heart skipped a beat.

There at the edge of a meadow against the hillside was the old cabin. "It's still here Emily!"

He parked the Cessna on the sandbar and walked to the cabin, where he hung his coat on a peg outside the door and pushed it inward. The old hinges groaned with rust. Shafts of light from the lone window fell on the potbellied stove that sat in the corner. A pile of neatly stacked wood and kindling had been left by a previous occupant. He checked the damper in the chimney, bent down and built a tipi of kindling and larger wood in the stove, then lit it. As the cheery crackle of the fire brightened the cabin, he sat on one of the bunks remembering. "It's been so many years," he said softly, stepping out onto the porch to survey his surroundings. "The last time we were here, we were sixteen-year-olds, weren't we Sis?"

Returning to the plane, he disconnected his phone from the charging system, checked the batteries on his satellite radio, and filled his canteens. Checking his ammunition, he loaded a few shells into his rifle and put the rest in his backpack. He carried his supplies up to the cabin, and dusted out a frying pan. After a lunch of bacon, eggs and hash-browns, he washed the dish, oiling the frying pan before returning it to its hook.

Then he rummaged in his pack sack, took out a small case and opened it with care. The flute had been a gift from Emily on their thirtieth birthday. He sat outside on a bench by the door and toyed with the flute for a moment. Soon the soft notes of the old tune *Tangerine* echoed across the valley. It was Emily's favorite.

Returning the flute to its case, he sat quietly, his eyes wet. Finally he got up and readied himself to climb the ridge above the cabin. He packed his bedroll and a pack-board with provisions along with the satellite phone, and his cell phone. After checking the rifle he climbed the ridge slowly, finally selecting a spot where he could lay and wait with a clear view of the cabin; a place where he could see but not be seen.

He'd settled in and was using his field glasses to watch a grizzly with her two cubs digging up a marmot hole on the hillside beyond the cabin when his phone buzzed. It was Niiqway. "Munson? Where are you?"

"In the Rockies, north of Jasper Park. I'm surprised I have cell service up here."

"What on earth are you doing there?"

"Watching a mama bear teaching her cubs how to find their lunch. Here; I'll zoom in on them for you. See that?"

"She looks big. Remember, you are not the top the food chain up there. It looks like a very beautiful, wild country."

"It is," he agreed. "How are you?"

"I'm okay. Just called to see how you're doing — I'm sure it's hard for you right now."

"Thanks. Yeah, that's why I came up here; to be alone with our memories for a bit."

"I understand."

"Any news?"

"Not much. We found nothing in Emily's email messages about Dragonclaw. She did say it was an email?"

"I think so… although I suppose she may have said 'message,' and I just assumed." Munson frowned. "Are you thinking *she* was targeted because of that message—that the explosion wasn't meant for me?"

"We don't know yet. Security footage from the hotel parking lot shows a man near your sister's rental car. It's fuzzy, but he's tall and lean, with a hawk-like nose, heavy eyebrows and dark eyes. We think it's a professional hit man they call the Hawk. I thought about capturing and sweating him, but he's a pro. He would die before revealing who he's working for."

"Hawk. I'll add him to my hit list."

"Look, I've got more news. Quite a few people of international importance were lost on the AC-990. A lot of the delegates from your convention."

"I knew about them," said Munson. "Huge loss to the scientific community, especially those involved in green energy research and climate change."

"Also on board was Adam Sayier, past vice president of Israel. And a French team negotiating for Canadian nuclear power plants."

"Any of them could have been the target."

"Yes," she said, "but we haven't yet confirmed that it was intentional. What *was* intentional was the murder of Dr. Fraser's boyfriend, Rolande Mercier. He was with her in London the day she was murdered, although he wasn't at the conference. His body was found in an alley behind the hotel. Time of death about an hour or so before Dr. Fraser died. There was no I.D. on the body, so it took a while to figure out who he was."

"Definitely murder?"

"Either that or the worst case of suicide I've ever seen: three bullet holes to the torso and another to the head. Looked like he was running away from someone who shot him down and then finished him off. Oh, and Munson— there was a key on the wristband Dr. Fraser left you. Looked like a yacht ignition key to me."

"It did."

"Mercier owned a yacht that is berthed somewhere in Saint Tropez, France."

"You think I have the key to Mercier's yacht?"

"He and Dr. Fraser were on a few days before the conference. Another development I should tell you about: Dr. Fraser's L.A. lab was blown up the day after our plane went down."

"Anybody hurt?"

"Not this time. But he Mercier seems to have been linked to WFFA."

"What do you have on them?"

"Just what we've already discussed—that they're a clandestine global fossil fuel lobbying group, a shadowy association of a few big oil and coal companies. We are not even sure which international conglomerates belong to it. We think it formed very recently."

"I had lunch with Martha Ambrose, the woman from the other raft. By the way, she's in Telford's cabinet."

"Energy minister, right?"

"Right. Remember the big guy in her raft?"

"Yeah," Niiqway chuckled. "She referred to him as an arrogant hippo. Apt, and it kind of stuck in my mind."

Munson grinned. "Well, he was bragging to her that he's the VP of some fossil fuel association, so you might want to see where that leads. She didn't refer to it as WFFA, so maybe they're not yet on her radar—or maybe she knows about them, but isn't sharing. Also, Walpender's on the board of directors for Centwenti, the company that build the AC-990."

"We had the Centwenti connection, but I hadn't tapped him for WFFA. I'll check it out."

"Cell service is going to be spotty up here. Anything else you need to tell me?"

"I learned that you and Emily paid for Kim Sorqaq's tuition and expenses at the University of Manitoba," she said. "You didn't mention that. Any particular reason?"

Her voice was light, but Munson wondered if it was some kind of accusation. "No," he said. "Kim thinks the government paid for his education, and we wanted it that way."

"Generous. You'll be interested to know that Kao has contacted Kim twice over the past couple of days. We know they've spoken, but we haven't been able to pick up their conversations. Any idea what that's all about?"

Damn. Kao was far too interested in the nuke. Was she trying to enlist Kim's help, grill him about it?

Surely he wouldn't have told her about the dunite! He shuddered. Dragonclaw could use that information, too.

"I'm not sure what that could be about," he said.

"It could be another example of that recurring connection between you and Dragonclaw," said Niiqway. "There's something there, Munson. Be careful. I have to go."

"Thanks. Oh, I should tell you: Martha Ambrose is under Ying Kao's spell."

"Too bad. I thought another woman wouldn't be quite so taken by Kao's charms."

"You know Telford's pulling assets out of the Arctic?"

"A little. Gotta go, Munson. We'll talk again soon. Stay safe."

Pocketing his phone, Munson wondered if he should have had Niiqway start looking for Whitey. No, he decided; he still couldn't shake the feeling she wasn't being honest with him.

As Munson set up his camp on the ridge, he realized he was at the bottom of the same steep cliff he'd fallen from as a teen. Abandoning his chores, he continued up the trail to the top of the cliff and found the spot where he'd lost his footing. Or had the ground had given way? He'd never been sure exactly how it had happened. From the bottom, it had seemed less dangerous and not nearly as high as he remembered.

He forced himself to approach the edge. As he peered over, the vertigo began again; his acrophobia had gradually grown worse since that near-death experience so long ago. Staggering back, he hugged the ground, slowly regaining his equilibrium.

"You warned me, Emily, didn't you? You said to stay back that day, but I didn't listen."

From this height, he could see that the grizzly and her cubs had wandered around back of the cabin. Sitting on a boulder, he got out his phone and inserted Dr. Fraser's USB drive. He imagined what she might have used for a password. The wristband had a small tag on it; squinting at it, he could make out the words *Saint-Tropez Y. C.* Probably Mercier's key, alright. He considered a few possible passwords, but nothing he had any confidence in. Too much to lose if he was wrong. Instead of gambling, he'd have to get back to Ottawa and get Addy to track Whitey down. None of his own attempts to find the man had yielded any success.

As the evening shadows lengthened, he made his way back down to his camp, had supper, and bedded down hoping the bears had not decided to follow his scent uphill. He checked his rifle again, then set it atop his pack, within easy reach of his pillow.

He watched the moon as it rose over the dark shadows of the mountains, feeling Emily's presence.

Was he imagining?

Yes, but she *was* there, if only in his mind.

CHAPTER 12

Munson awoke to a sound from the trail, and every nerve in his body came alert. The moon was bright, casting light on the cabin below. A man's voice, muffled, came from the trail, only a stone's throw below.

"Ya? Okay, okay, okay. *Hamburger.* Ya. … I am above da cabin. His plane is parked on sandbar. … No, he must be in da cabin. I burn him out. … Ya, but safest way is to torch him. If he comes out, I'll kill him. Then I'll torch da plane."

"Damn," Munson muttered, carefully reaching for his rifle. He watched the dark figure take a position where he could see both the cabin's window and the door. Munson heard a metallic click and watched the assassin lower a tripod from his own rifle, which he was training it on the cabin door. Then the man squatted down and took something from his pack. Some kind of incendiary device? The man stood and raised his arm to throwing position.

Munson squeezed the trigger. As the shot reverberated around the hills, the man dropped like a stone and never moved.

But had he come alone?

Keeping half an eye on the prone figure and half an eye on the trail, Munson pulled on his boots and waited, watching. After what felt like half an hour, he stood and, holding his rifle at the ready, walked down the trail to where the man lay sprawled in the dirt. He was obviously dead, his shattered head resting in a dark pool.

Squatting down, Munson tried to make out the man's

facial features. Niiqway had said the hawk was tall; this couldn't be him. Munson reached down and fished out a wallet and a satellite phone. The assassin had a small amount of Canadian cash along with an outdated international driver's license and two passports, one Iranian and one Canadian, all in the name of Ahmed Karim.

Munson pocketed the wallet and pressed the satellite phone's redial button.

"Yes?" A man's voice answered.

"It's me," Munson rasped.

"You're a dumb-ass, Karim. Gimme the friggin' *password!*"

"Hamburger," Munson guessed.

"You get it done?"

"Ya."

"I got another job for you. Orders are at the CN Tower, observation deck, men's room."

"Ya." Munson shut off the phone.

He checked Karim's backpack. A Glock, a couple of explosive devices. Standing, he searched the ground around Karim's body. Not far from his right hand was another of the small incendiary devices. He sighed. Lucky it hadn't blown him to bits as it fell.

Munson hauled Karim's belongings down to the cabin. There, he lit a lamp and typed out a text to Niiqway, but wasn't surprised to see he had no service. Saving it to his draft folder, he grabbed his flashlight, climbed the short distance back up to the ridge, and sent the message off.

The phone buzzed in his hand; voicemail from an undisclosed number. "I am a colleague of the late, great Doctor Caroline Fraser." The voice was so loud Munson nearly dropped the phone. "You have something for me. Call me the second you get this message, and for god's sake erase it from your phone. Number's two-five-oh..." Munson grabbed a stick and scratched it into the dirt.

He dialed, waited for the connection. "Solgren Canada."

"Sorry about the time," he said. "You texted me?"

"Ah, yes," boomed the voice. "Alexander Klutzky White-field McMurchy, at your service."

"Mr. McMurchy, I—"

"Nobody wants to be called Klutzky so my friends call me Whitey!"

"So you worked with—?"

"Doc Fraser? Yup, before she kicked off. Now I'm in charge, when I'm sober."

"I'd like to come visit you."

"Yup. You're the jasper she cursed with that damned jump stick. Leastwise, I'm hoping it's the one I think it is. Been following you in the news. Thought I'd best let you deal with your family stuff before I added any more crap to your life, but as it is you're on borrowed time."

"I had the distinct impression Dr. Fraser wanted me to give the USB drive to you."

"Of course she did, bless her." Whitey expelled a long, drawn out sigh. "Come to Kelowna, Doc Munson. I've got a small research lab here, and they haven't found me yet."

"You mean the assassins."

"Yup. Same ones that're after your sweet ass."

"Oh, joy," said Munson, unable to stifle a grin. "Are you an operating lab?"

"Certainly. Why else would we be here? When you come, bring the jump stick, a bottle of good Scotch, and dog food for the staff."

"Dog food—for the staff?"

"Yeah! Only three of us here, me, Winston Churchill and Eleanor Roosevelt."

"Churchill and Roosevelt?"

"Security guards. The huskies get the dog food. I get the Scotch."

"You sound like a highly qualified caretaker."

"Overqualified," he chuckled. "NASA-trained astronaut with a bunch of doctorates I don't even need for this job. Come on over to God's country and see us. Call me from the airport and I'll give you directions."

"I'll be there later today."

"Not a moment too soon."

Munson copied the number from the dirt into his cell phone, listing it under the name Eleanor Churchill, then checked his watch. Might as well get a little more sleep.

When he woke, he dialed Roger at the hangar. "Roger, I'm going on to British Columbia. What's the weather like?"

"Heather? Oh, she's good. Heard from her just this morning. But don't you be takin' that Cessna over the mountains, boy. Big storm brewing. Best get yerself on a commercial flight instead."

"I'll do that, Roger. See you shortly."

"Your buddy find you?"

"He did. Thanks, Roger."

Munson collected his camping gear and headed down the hill. He tidied up the cabin and made sure there was enough kindling and firewood for the next visitor. Closing up, he glanced up to where he'd left Karim's body.

The sow and her cubs were there. She'd probably bury the body and let it rot before they began feasting in earnest. He hoped Niiqway's people would retrieve the body before the bears developed too great an interest in human flesh.

Down at the plane he satisfied himself the Cessna had not been tampered with, started it up, taxied to the sandbar and took off in the pre-dawn light. As he banked in a lazy climbing turn, he shook his head. Too bad the bushwhacker was such small fry.

He had learned nothing about the big tiger's identity.

Munson left the Cessna and the rifle with Roger, telling him he would be flying back to Toronto after all. He stowed Karim's backpack, wallet and weapons in one of the hangar's lockers, then made his way to the main terminal. There, he was able to find a seat on an early morning flight to Kelowna, making it on board just a few minutes before takeoff.

"Good morning!"

Munson looked up from his aisle seat to see a ruddy-faced stranger. He wore a red plaid shirt with pants shortened below the knee, exposing high-topped hiking boots. "That'll be my seat."

"You're right," said Munson, standing. "They've put me at the window, but I prefer aisle. Can I swap you?"

"Sure," the man grinned, shedding his pack-board and stowing it overhead. "Name's John Stark. Pardon the get-up. I'm a forest ecologist from the University of Alberta. Doing field work; got out of the bush too late to change."

"Curtis Munson, marine geologist, Munson-Harrigan Consulting."

"Ah, yes." Stark glanced at him again before settling into the window seat. "You've been on the news lately. That was quite the bombshell you dropped. Fanning the flames of the oil debate was about the last thing we needed. Seems we'll never get people looking at the real problem."

Munson blinked. "The real problem?"

"Yup." Stark was emphatic. "No one wants to hear this, Dr. Munson, but right now the earth herself is spewing more greenhouse gas than the atmosphere can soak up."

"Interesting," said Munson. "What are you seeing?"

Stark's tone shifted. "There's a shift in the carbon balance in these boreal forests," he explained. "They blanket seven hundred and fifty million acres of the northern part of our Canadian provinces. The accelerating temperatures are resulting in more forest fires and beetle infestations. It's causing old-growth forests to die out faster. Until recently, these forests helped offset rising carbon concentrations; now they're adding to it. The planet's carbon sinks are eroding as global temperatures accelerate."

Munson nodded. "But we've recently realized this sudden acceleration is not impacted much by human generated CO_2. It's something else; changes in the sun?"

"Could be." John Stark snapped his seatbelt shut.

"And the bigger question is, what can we do about it?"

"That is indeed the billion dollar question," said Stark, growing enthusiastic. "I have a colleague working with British and American scientists on a project they're calling Astronomical Adaptive Optics. Big fancy name for it. This AAO involves firing billions of tiny wafer-thin reflective lenses into space, high above the earth, so they stay in line between the earth and the sun. They're like a cloud of tiny satellites that stay in space and deflect the sun's rays. My colleague, she's is working on a small part of the design."

"Interesting," said Munson. "Like a giant shade screen. Will they work with NASA to get the wafers up there?"

"Yup. They've tried using coil guns to fire them from the earth's surface. Unfortunately those ultra-thin reflective wafers are too delicate. They can't withstand the thousand Gs of sudden acceleration. Rockets also failed. The extreme vibration during lift-off destroys the fragile wafers."

"So it's dead in the water?"

"Nope; they're on to plan C. They'll manufacture the reflective wafers in the space station and deploy them with a space vehicle manned by an astronaut. And that presents the next problem. It will be difficult getting the astronaut back as he won't be in an earth-return orbit. He has go straight out there, deploy and position the mirrors and then power back and re-enter an earth orbit to return."

"So it's a suicide mission."

"It is, but what's one man's life to save billions? They'll do it alright, they just won't tell us when they do."

Munson frowned. "You'd think they could use remote detonation."

"No time to develop the robotics."

Munson shook his head. "But you'll probably face plenty of delays anyway—push-back from those still trying to get our heads around the complex intricacies of the myriad of systems that govern our environment. We can't predict what effect this kind of manipulation will have on—"

96

"Oh, they already have groups of protesters," Stark laughed. "But the folks on the AAO aren't going to do anything stupid. The first experiment will only cover a small area of the sky, just enough to measure the result. Maybe by the time that's done, they'll have the robotics they need for a mass deployment."

"If it turns out to be a good idea," said Munson.

Stark grinned. "Bit cynical, aren't you?"

Munson shrugged. "Cautious, I guess."

"Well, that's not a bad thing," said Stark. "We've jumped feet-first into too many technologies that proved useless or worse."

By the time they were airborne, they'd exchanged business cards. Munson was feeling the effects of having slept too little and with one eye open, and was relieved when Stark asked the flight attendant for a pillow. "Gotta get some shut-eye before Kelowna," he said, leaning against the window. Munson reclined his own seat and promptly fell asleep.

CHAPTER 13

It was a beautiful day in the Okanagan Valley. Munson rented a car, then called Whitey for directions. Driving through the hillside vineyards on the east slopes of the city, he passed one winery after another, some sporting elaborate gates. He pulled up at one set of gates, reaching through the rental car's window to press the buzzer. The intercom hummed. "We're sorry, the winery—"

As instructed, he interrupted the recording by punching in a series of numbers. The intercom hummed again. "Yeah?"

"Munson."

"Awntray voo."

The gates swung open, and Munson proceeded up the drive to a relatively industrial-looking building hidden in the trees. The door was opened by a tall, balding man with piercing blue eyes and a heavy white mustache; two huskies pushed their way out from behind him.

"So, the legendary Dr. Curtis Munson, in the flesh!"

"I am," said Munson, standing still while the dogs checked him out.

"White one's Eleanor Roosevelt, black one's Winston Churchill. May as well let 'em sniff ya good and get to know ya."

"Nice to meet you, Dr.McMur—"

"Good lord, laddie, just call me Whitey. C'mon in. Stay out of the dogs' way though. Roosevelt's in heat and Churchill's—well you get the picture."

The front of the lab had been converted to Whitey's living quarters. Overflowing bookshelves flanked a large oak desk. On the tiled floor, colorful carpets defined the rooms; one was surrounded by leather armchairs and dog dishes, the other piled with scientific journals alongside the neatly made bed.

Munson carried the dog food in and put two bottles of Glenfiddich on the kitchenette's small but tidy counter. "Here is the USB drive Dr. Fraser left you."

"Ah, Doc Fraser. Sweet Caroline. I warned her it wasn't time to tell the world. Okay, laddie. Let us put this here jump stick in my laptop and see what we've got." Adjusting his half-spectacles, he inserted the drive.

"It's password protected," warned Munson.

Whitey grinned and tapped the keys. "Not a problem."

Munson sighed, releasing the last of his reservations about his strange host.

While waiting for the files to transfer, Whitey reached for two water glasses and opened the Scotch.

"Afraid I can't join you," said Munson. "I'm driving."

"Water? Something—"

"I'm fine, thanks."

Whitey pushed the glasses aside and took a swig from the bottle. "Well, here's to the Doc." He stood. "Come see what we're up to, Munson. Don't let the dogs in. They're not allowed in here."

Whitey led the way into a bright, spotless lab. Although it was large, all of the floor space in use. A complex experiment was enclosed in a huge sealed Plexiglas room.

"Been working on this fer a bit, along with a colleague in England. What d'ya know about geo-engineering laddie?"

"Very little, but it's been in the news lately."

"The Greenland ice cap, the Antarctic—they're our coal mine canaries. We're watchin' the canaries die. We're near the tipping point. Things are gettin' desperate. Geo-engineering is the answer. We must manipulate the environment. Stop the canary from dyin'."

"What are you and your colleagues working on?"

"A major project, laddie, aimed at one thing. Deflecting the sun's rays back into space, to reverse the effect of a carbon dioxide-laden atmosphere. We're developing a white reflective covering for the Arctic islands and the world's deserts. It works the same as an ice cap."

"Deflecting the sun," Munson muttered. "Have you heard of a Dr. John Stark at the University of Alberta?"

"No, why?"

Munson dug out the card that Dr. Stark had given him and gave it to Whitey. "This scientist can connect you with someone who is working part of a project that I'm sure you would find interesting. Her project's written on the back."

"Astronomical Adaptive Optics," said Whitey, flipping to the card's front. "I'll contact Dr. Stark. Thanks laddie."

"So you weren't working on the hydrogen project?"

"Doc Fraser bounced ideas off me, but she was doing the work itself in her lab in L.A. Preferred to work alone, that one, so she kept me busy up here with this."

"You said that her hydrogen discovery should not yet have been made public."

"No," said Whitey. "No, definitely not. The auto industry has been working on this for some time. They have prototypes that cost six or seven million each. Doc Fraser's process is simpler and cheaper to build but it needs to be authenticated. And even though it's cheaper, it is still much too expensive to replace internal combustion engines. Hydrogen fuel cells need less expensive metallurgy to be viable for the general public."

"You're saying she got herself killed for nothing?"

"Not necessarily, laddie. Let's see what's on that jump drive." Whitey led the way back to his desk. "She was not a trusting woman, yet she entrusted you with her life's work. Incredible."

"She was dying," said Munson, shrugging. "I'm not sure it had anything to do with who I am. And she warned me that I'd be in danger. Her discovery has already ended her life, probably my sister's life, maybe the lives of two hundred and thirty passengers of our airliner in the Atlantic. I don't know yet."

"I know," said Whitey grimly. "It's big trouble." Unplugging the flash drive, he disconnected it from the wristband. "Here's your key ring."

"That was Dr. Fraser's," said Munson.

Whitey looked at it. "So it is, laddie. That's probably for her dead boyfriend's yacht."

"Rolande Mercier's?"

"So you are already aware of him." Whitey frowned. "Queer duck, that one. Seemed quite besotted with her—no surprise there. She was a great lookin' woman with a brain in her head; my kinda gal. If I'd been a couple decades younger..." He grinned, turning back to the screen. "But I really don't know what she saw in him. Now, what do we have here? Those files I'm familiar with, and that one, but this spreadsheet—hm. Well, well, well. That right there just might explain the attraction." He glanced up at Munson. "She was workin' on a WFFA membership list."

"You know about them?"

"Of course. Doc said they were on to her, pressuring her to quit what she was doing, 'or else.' So of course the obstinate woman was dead set on findin' out who they were. Take a look, Munson. See anyone familiar?"

"Roland Mercier," said Munson.

Whitey pointed a couple of names down. "And you, too, laddie."

Sure enough, there he was: Curtis Munson. In the column next to his name was an X. "What's the X mean?"

"Means she'd cleared you."

Scrolling down, Munson found Kim Sorqaq, Akira Tanaka. David Walpender was there, too, with VP alongside his name.

Scrolling back up, he found Ying Kao, Pavel Krotov and Irish Harrigan; alongside Kao and Harrigan was "?P?"; further up, with the same notation, were Nate Evans, the newly appointed CSIS director; his own former boss, Max Bolavar; and near the top of the list, Martha Ambrose.

The list contained 27 names in all, but the rest he didn't recognize. Most had just a question mark; a few had a combination of question marks and P or VP. Only Walpender's had no question mark, other than the few, like his, with an X alongside. He counted those. Only four.

"You're sure the Xs mean *cleared*?"

Whitey reached down to rub Winston Churchill's ears. "Aye; hypothesis eliminated. I am intimately familiar with Doc's shorthand. Good thing, or you would not be allowed to leave here alive."

Munson wasn't entirely sure he was kidding.

Whitey grinned. "So tell me what was happening when this came into your possession," he said. "The parts I wouldn't have seen on the televised feed. And what kind of chaos it's unleashed in your life."

Munson told Whitey the whole story; Dr. Fraser's death, Mercier's murder, the explosion aboard the AC-990, about Emily, the assassination attempt in the Rockies, Niiqway's involvement (although he kept her name out of it) and his suspicions. "I'm hoping I haven't led them here," he said.

"Not likely, laddie. Want to take a look at what all the fuss is about?"

"Sure."

"Take your time. I'll be toppin' up my scotch and takin' the security detail for their hourly stretch."

Munson scrolled through the files. They laid out the details of a complex on-board hydrogen system. Four U.S. patents were involved, each covering part of a process.

The hydrogen would be converted to electrical energy with a fuel cell and generator. The process cracked hydrogen molecules from water, but did it *on board* each fuel-cell equipped vehicle.

Hydrogen from water he understood. That was simple chemistry. But by applying a recent discovery using radio waves to generate a 3,000-degree-Fahrenheit flame in saltwater, she had developed a process where it was done on board the vehicle—generating hydrogen in small quantities at the demand of the driver, to feed a fuel cell that powered the vehicle.

That meant that a vehicle could run from a fuel tank of saltwater, emitting a residue of only clean water.

In automobile applications it would also eliminate the need to carry a fuel tank of hydrogen. Using Dr. Fraser's discovery, hydrogen would be generated from saltwater in small quantities, varying on the driver's command as needed to accelerate the vehicle. It would also eliminate hydrogen refueling stations, tanker truck delivery systems, pipelines and hydrogen generation plants.

Munson sat back, thinking. He had read somewhere about reclaiming hydrogen molecules from saltwater by weakening the bonds that hold sodium chloride, oxygen and hydrogen together, thereby creating a flame of intense heat as the hydrogen is released. This technology seemed to be based on that. The auto companies and American military had been working on two similar concepts, one involving conversion of H_2O to HHO. They had developed drive-by-wire prototypes that cost millions to build. In contrast, Dr. Fraser's process looked very simple, easy to build and economical to use.

There was one significant problem, though: fuel cells were expensive. To replace oil, it would require hundreds of millions of hydrogen fuel cells, each needing very expensive platinum components. That would put the cost of hydrogen fuel cells well beyond the financial reach of the masses. Finding a large new source of platinum could significantly lower the price of the exotic metal, but it would have to be massive.

How would Irish Harrigan feel about using their company's resources to drive down the cost of platinum? No doubt he'd be thrilled to think he could save the world.

Whitey's huskies bounded back into the room, and Munson turned to the scientist.

"Will this actually work?"

"Ah, laddie." Whitey grinned. "That's the billion-dollar question. Not my area of expertise, and I'm too close to the research to vet it. I'll head down to L.A.; gotta go there anyway to retrieve Doc Fraser's will. There's a scientist there who should be able to validate the work. I'll get in touch with her, and then I'll call you when we have the billion-dollar answer." He handed Munson the flash drive. "Here, you best keep this, laddie. I've copied it. But I don't want any copies going astray. These are the only two in existence. Promise me you won't make any copies until we've decided to make the discover public."

"I promise. Can I get a printout of the WFFA list, though? I'll want one for CSIS, and I don't want to pack the USB drive around."

Whitey printed the WFFA spreadsheet and handed it to Munson. "Just a minute, laddie." Stroking his mustache, he leaned forward to peer at something on his computer. "Best check out the boyfriend's yacht in France, Munson," he said. "That's the last place Doc Fraser was, and it's where she last saved changes to that WFFA file. Seems pretty likely someone on this list was out to destroy her, her work, or that list of names. Maybe all three."

CHAPTER 14

Niiqway slid into the booth across from Blake. "Telford's positioned his government to try to block the oil deal, but the provinces proceeded unilaterally," she told him. "China now has legal documents from the provinces guaranteeing them considerable access to the oil sands."

He grunted.

"China is rejecting our federal government position. It's now a real flashpoint for war between China and the U.S., with Canada squarely in the middle." She signaled the waitress for a coffee.

"Canada's attracting foreign armies, just like Kuwait, Iraq and Afghanistan did years ago."

"Bigger. All of our military assets are on high alert." The waitress approached with a carafe, and Niiqway paused until she'd moved on. "The huge Chinese military build-up has surpassed anything we've ever seen in Asia. The Americans have started a large build-up of troops and heavy armor in Washington State, Idaho, Montana and North Dakota. Canada can't defend herself from that kind of onslaught."

"What's Russia up to?"

"Russia?" Niiqway shrugged. "Our intelligence suggests they may be considering a more aggressive stance on the Arctic. Internationally, things are heating up on the Korean Peninsula, Iran is goading Israel and the Israel-West Bank problem has erupted again. God knows what will happen if the Middle East explodes."

"Telford's really in over his head, isn't he?" Blake reached for the carafe and poured himself a cup. "He probably hasn't really considered that China may have a powerful ally."

"Like the Russians? Unlikely. And they have been un-characteristically silent through all this. Only the Ukraine is still simmering."

Niiqway's phone buzzed. "Niiqway."

"Hi Niiqway."

"Hi, Munson." She glanced over at Blake. "Where are you?"

"En route to Toronto. Your people get the package I left you?"

"We have the one from the locker in Edmonton, and most of the package you left on the ridge. Apparently it was a rather grizzly scene."

Blake rolled his eyes at the bad pun.

Niiqway grinned. "We should talk when you get in."

"I'm thinking I'll spend the night in Toronto," he said.

"Okay," she said. "Call me."

She hung up. "He's staying in Toronto."

"Good," said Blake. "You know what to do."

Munson arrived from Edmonton in the evening. Walking past a newspaper kiosk at the base of the CN Tower, he read the headlines. *DROUGHT THREATENS HALF-BILLON WORLDWIDE. REAL CAUSE OF GLOBAL CLIMATE ACCELERATION MYSTIFIES.*

He stood for a moment gathering courage and then took the spectacular elevator ride upward to the observation deck, watching as the city of Toronto stretched out below. Fighting off a wave of vertigo and avoiding the elevator's glass floor area, he tried to reason with himself about his affliction. Acrophobia has been studied by scientists, he recited to himself. To maintain one's balance, one uses both vestibular and visual clues. With acrophobia, one over-relies on visual signals, causing the visual cortex to become overloaded, creating confusion and panic. This can be dangerous, because a person experiencing acrophobia in a high place could either freeze or jump.

You're not afraid when you're behind the controls of a Cessna, he told himself. You feel perfectly safe in a helicopter. This is perfectly safe, too.

Just stay calm.

But as the elevator sped up through the soaring structure, he already felt the creeping panic. Fighting back the vertigo as the elevator came to a stop one hundred and fourteen stories above the city, he staggered forward, clinging to the walls for support. Making his way unsteadily down the inner hallway, he found men's room. The toilets had no lids; the hand dryer was a solid unit. He checked under the sink counter. There it was. He stuffed the note into his pocket and steeled himself for the return journey to good old terra firma.

Retrieving the note, he read it with alarm. It was a photograph of Martha Ambrose, along with what appeared to be the attractive Member of Parliament's home address.

Why were they targeting the minister of energy? Fraser had her pegged as a possible WFFA member. Were they cleaning house? Or had she been included on Dr. Fraser's list by mistake? Was she being targeted for what she knew? Or was she being picked off because—because of her association with him?

He shuddered.

No, probably not. Martha had been with Walpender on the raft, and the arrogant hippo had shot his mouth off. Most likely, Walpender was with WFFA, and behind this.

Niiqway still wasn't answering her phone. He left a message letting her know Ambrose might be in danger, then hailed a cab, hoping there would still be a seat on a late flight back to Ottawa.

Exhausted by the long hours he'd been keeping, Munson pulled into his driveway well past midnight. Glancing upward, he was instantly on alert. Bloody hell! Over on Emily's side of the duplex—was that a beam of light in her bedroom?

Unlocking the door to his own home, he entered, unholstered his gun and inserted his key into the door they'd had installed between the apartments. He held his breath as the lock clicked. Easing the door open, he took off his shoes and, in the darkness, crept upstairs.

At the door to Emily's bedroom, he snapped on the lights. Standing at the foot of the bed was Niiqway, her Colt aimed.

"Niiqway! What the hell?"

She lowered her weapon. "Munson, you must let me explain. Shut off the lights."

"Why?"

"Please, just do it," she said. "And please, point that somewhere else."

"Fine." The streetlights cast strange patterns through the windows. Munson watched Niiqway holster her gun, then he holstered his.

Niiqway sighed. "Munson, since yesterday afternoon I've been trying to clear your sister's name."

"What?"

"The Canadian Transportation Safety Board's preliminary reports state that our flight was bombed. The RCMP and FBI are following a lead that your sister Emily blew up our flight to kill one of the passengers, Adam Sayier, the past vice president of Israel."

What the hell was she talking about?

"They are investigating Emily to see if she bombed the plane. The lead suggests she smuggled a bomb on board our plane in a piece of pre-checked luggage. It has been alleged that she was an undercover Palestinian operative."

Munson found his voice. "But that makes no sense. It's … it's absurd."

"They claim that she was involved with the Palestinians. They say they have evidence of this. They say she hated the Israelis with a passion."

"Preposterous!" He tried to read her expression in the dim light. "Emily was involved with the Palestinians, helping them with poverty issues and education in areas others won't touch because of the politics. She was no terrorist. Her views were moderate. How could anyone make such an allegation? She supported the Palestinian-Israeli peace initiatives. And she knew I was on that flight."

"The lead that they are working from suggests Emily transferred to a different flight at the last minute and thought that you were flying with her—in fact, there was a second seat reserved on her flight in your name. She didn't expect you to be on the AC-990. It boarded at an adjoining gate just before ours—"

"But the whole idea is outrageous! How could she have gotten her luggage on... It makes no sense. They've got their heads up their asses."

"I know. I don't believe this for one second. You are not an insensitive man. You would have suspected something. You would have known."

"Well, thank you for that," Munson said, bitterness rising in his throat. "So, why were you searching Emily's home?"

"The RCMP have requested a search warrant for her unit," she said. "Blake got wind of it and tied it up in red tape for a while, but it *will* be granted tomorrow. I wanted to get here first and see what they're after. Have you ever looked in this locked cedar chest?"

"Hell, no. Emily never locked except her front door. Why would I ever look in her cedar chest?"

"It's locked, Munson. And I haven't found anything else of interest."

Munson reached down to lift the lid.

It was locked.

"Wait! Put on these gloves." She passed him a pair, then knelt in front of the chest. "Hold the penlight on the lock," she said, handing it to him. "Try not to flash it anywhere it can be seen from outside." Carefully, she picked the lock open and raised the lid.

Munson shone the penlight beam over the top tray: newspaper clippings of Israeli army incursions into Lebanon, and vice president Adam Sayier's ordering of the army to retaliate against Lebanese military leaders. There were also papers on bomb-making and terrorist tactics.

Munson stared. "These papers have been planted." He removed the tray. The lower portion of the trunk contained a handgun, grenades and detonator systems, and an incendiary device similar to the ones he'd found on Karim. At the bottom, encased in its original box was a new semi-automatic rifle with several clips of ammunition. "She kept her treasures in here, schooldays stuff and family heirlooms and whatnot. This is a set-up," he said grimly. "Why? By whom? Dragonclaw?"

"Possibly, but the RCMP was tipped off about this by Nate Evans at CSIS. Pretty sure Evans was acting for Walpender. I think they set you up, but I'm not sure why."

"Evans. He's on Fraser's WFFA list."

"Seriously?"

"Yeah, we need to get caught up. First, we'll inventory this stuff."

"You're not going to remove it?" Niiqway put a hand on his arm. "You must!"

"If I remove it, that will just tip them off and they'll try something else. And if they stay one step ahead, I'll never bring them to justice. No, we'll inventory it and leave it. Ah, holy Murphy!" He sat on the bed trying to gather himself. "Thank you Ellen Niiqway. Twenty minutes ago I was ready to throttle you for breaking into my home."

Setting his phone's camera for low-light conditions and turning off the flash, he photographed everything, focusing on the markings on the hardware. Then they refilled the cedar chest as they'd found it.

"Come next door," he said. "We really need to talk."

On his side of the duplex, he put on the kettle and got out a couple of mugs.

"So Dr. Fraser was aware of the WFFA?"

"Whitey says they were hassling her. At least, that's who she thought it was." Munson pushed the basket of teabags over to Niiqway, and she selected a chocolate chai. "There was a list of possible WFFA members on her USB drive."

"And Nate Evans was on her list?"

"As a possibility, along with a bunch of my people." He dug the printout from his pocket and passed it to her. "And Ambrose—oh, did you get my message?"

"Yeah," said Niiqway. "You said she might be in danger. What's that about?"

"Karim's orders." He felt himself reddening. "I didn't tell you—I got his next assignment from his phone. Did you get to his body before the bears?"

She gave him a strange look. "It's been taken care of."

"Well, what about Ambrose?"

"I called Blake when I got your message. He has a detail on her. You'd better fill him in tomorrow. You think there was a reason for her to be on Fraser's WFFA list?"

"Looked pretty speculative to me. Heck, I'm on it." He grinned. "She'd ruled me out, though. Nice little x beside my name. Whitey translated. Oh, Mercier was on it, too."

She glanced down at the list. "Roland Mercier, her boy-friend?"

"Yeah, although from what Whitey was telling me, she might have been using Mercier to figure out who else was involved. She was in Saint-Tropez on his yacht with him, and Whitey says that key with Fraser's USB drive was probably for his yacht."

Niiqway nodded. "The *Cannelle*."

"Whitey's pretty sure Dr. Fraser found out something down there that got her killed."

"So it wasn't about her discovery itself?"

"Could have been both. Whitey was trying to get her to hold off on announcing it until she'd had it vetted, and he says it would still have been too expensive to give fossil fuels a run for their money."

Niiqway frowned. "Is he vetting it?"

"No, he's taking it to someone better qualified, down in California."

"Where did you find Whitey?"

"I promised him I wouldn't tell," said Munson, although he wouldn't have been surprised she already knew.

"We need to bring Blake up to speed." Niiqway sipped her tea. "Can you meet me at CSIS headquarters tomorrow, say 1:00?"

"Sure."

"Although with Nate Evans in charge of CSIS now—Blake and I have our suspicions about him, and it looks like Fraser did, too. Maybe we should have Blake meet us somewhere else. I want his permission to follow up on this Saint-Tropez connection."

"Bring him by my office instead."

She nodded. "Good idea. No, wait. I'm in Toronto tomorrow."

"Well, send him by and I'll fill him in." Munson ran the list through his scanner and handed her a copy. "Want some company in Saint-Tropez? I might have a line on a yacht there."

She grinned. "I'll try to book us out of Toronto"—she looked at her watch—"tomorrow morning. Good lord, I need to get home and get some sleep."

"Guest bed's available if you want it."

She winked at him. "What would the neighbors think?"

Whatever they want, thought Munson as he watched her cross the street to her SUV. Let 'em think whatever they want.

CHAPTER 15

Munson's line buzzed just ahead of 10:00. "Munson, Scott Blake is here to see you."

"Thanks, Addy. Send him on in."

He waved the deputy director to a chair. Blake had lost weight and his skin had an unhealthy pallor. He read Munson's concern. "Pneumonia. Can't seem to shake it. Guess I should have taken a few weeks off, but there's too much going on, and as I'm sure Niiqway told you, we just don't know who to trust."

Munson nodded.

"Thanks for adjusting your schedule. Niiqway said we needed to talk. What's on your mind?"

Munson handed over the note from the CN Tower. He'd encased it in a clear plastic sheet protector. "I've tried not to handle it too much."

"This does seem to imply a threat to Martha Ambrose," said Blake.

"You think it's WFFA?"

"More likely Dragonclaw," said Blake.

"I don't get the relationship," said Munson. "Who is pulling the strings?"

"Dragonclaw seems to be manipulating Kao and the WFFA, among others. His primary objective seems to be helping China get whatever they want. Arable land, fresh water, and oil are at the top of that list, and Canada has them all—in spades. The Saudi problem only makes our resources even more valuable to China."

"Yeah, and Russia wants Canada's Arctic for its oil, too. Is Dragonclaw likely to be someone I worked with in the oil industry?"

"Maybe." Blake grinned. "Some think it could be you."

"Yeah, right. I'm a goddamned Chinese spy!"

"You think I'm kidding," said Blake. "Dragonclaw came from California fairly recently, just as you did. Of course, your own rather sudden relocation to Ottawa may be pure coincidence."

"It wasn't sudden," Munson assured him. "We'd been hashing over the pros and cons for some time. It was getting too complicated to get work visas for our Canadian team members."

"Mm. Also, Dragonclaw has access to the same kind of confidential government information that your firm has acquired." Blake eyed Munson carefully. "You fit our profile, and so does your partner, Harrigan."

"But you know that's preposterous! I am a scientist, a marine geologist, not a bloody political extremist—or a terrorist. And neither is Irish Harrigan."

"We looked at your young geologists—Akira Tanaka, a clever and capable young woman who seems passionate about global climate change; Kim Sorqaq, who seems to believe that the rest of the world is hell-bent on destroying the Inuit way of life; and Pavel Krotov, who is by far the most ambitious of the three."

Munson nodded; the descriptions were apt.

"But none of you fit perfectly. By the way, Sorqaq's been in contact with Kao."

"Kao called *him*, right?" Munson realized he was being defensive, and adjusted his tone of voice. "That's not Kim's doing."

"Well, as I said, none of you fit perfectly." Blake smiled reassuringly. "I know it isn't you. If I still had any suspicions I would never have given you a CSIS identity. Have you gotten anywhere with Telford?"

Munson shook his head. "He's totally under Kao's

114

shapely thumb. The woman's brilliant, and she strikes me as cold as ice."

"Are they … involved?"

"That's the impression I got."

Blake grimaced. "Well, see what you can do. Now." He leaned forward and lowered his voice. "I'm struggling with my health, and as Niiqway's already told you, I don't trust my chain of command. She's going to need some help if I'm knocked flat on my back again, and she seems to trust you."

Well, that was something.

"In Washington last week there was a cabinet meeting," Blake said. "U.S. Vice President Diane Stone delivered a concise message: the American policy of reducing dependency on offshore oil had resulted in their loss of control over foreign reserves. She said an exception was their continuing reliance on Saudi imports, so for the Americans the imminent failure of Saudi oil production was catastrophic."

Munson nodded. "Go on."

"Stone claimed that to offset such a loss, the Americans would need *all* of Canada's oil. This would force curtailment of Canada's western province negotiations to export oil to China. At that point the Americans would be head-to-head with China, who will be desperate for the same oil. Further, she said it was now urgent that the Americans have us ramp up our oil sands production, over-riding stiff worldwide environmental opp … opp—excuse me—opposition." Blake leaned back, struggling with a fit of coughing.

Munson pushed a tissue box across the desk.

"Thanks. And here's the kicker," Blake continued. "If China doesn't back off, she said, the Americans would be forced to seize control of our oilfields."

Munson frowned. "They mean to *invade* Canada."

"Yes. Stone told the Cabinet that Canada has a weak and inexperienced prime minister with a novice, unpredictable minority government. The U.S. State Department has told them that Telford and his Cabinet are dangerously pro-China. They already know for a fact that he is very strongly anti-American, and they don't trust him at all under these circumstances." Blake managed to suppress another coughing fit. "Here is the most troubling part. For now, the U.S. president has ordered that they stop sharing military intelligence with our government."

"That really *is* ominous." Munson shook his head. "Especially with the Saudi oil failure, since Russia is now such a threat to our Arctic. Has the prime minister been briefed on all this?"

Blake groaned. "I have no way of knowing. Our new director, Nate Evans, has taken over the file." He glanced at his watch. "I have an 11:00 meeting with the minister of defense today. I understand one of your crews is doing some research on Ellesmere Island?"

Munson nodded. "Smith Sound area. Why?"

"A local climate researcher called in a report of a submarine with jihadist symbols on its turret, skulking around just north of Smith Bay. Interesting timing, given that we're trying to convince the government not to leave our northern borders unprotected. Your expertise in the area could be helpful. How about coming along?"

"Sure. I'm really troubled by this new policy." Munson buzzed Addy and told her he'd be out for the rest of the afternoon.

The meeting was in the east wing of the Parliament Buildings. As they arrived, Blake made the introductions.

"Dr. Munson, a marine geologist who specializes in the Arctic, is a principal of Munson-Harrigan Associates here in Ottawa. I've asked him to join us." With a wave of his arm he introduced the table. "Rosaire Lacroix, our Minister of Defense; Colonel Frank Raigan, Arctic Command C.O.; Assistant Commissioner Andrew Talbot, RCMP; our new director here at CSIS, Nate Evans; and Martha Ambrose, our Minister of Energy and Northern Affairs. Please be seated. We are here to discuss the sighting of a foreign sub in Baffin Bay."

Minister of Defense Rosaire Lacroix turned to Munson. "So you are the notorious Dr. Munson who revealed the end of Saudi oil. You spiked oil prices to over two hundred dollars a barrel and edged us toward an oil war."

"I'll certainly agree that I could have handled that disclosure better," said Munson evenly.

"You *certainly* could have warned us first."

"Ideally, I would have," Munson agreed.

Blake sighed. "That's not what we're here for. Let's get on with it. Raigan?"

Colonel Raigan stood and switched on the projection screen, revealing a photo of a sub barely visible through cloud cover. "This is the sub we've been told about," he said. "It's an older Russian sub. Given the markings eyewitnesses saw on its turret, we believe it's in the hands of jihadists." He scrolled to another slide. "It was spotted late yesterday, about here." He pointed to Cadogan Inlet, on the eastern coast of Ellesmere Island. "Our satellite images show several unidentified camps in the area." The map showed a smattering of red dots from Cape Mouat north to Pim Island. "Here's a close-up view of the one we're most concerned with." He zoomed in to show one near Easter Island.

Blake turned to Munson. "Dr. Munson, you've spent time in the north. Any idea what they're up to?"

Munson got up and walked to the screen. "On shore, I make out four two-man tents. This—" he pointed — "looks like an ROV with underwater imaging equipment. It's probably an eight-man camp. My guess is an exploration crew. No paperwork filed?"

Blake shook his head. "That's what concerns us."

"Might just be a filing issue," said Munson, making a mental note to have Addy confirm Sorqaq's paperwork was properly done. "I'd be more concerned about the sub. It's actually one of Russia's newer models. They have enormous on-deck fire power. Their deck cannon is a super-gun that can fire a thousand rounds per minute."

Colonel Raigan frowned. "You are not a trained military observer. I'm afraid you are mistaken, Dr. Munson."

Raigan had chosen to misidentify the sub. Why? Munson recalled where he'd seen Raigan's name: Dr. Fraser's list of potential WFFA members. He raised his chin. "With all due respect, Colonel, as a Canadian military veteran and an Arctic scientist, I've made it my business to recognize vessels of neighboring Arctic countries."

"Colonel?" Minister Lacroix leaned forward. "Are you certain of your identification?"

"Of course, Minister."

Lacroix turned back to Munson. "In your opinion, what are they after?"

"I can't say for sure, Mr. Minister. That looks like the equipment we use for mapping underwater gas hydrate concentrations. It may be completely unrelated to the sub, but if does appear the Russians are up to something. That's some big firepower to be—"

CSIS Director Evans shook his head. "Colon Raigan disagrees, Dr. Munson."

"Let me clarify, then," said Munson. "The reason this can be identified as a newer sub is the remotely operated vessel clamps on its aft deck. If you'll go back to that image..." He waited while Raigan grudgingly clicked back through the slides, then pointed to the dark spots on the sub's flat afterdeck. "The older ones didn't have those."

Evans frowned. "Those look like shadows."

"The image is fuzzy, but that's what—"

"I'll go with Raigan's word," said Evans.

"Let that go, and think!" Lacroix urged. "What could they be after in our Arctic waters? Does anyone have other theories? For example, could it be a scientific study?"

"There *is* an Arctic study going on," said Munson. "It

may be part of the scientific exploration to check for the presence of underwater methyl hydrates. The Russians, along with other NORC nations including ourselves are studying this. However this doesn't answer the report of painted jihadist symbols on the sub's decks. What's that about?"

Raigan snorted. "We are not going to base this on the word of some Eskimo hunter."

"I'm told the Inuit man that you speak of is a climate researcher," Munson said evenly. "He is likely a university graduate."

"Your brilliant researcher probably *misidentified* the markings," said Raigan.

Martha Ambrose leaned forward. "So the camp at Easter Island may or may not be connected to the sub, which may or may not be Russian. If they're connected, it could be a scientific study. Or, could it be a clever ploy to have us watch their sub while they're up to something else? A distraction, to keep us focused on the wrong thing." She glanced pointedly around the table, her eyes resting on the Minister of Defense. "We should properly identify the trespassers and determine why they are violating our territory. Then we can respond appropriately."

"That is my preference." Lacroix agreed. "Yes. We'll observe them and have an Integrated National Security Enforcement Team investigate. INSET will positively identify both the sub, and the camp. The team will include RCMP and CSIS."

Talbot and Evans nodded.

Lacroix turned to Munson. "I apologize for my harsh comments, earlier, Dr. Munson. Given your Arctic experience, perhaps you could assess whether or not their purpose is scientific. Would you agree to go along with the team?"

"Good idea," Blake nodded. "I'm puzzled by the underwater imaging equipment. We also need an oceanographer to assess what that camp's up to."

Munson glanced at Blake. Smooth.

"We have one." Blake continued. "Agent Niiqway is an oceanographer."

Defense Minister Lacroix leaned forward. "Will you agree to go along, Dr. Munson?"

"When will you leave?" Munson asked.

"Tomorrow."

"Tomorrow?" Evans shook his head. "Not a chance we'll be ready that soon. Three days at the earliest."

"Three days?" Lacroix scowled. "That's—"

"In the meantime," Evans interrupted smoothly, "we'll continue to monitor them by satellite."

Lacroix looked skeptical, but he turned to Munson. "Munson?"

Munson considered. He and Niiqway were on their way to France, so Evans' delay could work in his favor. Would there be time? But he was very curious about the sub, and about why Raigan was so obviously misleading the committee. "Okay," he said, "I'll clear my calendar."

As the meeting ended, Martha approached. "I'm simply delighted to see you here," she began, tossing her red hair and taking Munson's arm. "You're comin' to my place for lunch. You're goin' to tell me about Saudi Arabia over a bottle of Chablis." She pressed a slip of paper into his hand. "It's just five minutes from here, so I'll be expectin' you in no more than fifteen. And no, I'm not taking no for an answer."

It was difficult to object to Martha Ambrose when she had the bit in her teeth, and anyway he wanted to talk to her about the threat to her life. He nodded, and she grinned, turning to one of her security detail. "See this good-lookin' man, here? Ya'll be lettin' him in when he shows up at my apartment. Now let's get a-movin', boys, 'cause I have company comin' and I need a couple minutes to prepare."

Minutes later, while they prepared a salad and sandwiches in Martha's swank Ottawa apartment, she broached the subject. "So, I understand you're responsible for my new security detail. How'd that come about?"

"Just in the right place at the right time," he said. "From what I understand, the hit man's been linked to Chinese intelligence. Why would they be after you, Martha?"

"Probably because I'm one of the people proposin' new federal environmental controls on the huge new pipeline construction project to the western coast. It's delayin' the project. In fact, it's pretty much stopped it."

She moved to top up his wine glass, but he shook his head. "Thanks, I'm driving. What are you going to do about the threat?"

"Nothin'. I'm not gonna be swayed by some crazy in big oil. That reminds me, you were an oilman. You ever hear of an organization by the name of WFFA? Stands for World Fossil Fuel Association, I think."

He nodded. "Just recently."

"Me, too. What's your take on them?"

"From the little I know, they're an international lobbying group. Big oil, of course."

"That's what I'm hearin'." She passed him the plate of cookies. "I'm also hearin' they're not too concerned with keepin' it legal."

"Think they're behind the threat on your life?"

She tilted her head. "Maybe. I suppose it makes more sense than Chinese intelligence, although maybe they're one and the same. Speaking of intelligence: Funny coincidence, Agent Niiqway being on the raft and all."

He shrugged. "She was tailing me at the time."

She raised her eyebrows. "You like her?"

Munson felt himself redden. "I'm not sure I trust her."

"I see," said Martha. "Well, that gives me the perfect reason to check out my competition."

Munson choked on his cookie, and she grinned, passing him his water glass. "Gal's always gotta know what she's up against. Now, that's enough about me. How are you, really?"

He tried to keep it light, but by the time Martha was loading the dishwasher, Munson found himself talking about Emily. "I never considered not having her in my life," he said, handing her the last of the plates.

Martha gave his arm a gentle squeeze. "I can't imagine what it must be like to lose someone so close to you," she said, regarding him seriously for a moment.

Munson swallowed hard, concentrating on wiping the counter while Martha leaned over the dishwasher, shuffled a few dishes and pulled the door closed. "Thanks for the help," she said lightly. "Coffee?"

He considered, then shook his head. "I should be on my way," he said. "You've listened to me ramble enough for one day."

"My absolute pleasure," she smiled. "Come ramble any ol' time."

He collected his jacket and said goodbye, suppressing an urge to kiss her.

CHAPTER 16

It was late when Niiqway called Munson's cell. "Have you checked in?"

"Yes," he said. "I'm at the Four Seasons. You somewhere nearby?"

"I live not too far away." She considered a moment. "Why don't I meet you in the lounge at your hotel? Save you having to go out again."

"Sure," he said.

"Great. I'll be there in fifteen." She hung up.

She found him seated in a booth with his back to the wall, and settled in alongside him.

"Hi," he said. "What can they get you?"

"A decaf, thanks. How did your meeting go?"

He motioned to the waiter. "Not great."

"I'm not surprised," said Niiqway. "That deck was stacked against you. I did some digging. I've confirmed that Nate Evans was propelled into the influential position of director at CSIS by our friend, Ying Kao. She recommended Evans for the position and after some quick vetting, Joe Telford confirmed it."

"Kao has her long and ever-so-elegant fingers in every pie." Munson's eyes narrowed. "Are you sure she's not Dragonclaw?"

"Not sure of anything at this point," said Niiqway. "Nate Evans is formerly Nate Evanishyn, who immigrated to Canada from Hong Kong with his family as a teenager. His father was a member of the Russian Consulate in Hong

123

Kong in the nineties. Over the years he became a well-educated and trusted member of the Ontario elite. Remade himself as Nate Evans just before entering university."

"Russian, huh?" Munson stroked his chin. "And there's a Russian sub in the Arctic right now."

"Russia has designs on Canada's oil-bearing Arctic to add to their production capacity."

"Yeah, but try telling Telford that." Munson shook his head. "What else did you find out about Nate Evans?"

Niiqway sipped her coffee. "In his youth, he was a radical left-winger who spoke fluent English, Russian and Cantonese. His subversive leanings had been ingrained from childhood. He still has contacts with the Russians. As Nate Evans, he became a successful Ontario criminal lawyer. He's kept his track record beyond reproach."

"What's with this Colonel Raigan fellow?"

She'd heard from Blake about the two men's disagreement over the sub; clearly, anyone inspecting the photos could see that Munson was right.

"We don't know if he's being threatened and lying out of fear. I suppose he may believe what he's saying, in which case he's suffering early-onset dementia and ought to be relieved of his post."

"Oh. No, I doubt that's the case," said Munson.

"Lighten up, I was kidding. Anyway, he's been on our radar for a while. Fraser had an X beside his name on her WFFA list; I'm not sure why she'd ruled him out for that. His name has also come up in connection to Dragonclaw."

Munson shook his head. "So now we have Nate Evans heading up CSIS, Ying Kao influencing the government, and Colonel Raigan controlling the Arctic military. And they all have connections to WFFA, Dragonclaw, or both. But who the hell is this Dragonclaw?"

"That's the question."

"Your source of all this?"

"My sources are solid."

"Are you sure?"

She studied him. "Of course I'm sure." Munson really needed to deal with his trust issues. "Oh, and by the way, for the past few days I have been followed by someone. I caught a glimpse of him, but that's all. I'm reasonably certain it's Hawk."

Munson cursed under his breath. "I was hoping he'd tail me. I want to lure him out into the open."

"Apparently he hangs around the strip clubs when he's in a city," said Niiqway. "He favors the crowded, dingy ones frequented by druggies and prostitutes."

"Like the Fallen Figleaf?"

That was a surprise. "He's damned dangerous, Munson. Don't do anything rash."

He said nothing.

She passed him an envelope. "Our flight information's in here. We need to be at Pearson by 4:15." She grinned. "That's a.m."

He glanced at his watch. "Better get some shut-eye, then. You have far to drive?"

"Nope." She stood. "See you bright and early."

Munson slid some cash under his saucer. "I'll walk you to your car."

"No need."

"Ah, but I insist," he said, placing his hand on the small of her back. "I need to stretch my legs."

Damn, he was persistent. Might as well get on with it. No shaking him at the parkade, either; he had to come over and admire her Mustang. "Looks good in white," he said. "How often do you get to run her with the top down?"

"Not often," she confessed. "Spending too much time in Ottawa. Might be time for a career change."

"Back to oceanography?"

"My first love." She fired it up.

"Sounds great," he said, and it took her a moment to realize he meant the engine.

"Have a good night, Munson."

"You, too."

The Fallen Figleaf was dark and crowded and the band was loud, but as Munson sat watching the dancers, he was oblivious to the oppressive noise. He had chosen a table in the deep shadows on the mezzanine where he had a good view of the dance floor, as well as the main entry to the club. If he was lucky, the Hawk should arrive anytime now.

He didn't have long to wait. The tall lean man with the hawk-like face appeared on the mezzanine from the rear hallway and took a seat in the far corner. Munson had slipped his gun from its holster and was edging nearer when an unusual movement on the dance floor caught his eye. A hooded figure wove through the crowd toward the mezzanine stairway, then up the stairs, pausing directly in front of the Hawk's table. The Hawk glanced up, reached into his coat and began to rise, gun in hand, then jerked backwards and settled back into his booth, his gun dropping unfired to the floor. His assassin continued across the mezzanine, down the stairs and out the exit.

Shaking off his shock, Munson strode after the shooter, arriving in the parking lot to catch a glimpse of a white ragtop Mustang, tires chirping as it sped toward the freeway.

Watching the tail lights disappear, he considered the speed with which the Hawk had pulled his weapon and whistled softly.

Niiqway had probably saved his life.

It was still dark when Munson arrived at Pearson International. Niiqway was there to meet him. "Munson, I have news."

"At this hour?"

"CSIS never sleeps." She grinned. "They lifted prints from a couple of items in Emily's cedar chest. Hawk's."

126

"So she's cleared?"

"No, because she could have gotten those items from him. But there's no evidence she did."

"Maybe he'll tell us where he got them from." Munson's tone was more sarcastic than he'd meant it to be.

Her eyes narrowed. "Not likely."

"You've probably taken out one the person who could have cleared Emily."

"And if I hadn't?"

She was right, of course. He would have done it himself. Or died trying.

She nudged him. "Hawk would never have talked," she said. "There was a second set of prints, and they weren't Emily's. We'll find a way to prove her innocence." Their boarding area was coming to life, and she lowered her voice. "There's more. We have uncovered evidence of a pending lawsuit involving the use of melded fiber used on the wings of the AC-990. It may have been lighting strike."

Munson thought back. That flash of light as the cabin blew apart. Was it a lightning strike, or an explosion?

"I think the aircraft design was flawed and Walpender wants to derail that part of the investigation with this plot to involve Emily."

"Hmm."

"Now," she said, "about your protégé, Kim Sorqaq, we've been following up on him too. You arranged his summer jobs while he attended U of M."

Munson felt tired. "I helped him get summer jobs. Yes. He worked on a survey vessel in the high Arctic."

"What was he doing?"

"They were mapping underwater gas hydrate concentrations along the coast and—" He stopped short.

That equipment he'd seen on the satellite images of the Russian sub.

Kao had been altogether too interested in his father's story of the missing nuke.

And Kao had been trying to contact Kim. "You may be

right about Kim, but this is not the best subject for airport talk," said Munson. "I'll explain on the way to the yacht."

Niiqway, who had been leading the way along the pier, stopped counting slips and looked up. "Wow," she said. There in all her glory was the *Cannelle*. Her hull color was striking—a soft, creamy butterscotch. She was a sleek, modern eighty foot motor yacht, hatches secured, rigging stored.

They climbed aboard and Munson inserted the key in the lock. The door swung open to a luxurious salon, dining area, galley and pilot house, all at deck level. Below were crew quarters and the staterooms, one of which had been used recently.

"Looks pretty new," said Niiqway.

In the pilothouse, chart storage held registration documents. The owner was Rolande Mercier of Marseilles. "You were right about it being new, Niiqway," said Munson. The yacht had only a few hours on its diesels. "Built in Italy, purchased by a numbered company and transferred to Rolande Mercier for a sum of one U.S. dollar."

"Payoff," she said. "The log says Mercier and Fraser took a little cruise two days before the AC-990 crash."

"Can't have gone far," he said. "Damn, the yacht's GPS has been erased."

A thorough search turned up nothing more. Niiqway had already disembarked while Munson did one last pass, and locked up.

He found Niiqway talking to an elderly woman on the neighboring yacht. She eyed him suspiciously.

"Hello," said Munson.

Niiqway took his elbow. "Honey, I was just telling Marge how kind it was of Uncle Roland to let us use his yacht for the weekend."

Munson eyed her. "Very generous," he agreed, turning to the woman. "Good old Uncle Roland."

"Well," said Marge, "you tell your uncle for me that he better not let that last bunch aboard again."

"Oh, dear," said Munson. "Was there a problem?"

"Big argument," said Marge, darkly. "Thought for sure someone was going to go overboard. Lucky there wasn't any damage."

Niiqway looked at Munson. "Oh, I hope it wasn't Cousin Fred. He has such low-life friends."

"This bunch looked pretty darned high-falutin," said Marge. "Just *acted* low-life, fighting over that woman."

"A woman!" Niiqway shook her head. "Well, now, that doesn't sound like Fred. Tall, skinny guy with a really bad complexion?"

"One of them was tall, but hardly what anyone would call skinny," said Marge. "Great big fat man. Other guy was skinny, but real short."

"Could have been Uncle James," suggested Munson.

"Or Ralph," said Niiqway. "You know how he gets."

Munson frowned. "Maybe." He turned to Marge. "Did you get a good look at the woman?"

"Sure did," said Marge, pulling her cell phone from her pocket. "Took a couple photos just in case the police came to ask questions. Just let me… no, not …there, that's them." She held out her phone for Niiqway.

"That's Ralph, alright," said Niiqway triumphantly. "With another woman. Poor Celia. Of course, she'll never believe it. Marge, can I take a photo of this?"

"Why sure, honey," said Marge. "Here, I'll zoom it in. Got it? There's a couple more here, too."

Munson looked on as Marge gleefully showed Niiqway a few more photos of his former boss, Max Bolavar, on board the *Cannelle* with David Walpender and the beautiful Ying Kao.

During the drive back to the airport, Niiqway considered passing her phone to Munson so he could download the photos. Better not, she thought; she needed to clear a few things off it first. "Tell me about Max Bolavar," she said.

"Not a lot to tell," said Munson. "He's brilliant, creative and resourceful; great strategist. Galaxy-21 was rocketing to the top of the industry, thanks largely to him. But he had a bit of a ruthless streak, too. The longer I was there, the less comfortable I was with his methods."

"Illegal?"

"No; just immoral. Well, in my book. You know something funny, though? He helped fund Emily's work, gave her seed money for some of her projects. Even acted as consultant for a couple of them."

"What kind of projects?"

"A couple of green energy initiatives that didn't work out, and a couple of humanitarian initiatives that did."

Niiqway glanced at him. "Why did the green initiatives fail?"

"Good question. There seemed to be terrible luck with roadblocks—"Munson scowled. "You're suggesting he was actually in it to keep her from succeeding?"

"Maybe." Traffic was light on the freeway, and Niiqway glanced in the mirror. The black SUV that had been tailing them was still there, still keeping its distance. "How about the humanitarian projects—where were they?"

"Palestine, and the Arctic. She was—"

"Get down!" The SUV had accelerated suddenly and was pulling alongside. As bullets smashed through the side window Niiqway braked hard, then swerved through traffic and down an off-ramp, zigzagging through a busy intersection and onto the secondary highway.

Munson swiveled to look back at the overpass. "Looks like they've been in a fender-bender," he said.

An approaching police car's emergency lights flashed on and Niiqway pulled over, watching her mirrors as it sped toward the accident scene on the overpass.

"That'll hold 'em a while," said Munson. "WFFA, you figure?"

"Maybe," said Niiqway. "Maybe Dragonclaw." Maybe even CSIS. Munson had very visibly stowed Fraser's flash drive at his bank in Ottawa, so wasn't about that. They'd probably drawn fire for what Marge had told them.

Shit.

She hoped Marge was okay.

In the boarding area for their connecting flight from Paris, Munson's junior partner Akira Tanaka joined them. Earnest and passionate, she reminded Niiqway of a hippy aunt she'd loved as a child.

"Where's Irish?" Munson asked.

"He's staying on," said Akira. "Met up with some people he wanted to talk shop with, and figured he'd extend his stay."

"Conference worthwhile?"

"Totally!"

As Akira launched into a long and enthusiastic description, Niiqway reached for Munson's cell phone and mimed transferring photos. He nodded.

Niiqway took the opportunity to thumb through his phone's contact list. Nothing surprising. She wondered if he had more than one phone.

She finished the transfer, passed his phone back, and waited for their flight to be called.

CHAPTER 17

The connection from Toronto was delayed. Munson arrived home in the wee hours, downed a couple of drinks while browsing the news headlines, and dragged himself to the shower.

There was no hot water. Cursing, he wrapped himself in a towel and checked the breaker box; nothing amiss. He checked Emily's side of the duplex to make sure nothing was leaking from their shared hot water system; no sign of a problem. Probably a burned-out element. Exasperated, he called a cab. While pulling on clothes and packing a bag, he downed yet another Scotch.

At the hotel he took a long, hot shower and slept until the alarm woke him. After a quick breakfast he hailed a cab to take him back for his car. Arriving at his street, he saw a smoking ruin with police tape blocking entry.

He stood with his neighbors, staring at the burned rubble that had been the home he'd once shared with Emily. The explosion had blown the lower level walls out, dropping the second floor of both units to the foundation. It had all burned to ash, leaving only scorched freestanding masonry. The shell of his fifteen-year-old Chevrolet still sat in the driveway.

Was this a freak accident—something related to the hot water tank? Somehow, he doubted it.

"We thought you was a-goner." Munson turned to a small cluster of neighbors. "She blew up at three in the morning. Bet it was a gas leak."

"Nah, cops say it was a bomb," argued the woman who lived next door to Emily's side.

"Yeah," an old fellow from down the street added. "I was up havin' a pee when I heard the 'splosion. I mighta seen the guy that done it."

"What kind of car?" Munson asked.

"Lincoln Navigator," the man nodded gravely, enjoying the importance of his disclosure. "Light grey, maybe silver."

Munson frowned as he climbed back into the cab. Irish drove an old silver Navigator.

Bomb or no bomb, he was mighty lucky—if luck had anything to do with it. "Might as well head to the office," he said to the cabbie. "There's nothing left here."

Irish's Navigator sat in its usual spot in the company's parking lot; the keys were on their hook in the executive men's room. Munson tried to reach Irish, but could not make contact. He shook his head, refusing to believe his partner had been responsible for the explosion.

He spent the few hours working at his office, ensuring that everything was running smoothly while he once again re-adjusted his shattered life. He was just leaving the office for an appointment with Telford when Whitey called.

"I saw the news, Munson. Sorry about your home. I have a suggestion."

"Are you okay Whitey? I tried to contact—"

"I'm fine so far, but things are getting sticky. Is this connection secure?"

"I don't know. I think so."

After a hesitation, Whitey said, "I'm keeping *it* on me. Are you?"

"No; I put mine in a safe place a while back."

"We may have to release it quickly on the net if something happens to one of us," Whitey said. "I'm sending a list of addresses to your phone. In an emergency, you can plug in the jump stick and send it out to my address list."

"Okay. Who's on the list?"

"Twenty of the world's leading universities."

"Okay, I read you."

"Good. You take care."

As Munson debated heading to the bank on his way to the Parliament Buildings, his phone rang again: Martha Ambrose. She was her usual flamboyant self, but he found he was not in the mood for her upbeat personality. Adding to his black mood, his cell phone cut out. He called her back.

"Sorry, Martha, I'm in a miserable mood," he said.

"Nonsense. Nothin' can be that bad. What the heck is that buzzin' noise?"

"My phone's in a bad mood, too. I'll have to—Hello?"

The line had gone dead again. Addy wasn't at her desk; he'd have to ask her to deal with it when he got back.

Munson strode down the steps of the Parliament Buildings, shaking his head. Telford was a damned stubborn man. The photos of Kao with Walpender and Bolavar meant nothing, he insisted—nothing at all. Although Munson thought he'd detected a bit of jealousy, Telford certainly gave no sign he thought Kao was involved in any kind of conspiracy. When Munson suggested it, Telford had laughed in his face, flipped his desk calendar open, said he'd forgotten a meeting, and effectively evicted Munson from his office.

"Well, there's a sight for sore eyes!"

He turned to see Martha Ambrose exiting the building behind him, flanked by a couple of men in dark suits.

She raised her eyebrows. "My, my. What's got you all hot and bothered? And can I be of any help?"

Munson couldn't help grinning at her suggestive tone.

"That's better," she said, hooking her arm through his. "Come for lunch, Munson. These bodyguard types don't get to fraternize at all—it's not one bit like the movies. I need the pleasure of your company."

One of the bodyguards was beginning to intervene, so

Munson flashed his CSIS badge, then allowed Ambrose to lead him to the waiting SUV. "Martha, I need cheering up," he said. "You are perfect."

She beamed, tossing her red hair happily and pulling him closer. "What a wonderful thing to say."

At her apartment, she told the suits to wait outside. "Ya'll don't contribute to the conversation anyway." She closed the door and helped Munson out of his jacket. "Don't worry, they'll be just fine. I'll send them out some sandwiches and coffee. Maybe even a chair so they can quit standin' at attention for a while."

He grinned happily. "It's good to see you, Martha."

"Where *have* you been? I was expecting to hear from you, and then you said you were in a bad mood before your phone cut out. I'm gonna trust you that's what happened. Let's see, we have some biscuits..." After waving him to a stool, she bustled around her kitchen. Her moss green suit hugged her curves.

"That's a great color on you," he said. Lame. What he meant was that she was very, very attractive. "So, has anyone figured out why you're on a hit list?"

"Nah, not yet."

"Should you be going out?"

"My place of work is pretty darned secure, and I have my lovely security escort. Pretty sure I'll be fine."

"It's not enough Martha."

"I won't be intimidated." She brushed it off with a wave of her hand. "Now, where have you been?"

Munson told her about his apartment.

"That was your place?" Her eyes were wide. "My god, Munson. You could have been killed! Was it an accident?"

He shrugged. "My hot water tank was on the fritz, which was why I'd gone to a hotel for the night. Guess they'll let me know when they've finished their investigation. Who knows how long that'll take."

"Where will you stay? Want to crash here?"

He shook his head. "What will the neighbors think?"

"Who cares?" She grinned. "We could always give 'em somethin' to talk about. But I've been trying to reach you for a couple of days, make sure you're eatin' an' all that." She pulled her lips into a very attractive pout. "You been screenin' my calls?"

Munson filled her in on the trip to Saint Tropez and the attempt on his life. Once he started spilling, he couldn't seem to stop; he told her about Dragonclaw, Kao, Walpender, the discovery, everything.

"My god, Munson, what have *I* got that they want to eliminate me for? It must be more than just my position on the pipe line."

"In your case, I'm not sure—but be careful, and don't trust Kao."

"I'll be careful."

"And…" Munson paused. "Martha, I don't know if there's a way to do this discreetly, but…there's something about Niiqway."

She raised her eyebrows.

"I don't entirely trust her. I know you were kidding about checking her out, but can you—"

"I'll see what I can do."

"Thanks for lunch." He stood, and she came to put her arms around him.

"Oh, you're not goin' are you?"

"I must." She was soft and warm, and if he didn't get out of here soon he really would be giving her bodyguards something to talk about.

"Let me give you a lift," she said, kissing his cheek.

He grinned. "You give me a huge lift when I see you. I do have to go, but I would like to call you. Perhaps we could have dinner soon—"

"Alright, alright." She released him and followed him to the door. "You call me soon, Munson. And stay safe."

Back at the office, Munson stopped at Addy's tidy desk.

"Can you do something with this?" He handed her his phone. "Damn thing's messed up. Is Irish back yet?"

She nodded toward his door. "Got in about an hour ago. He's alone."

Munson headed into in his office. "Irish, welcome back. Good trip?"

Irish shrugged. "Paris was Paris. Not half as exciting as your neighborhood, I hear."

"Yeah," said Munson, dropping into a chair.

"You need a place to stay for a couple of days?"

Munson shook his head. "I'm headed north anyway. Addy's already bought me a new wardrobe; tailor's just making a few adjustments. So, what's the latest scuttlebutt on geo-engineering?"

"It is a ridiculous manipulation of the environment, what else?" Irish grinned. "They're worried about human survival following what they continue to call 'the acceleration.' They talk about rising sea levels, flooding coastal cities, drought and severe weather events like the U.S. is now experiencing. They're obsessed with earthquakes, tornados changing ocean currents, CO_2 and stuff. Bunch of crazies—"

"Okay, okay, skip the sarcastic introduction."

"They're looking at ways of slowing the warming process to enable world populations to adapt. These guys are working on solar umbrellas and other ridiculous things."

"Akira seemed much more impressed than you are."

"Yeah." Irish waved a hand. "The naiveté of youth. They're talking of creating more marine strata-cumulous clouds over oceans, to reflect sunlight back into space. They're seeding the oceans with billions of iron particles to beef up plankton growth. I'm sick of it. We should focus on creating efficient, sustainable systems that don't impoverish third world countries, and that don't cause more environmental problems than they solve."

Munson nodded sagely, and Irish grinned.

"On a more pressing matter, we have to talk. Our business has been spending way too much looking for that platinum source."

"I'm sorry you think so."

"Just facing facts, Munson. We need to call it off."

Munson sighed. "I have to go north within the next couple of days," he said. "Maybe let me see what they've done, spend a couple more days and some of my own time."

Irish shook his head. "You're a dreamer, Munson."

Munson stood. "Maybe. But maybe we'll find that efficient, sustainable energy system you're looking for."

Irish grunted. "Like I said, dreamer."

CHAPTER 18

Munson's phone rang. It seemed fine since Addy had charged it. "Munson? Whitey. I have someone here who wants to speak with you."

"Okay, I—"

"Dr. Munson? This is Sylvia Tomlinson."

"Hello, Dr. Tomlinson." He got up to close his door.

"I have to tell you, hydrogen technology was off my radar. Too many major hurdles ahead. A hydrogen-powered car has been developed using new sodium technology, but it's years from going into mass production. The first prototype cost millions."

"Not a solution, then?" Munson ventured.

"Pound for pound, hydrogen contains almost three times as much energy as natural gas, but unlike oil or gas, it is not really a fuel," Dr. Tomlinson replied. "It is a way of storing energy. Incredibly challenging."

"Sounds bad."

"But Dr. Fraser's patented process deals with solid state storage of hydrogen, using palladium to trap hydrogen molecules at room temperature and then release them on demand using metal hydrides."

"Is that good?"

"Very exciting!" Dr. Tomlinson's voice rose, then dropped again. "But a forty-ton tanker truck that can carry enough gasoline to fuel *eight hundred* cars can only carry enough hydrogen to fuel *eighty* cars. The only economical way is to manufacture hydrogen right where you need it in the exact amounts that you need. We were still working on that."

"So it's—"

"That's where her brilliant seafire solution comes in! Producing hydrogen requires temperatures well in excess of twelve hundred degrees Fahrenheit. Normally this would require a nuclear reactor or fossil fuels. Research developed by others used radio waves to weaken the bonds which hold sodium, oxygen and hydrogen together. The radio waves cause the hydrogen in the saltwater to burn off with a flame of near three thousand degrees."

Munson's head was swimming.

"Dr. Fraser found the way to control the process without burning off the hydrogen so it could be captured and stored in a palladium compound. From there it can be drawn down as it is needed. The key is her initial discovery that saltwater can be made to burn."

Munson nodded thoughtfully. "Sea fire."

"It can be used in any power system, in any engine, as it is needed. This will eliminate transporting the stuff. It will be created within each automobile and available at the very moment you step on its accelerator pedal. All you would need is a fuel tank full of saltwater for the hydrogen conversion to a fuel cell. If she was right."

"If?"

"Dr. Fraser made a huge breakthrough." Dr. Tomlinson's voice had risen again. "This is an unbelievable day for our planet. I'm certain her protocols are valid. I've pulled out all the stops to build a model from her blueprints, but as I'm sure you can appreciate, the trick is to make sure I'm only dealing with people I can fully trust. Once we've replicated her results, we'll—"

Whitey was saying something in the background.

"I'll let you talk to Whitey again, Dr. Munson. But yes, this is very, very good news."

"Thanks, Dr. Tomlinson. I—"

"Guess who holds the patents, laddie?"

"Hi again, Whitey. You?"

"Yup. I retrieved the Doc's will from her safety deposit box. She left the patents to old Whitey alright. If seafire is successful, you and I are goin' to need more personal security than Roosevelt and Churchill can give us."

Munson nodded. The discovery would be worth hundreds of billions, maybe trillions, except for one thing; it would be too expensive. "Wait—you and I. Us?"

"Yeh, laddie, us," said Whitey. "I'm getting old, and I need a partner. Don't spend your millions yet, though. We have some wrinkles to work out, not the least of which is a source for that palladium. Keep mum about this. I've sworn Dr. Tomlinson to secrecy. We'll talk soon."

"But—"

Whitey had already hung up.

———————————————

Munson met Niiqway in the lounge at his hotel. He seemed tired, but not unhappy. "We've got to stop meeting like this," he quipped.

"Munson, your apartment."

He shrugged. "It was either a ridiculous coincidence, or someone's playing for keeps."

"We got our orders. INSET team's leaving to look into the sub tomorrow morning. You still in?"

He nodded.

She slid their itinerary across the table to him. "You need to replace any of your gear? Cold-weather clothing?"

"That stuff was stored at the office," he said. "You look miserable. What's the problem?"

She sighed. "I'm not cut out for this, Munson. I think it's time I gave it up."

He raised his eyebrows. "Niiqway, you surprise me. What will you do?"

She hesitated. "Why do you ask?"

"Just wondered."

What should she tell him?

She realized the ensuing silence had grown uncomfortable. "Sorry, Munson. Just feeling a little whiny. Ridiculous of me, after what you've been through."

He narrowed his eyes, then shrugged. "Okay, Niiqway, maybe it's none of my business. Instead I'll tell you about the rock I picked up near our iceberg." He lowered his voice. "It could be a very significant find, Niiqway. My team's up in the Arctic right now, trying to find out where the iceberg came from. When we've finished checking out the sub, want to come prospecting with me? Your knowledge of ocean currents would be..." he let the sentence hang.

Oh, god, what should she do?

"So, what do you say?" he asked finally.

She looked up and smiled. "I can't think of anything I'd rather do than spend time in the high Arctic." She finished her drink, paid the check. "See you in the morning."

From the car she called Blake. "After we check out the sub, Munson wants me to do a little exploring with him."

"Where?"

"In the Arctic. We'll stay on after the INSET team leaves."

"The north's a big and dangerous place, Niiqway. You know your orders."

She nodded. "I'll take care of him."

Dusk was falling at Nanisivik airport on Baffin Island as the two Twin Otter aircraft arrived and shut down their engines. Munson peered through the cabin window. Unbuckling his seat belt and preceding the others off the plane, he was the first to feel the wind's warmth as he stepped through the doorway. The tundra was clear of snow and the ocean was almost completely free of ice.

The ocean sparkled in refracted sunlight, overshadowed by the rocky bluffs across the bay. Icebergs floated outside the bay amid broken bits of pack ice. The cliffs reached upward toward a brilliant red-tinged sky. Further up the sound, the bed of what had once had been a glacier receded back into the hills where rocky tundra stretched inland as far as the eye could see. Along the near shore, seals played among the rocks.

Beyond the recently closed Canadian naval base, the old village, seen earlier from the air, lay fifteen miles away in Arctic Bay, its buildings clustered around the shoreline.

"I'm spellbound," said Staff Sergeant Nancy Potter, catching up to Munson as they walked to the village. "I think our Canadian national anthem phrase *home and native land* just took on new meaning for me. But why the red sky?"

"The sun shines through an Arctic haze," Munson explained. "At times it's like the smog over Los Angeles. It's made up of soot, hydrocarbons, heavy metals and a range of greenhouse gasses."

Potter frowned. "Is that dangerous?"

"It's a problem, alright. We've known about it for years, but it's been difficult to make any progress in rectifying it. Now temperatures are accelerating even faster."

"So we're up close and personal with the effects of man-made climate change."

Munson winced, but nodded. "In simplistic terms, yes. And you'll find that up here, there's a certain amount of resentment because of what we southerners are doing to the north."

Sergeant Potter looked at Niiqway. "I see."

"It is a big problem, and not easily solved," said Niiqway. "This is ground zero, and yet few people give it the attention we feel it deserves." She turned to the others. "Our people's main tongue is Inuit, but everyone also speaks English. The Inuit schools are computer equipped, so children have access to the internet and receive a modern education. Some of our traditional ways are still in evidence, but don't be deceived: over the centuries our people have not been treated well. The south brought tuberculosis, drugs and many other problems to the Inuit. It is not only the sudden acceleration of global warming that threatens our future. It's our modern civilization."

As they neared the inn, a group of villagers gathered in their path. "Munson, welcome!" Village leader Lodi Ipeeli stepped forward. "We are so sorry to hear of our Emily," he said, clasping Munson's hand.

"Thank you, Lodi. This is Inspector Robertson." Ipeeli shook hands with the policeman cautiously. "Staff Sergeant Potter, RCMP; Corporal Smith, one of our pilots; and I think you already know our oceanographer, Ms. Ellen Niiqway."

Ipeeli greeted each member of the INSET team as they entered the inn, but Munson stayed outside. One after another, the villagers filed by, paying their condolences, most with a story to tell of Emily's kindness, her compassion, her sense of humor.

By the time they'd all paid their respects, it was growing late. Niiqway approached. "Come have a bite to eat, and I'll show you to our quarters."

Munson filled a plate with ptarmigan and rice, then joined the others. Sergeant Potter was asking, "How many Inuit live in the north?" All eyes turned to Niiqway.

"Nearly a hundred and fifty thousand, across Greenland, Canada and Alaska," she responded. "They live in small villages, along the coastal islands all across the north. About forty thousand live in Canada."

"Along the Northwest Passage?"

"Some do. It's now free of ice most of the year, and navigable."

Potter's eyes were wide. "Where does it go?"

"It stretches through Lancaster Sound and Viscount Melville Sound across the high Arctic," said Niiqway. "But where it goes has never been what's most important. It is what some us refer to as our 'grocery store.' We have always depended on seals, whales and walrus for survival."

Potter fell silent, and Niiqway glanced around the deserted restaurant. She turned to the Inspector. "So, what happens tomorrow?"

"We split up," he replied. "Potter and I will be explore the coastline along Devon Island, where the government had some concerns about a couple of sensitive areas. Smith will fly you and Munson up the east coast of Devon and then on up the southeast coast of Ellesmere Island." The inspector paused. "Thanks for making arrangements for us to fuel at your company's base, Munson. They're still good with that?"

Munson nodded. "The team can overnight there too, if need be. What's our priority?"

"We'll want you to check out the sub's last position and the campsite on Easter Island, preferably without attracting attention. Potter and I expect to be overnighting back here or in Resolute, depending on what we see along the way."

The door opened and a couple came in and helped themselves to coffee, settling at a nearby table. As a few more people entered the restaurant talk at the INSET table returned to life in the north. Munson tuned them out, mulling over what the villagers had said about Emily, remembering how she'd told him to make a difference. And not to repeat the mistake he'd made with Kristin. If she was still alive, where would she be now? On a volcano, perhaps back in her native Iceland?

As Munson finished his meal, a few more villagers stopped by to pay their respects. Well, Emily had certainly made a difference in this part of the world. Perhaps there would be time for him to do the same.

He stood and stretched. "I'm going for a walk."

———————+———————

Munson's morning shave was interrupted by an insistent knock at the bedroom door, and he opened it to find Inspector Robertson. "Sorry for the early hour, Munson," he said. "Smith's tossing his cookies. Are you able to fly the Twin Otter?"

"Sure," said Munson. "I'll grab a bite and head over to do the pre-flight."

Robertson nodded. "I'll send Niiqway over after she's eaten."

She was already there as he finished the pre-flight, and he helped her stow her bag before settling into the cockpit. It was a beautiful morning to be in flight. Once over the open ocean, they watched beluga whales swim playfully below. Along the eastern coastline of Devon Island, the glistening bodies of hundreds of walrus could be seen as they heaved-out along the rocky shore. Further along, the coast harp seals congregated.

"Poor creatures," she said. "They're being poisoned."

Munson glanced at her. "How's that?"

"Violent weather events transport our pollutants north, and once they're here they quickly make their way to the top of the food chain. They're toxic to seals and polar bears. The Inuit people are vulnerable, too. Cadmium, mercury, lead, arsenic—they are all increasing in the Barents Sea and the Arctic Ocean."

"The oceanographer emerges," he grinned, but she stayed somber. He flew briefly west toward the former Galaxy-21 camp near Craig Harbour, now repurposed as a research station. From the air, the old rock and earthen igloo sat lonely and forgotten.

Niiqway continued snapping photos of the terrain as they passed Cape Norton Shaw, then Cape Combermere. At Smith Bay, they followed the water inland, checking each of the many inlets before continuing back out around Cape Mouat. The camp near Easter Island had vanished; no sign of the sub. This was like looking for a needle in a haystack. Eventually Niiqway sighed and put her camera away.

After a fruitless day searching the coastlines, Munson set down at the Munson-Harrigan base near Smith Sound. As expected, the base was deserted; the crew was out in the field. Munson retrieved a drum of jet fuel from the cache and re-fuelled the aircraft while Niiqway made a quick supper over a propane camp stove.

"Come and get it," she said. She seemed dejected. They had both been stunned at the change in the landscape, and there was little conversation over supper.

Munson helped her clean up, and they went down to the water where they shared Niiqway's flask of brandy. A snowy owl flew past in search of lemmings on the coastal tundra. Munson had brought along his flute, and the soft notes of *Night Theme* gained clarity across the water.

"Mmm," said Niiqway as gloom melted into serenity. "Like pouring honey on the ocean."

CHAPTER 19

The next morning they were heading south, flying low near Easter Island under heavy cloud, looking for a place to land from which they could check out the deserted campsite.

"Munson, the sub!" She was pointing ahead and to their right. It lay in deep water surrounded by grease ice, not far from the coast. "Drop down a bit while I get some photos."

"Colonel Raigan is wrong, said Munson. "It is definitely a new Russian sub."

"Can you get lower?" Niiqway asked.

"We already too low," said Munson. "Get what you need, Niiqway. If he's hostile, we're sitting ducks."

"There is no one on deck," said Niiqway. "We're—oh, shit. Take it up, quick!"

Munson pulled back on the yoke and reset the flaps, pushing all the power in.

"Up, damn it," shouted Niiqway. "Faster!"

The first volley from the sub's super-cannon went under them; the second burst hit a wingtip and several rounds went through the wind-screen. Munson banked quickly, flying away at right angles and climbing fast to give the gunner less to shoot at.

"Unh!" Niiqway exclaimed. "I'm hit."

Munson glanced over. Niiqway was bleeding profusely. "Something struck your head," he hollered above the roar of the climbing Otter. "You hit anywhere else?"

"Don't think so."

148

Munson held them in a steady climb. "We're losing oil pressure in the starboard engine," he said grimly, watching a trail of blue smoke from the right turbo prop. "I'm going to shut it down before it catches fire." Struggling to keep control, he shut down the engine and watched the propeller slow to a stop.

Niiqway left her seat, returning with the first aid kit.

The plane still had an alarming vibration. Munson glanced down out the side window where he could see the left side pontoon hanging at an odd angle. The front strut must have been broken by the sub's fire. To land on water was out of the question. He may be able to ease it down on a hard-packed runway. He did some quick thinking. The tiny strip at Grise Fiord was closest, but landing there was tricky under the best of conditions. Nanisivik might be a little closer than Resolute, but they'd be over open water much of the time. Resolute had a hard packed runway and hangars, and there'd be medical assistance for Niiqway. He checked his fuel gauges. If he could nurse them in on one engine, they might make it. He headed southwest.

Niiqway closed the first aid kit. Her color looked better. "You okay?" he asked.

"Not as bad as it looks, I don't think," she said. "The bandages will stop the bleeding, anyway. Bet that's what got me." She pointed to the shattered radio.

He nodded. "We'll try to lock in on the Resolute beacon and hope for the best."

"How far?"

"Too far. It'll be touch-and-go." If the fuel tanks were ruptured it was all over. If they weren't, they'd be flying on fumes for the last few minutes. "I'm not familiar with this particular kite. It will be rough just keeping it in the air on one engine."

"Why not just land on the water?"

He shook his head. "Pontoon's out of commission. That's what's shaking us up. We'll be lucky to land safely on hardpack."

The fuel in the starboard wing tank had already been transferred to the leaking port tank to fuel the port engine. Now both tanks registered empty. They'd made it to Cornwall Island, but were flying low and losing altitude. Munson struggled with the controls, feeling helpless as the sputtering engine starved for fuel. They were not going make it. Below, the rugged shale-covered island offered instant death; on impact, the broken gear would catch and catapult the plane onto its back.

Niiqway gazed at the rugged, seemingly endless landscape. Watching a polar bear ambling along below, she shook her head. "What a wild, beautiful place to die."

"Say prayers to your God," he told her. "It's game over." Munson's thoughts turned to Emily, his parents. Kristin. He should have found her, should have gone to Iceland, at least tried to see her, to find out why she had cut him off without a word.

Niiqway raised her head. "Are there parachutes in this thing?"

"No."

"That's a drag." Niiqway giggled. "Drag—drag chute. Get it?"

He shot her a look and realized her face had lost all color. Was fear taking its toll, or was it her head injury?

He continued to struggle, trying to will the machine to fly. "We're losing it." The turbo-prop coughed, sputtered and died. There was an eerie silence with only the whistle of wind in the struts and the pounding of his pulse.

As Munson held the controls steady, the rocky hills of Cornwallis Island were coming up to meet them. "I can keep it in a glide for a few seconds. This is it." He felt calm, almost serene. He'd done everything he could.

"Start the other engine!"

"What?"

"We're not meant to die. Start the other engine!"

Suddenly her request registered.

He punched the starter of the disabled starboard engine and heard the turbo-prop cough. He held his breath, punched it again and held it. To his amazement it fired up, belching smoke. Within seconds it began to lift the aircraft. "Residual fuel. You're a bloody genius," he said. "The question now is, how much? And will she catch fire?"

He held the power down, barely enough to keep them airborne. Continuing to lose altitude, they headed in against the wind. There! The beacon was strong, atop a hill overlooking the hamlet. He'd never felt such elation.

"We'll take it straight in on the right side. Hang onto your britches, at some point she'll skew around sideways if the left side gear digs in and fails."

They touched down, skidding slightly sideways. Sparks flying, the left side pontoon skidded along until they stopped at the far end of the runway. Munson stared at the smoking engine. "Guess it wasn't our time."

She smiled. "Well done."

"And you, Niiqway," he smiled. "And you."

Over the next few hours he made arrangements for repairs to the airplane, then met Niiqway for supper. "I told the hotel staff about Emily's death," she said. "They were horrified, as I knew they would be. They hadn't heard."

"They all loved her," he said. "How's your head?"

"Nothing serious," she said. "They gave me some blood, but I'd rather have had it in the form of a nice juicy steak."

Ravenous, they made do with the dinner special. Munson walked her to her room at the hotel, then went across the hall, had a quick shower and gratefully flaked out.

The next morning he met Niiqway in the restaurant for breakfast. "You look rested," he greeted her.

"You, too." She led him to a table. "Blake sent us an encrypted message." Niiqway pushed it across the table.

Jihadist sub sunk by JSF jet.

"My god." Munson lowered his voice. "We just declared war on Russia."

"Maybe not," Niiqway said, folding the note and tucking it into her pocket. "The seas are deep in that sound. If we hit it amidships and knocked out the radio, it may have sunk without communicating its position. And we still don't know whether it was the Russians. They claim it was stolen."

Munson snorted and slid his coffee cup toward the approaching waitress. She set down menus and filled their coffee cups. "You need a minute?"

"Breakfast special looks good," said Munson.

"Make that two," said Niiqway.

The waitress nodded, collecting the menus and retreating to the kitchen.

Niiqway leaned forward. "We've also had some news about the AC-990," she said quietly. "CSIS has confirmed that Centwenti Aircraft is fighting the National Traffic Safety Board's findings that the aircraft was struck by lightning. We know they're refuting the metallurgy. They simply won't admit the design flaw." She stirred some cream into her coffee. "There was a similar case in Norway, where a helicopter was struck by a micro-burst and downed in the Atlantic. On our plane, they found that an experimental lightweight melded fiber used in the wings failed as an electrical conductor in a lightning strike and penetrated the airframe."

"Okay..." Munson wrinkled his brow.

"It is a recent discovery. The fiber has been introduced in aircraft design because it is even stronger and lighter than carbon fiber or aluminum. When lightning strikes an aircraft, it travels over the aluminum skin and is dissipated harmlessly."

He nodded.

"But in our case, the NTSB suspects that a lightning bolt struck the left wingtip. It traveled along the melded fiber through the plane's fuselage, weakening a section of the right cabin wall. The cabin wall may have then broken out, due to the inside pressurization. It's also possible that instead, the lightning may have triggered an explosive device in the luggage compartment."

"The hell you say."

"Either way, the flaw should have been understood by Centwenti engineers. In fact, the RCMP think they knew about it. There was no aluminum skin on the leading edges for the lighting to travel over to where it could dissipate. "

"Our flight was just ahead of a hurricane," said Munson. "There were perfect climatic conditions for a micro-burst. Were the fuel tanks left intact?"

She nodded.

"So the microburst may have blown out the side of the aircraft? I'll bet Walpender guessed what had happened as we ditched."

"Yes, our WFFA tycoon is into this up to his armpits. If there *was* a bomb on the plane, I'm betting it was set to go off after Walpender deplaned in Toronto. The fact he'd been on the plane just before would tend to 'clear' Centwenti, and possibly even WFFA."

"But why on earth would they blow it up?"

"My guess is they were targeting the scientists on board. In effect, Walpender was killing off his competitors." She sipped her coffee and made a face. "Oh, this is wicked strong." She stirred in more cream, then licked her spoon.

"So the explosion on the AC-990 may have had nothing to do with me?"

She shrugged. "That *is* another angle. Walpender is big oil. His boss wanted to destroy the discovery. Once you'd transferred to that flight, they probably thought you were travelling right through to Vancouver with the rest of the delegates. After we went down, they learned you were on the raft from the media and came after us on the island, which would mean someone else killed your sister, thinking you had made it to Toronto."

"Unless they'd already set the wheels in motion," he

said. "Even once they knew I wasn't in Toronto, they might not have bothered to call it off. They're not exactly sane."

"It also fits that Walpender engineered the set-up of your sister as a terrorist to cover Centwenti's butt," she said. "We'll get it out of him. It looks like they'll have enough for a Walpender indictment, so they're picking him up."

Munson clenched his fist. "I'd like to be there when they're questioning him."

She shook her head. "Not gonna happen," she said. "So Dragonclaw may not have had his fingerprints on our plane going down."

He sighed. "You reach Robertson?"

"They ended up back in Nanisivik," she said.

"Figure there's any point checking out that abandoned campsite?"

She shrugged. "Robertson's on his way there. If they find anything, they'll want us to come take a look. We could go either way, if you like. I asked for leave when this mission was done."

"I've arranged for one of our planes to be in Nanisivik. Unless CSIS has already made other arrangements, maybe we should just take the next commercial flight back there and pick it up. Oh, did you get any decent photos of the camp, or the—?"

"Yup." She leaned back so the waitress could set their plates down. "Show you after breakfast."

"Here you go," said the waitress. "Did I hear you're looking for a flight out?"

Munson nodded. "

"Fellows over there are a couple of journalist types, headed for Nanisivik," she said. "Might give you a ride if you pay for the extra fuel."

They'd been airborne for half an hour when one of the journalists, an earnest young photographer, discovered

Niiqway was an oceanographer. He lit up. "An oceanographer? What's your perspective on this acceleration mess we're in?"

Before she could answer, the writer jumped in. "We need to stop emissions of carbon dioxide from all of our energy systems worldwide before we kill all life in our seas."

Munson swiveled to look at the speaker: a bearded, bespectacled fellow of indeterminate age, his hair pulled into a ponytail.

The photographer looked at Niiqway. "Is that true?"

"You want the scientific version?"

He nodded.

"Okay." She pulled out a notebook and pen and started drawing molecules. "Carbon dioxide—that's CO_2—mixes with rainwater, H_2O, and forms H_2CO_3, which is carbonic acid." She circled her last scribble, tore the page from the notebook and handed it to him. "You follow?"

He nodded again.

"The carbonic acid falls into the oceans. In the past, over thousands of years it formed calcium carbonate, but the acid levels are rising at such a fast rate that the oceans can't keep pace. Hundreds of billions of tons of carbon are being absorbed into them. Sea life will disappear. The oceans are now able to absorb only half the CO_2 that they did forty years ago."

Munson wondered if the photographer was still actually following, or just nodding agreeably.

"The sea's ability to absorb carbon is reaching the saturation point," she continued. "When acidification occurs, it causes carbon dioxide molecules to react with water. This releases hydrogen ions in huge quantities, lowering the water's pH and increasing acidity."

The photographer rubbed his chin. "But, what does that *mean?*"

The writer spoke up again. "Ocean acidity is already killing Australia's Great Barrier Reef," he said. "Many species of fish are disappearing. Eventually, the oceans will be a huge dead zone. We must stop using fossil fuels."

Munson turned to him.

"You paint a gloomy picture."

"It's sound science," said the writer. "The oceans control our destiny. They absorb the sun's heat. Studies show that rising sea temperatures are killing the microscopic sea algae called phytoplankton. The warming oceans are reducing their nutrients. In the sixty years 1950 to 2010 they had reduced by a whopping forty percent. Since then we've been unable to stop the decline. Phytoplankton is critical to the planet's life support system because they produce half of the planet's oxygen that we breathe."

Munson looked at Niiqway, who nodded. "These dying sea algae are more valuable to our survival than all the vegetation on the land combined," she said.

"I guess I sort of understood the sea algae-oxygen link," said Munson. "I hadn't thought about it for years."

The photographer frowned. "So you agree with what he's saying?"

Niiqway shrugged. "Pretty much. Unless we reverse this, without their oxygen all the fish and marine life will die and eventually so will we."

"Human-generated CO_2 may be part of the picture, but it is not our current acceleration problem," said Munson. "What you're describing still points to increases in heat from the sun itself."

The writer snorted. "Denier," he said, dismissively.

The photographer sent Munson a worried glance, and Munson winked at him. "I'm not saying we're not contributing," he said evenly. "We are. Just pointing out that there's more than one factor in play."

CHAPTER 20

By the time Munson and Niiqway had reached Nanisivik, Robertson and Potter had already searched the deserted campsite. They'd radioed back to the airport with a message for Niiqway: Nothing worth examining.

Niiqway used the airport phone to get in touch with Blake. "We've wrapped her up here," she said. "What do you want me to do?"

"Carry on as planned," he said.

"Are you sure?"

"Orders are orders, Niiqway."

Sighing, she went in search of Munson and spotted him through the airport window, talking to someone. She headed outside and found him striding toward her.

"I'm on leave," she said.

"Great," he grinned. "Our bird's here. Got your gear?"

She nodded. "Let's go exploring."

"Is there time?"

He glanced at his watch. "We can make it to our base at Smith Sound if we don't dawdle."

They were soon airborne again, flying under heavy cloud in a direct line. "Much faster when you're not zigzagging in and out along the coast," mused Niiqway. Their route took them over Easter Island, and she peered down.

"Odd." There was nothing in the open water's surface or below the thin ice layer close to shore. "No sign of a slick."

"Very odd," agreed Munson. "I suppose it could have been on the other side of the island."

Niiqway craned her neck. "Do we have time to circle?"

Munson shook his head. "We're cutting it too close as it is. You think we've been lied to?"

"Roberston and Potter were here earlier; they might have seen something," she said. "Or not. You can bet I'll be asking."

Munson grinned. "You're on leave, Agent. Try to relax."

Relax. She sighed. Yeah, sure.

They settled the Twin Otter on open water in the fading light, taxied to the beach, anchored and tied down. The sleeping tents, facing each other, went up easily. Nearby Arctic ground squirrels, shik-shiks, peeked from their tunnels in the ground. A willow ptarmigan scurried for cover. The clouds had vanished, and as they made dinner the moon rose, its brilliance reflecting off the water. Somewhere nearby a seal splashed. They sat in silence until Niiqway spoke.

"I think it's time you tell me *why* we're chasing icebergs."

He hesitated. "Dr. Fraser's discovery is in the final stages of validation," he said. "It could begin shifting the world away from fossil fuels within months, except for one thing: It requires fuel cells to convert the hydrogen to electrical energy. Millions of fuel cells will be needed. And fuel cells need platinum and palladium components."

"Platinum is expensive."

"Prohibitively, but that's only because it's in very short supply. If we can find a large new platinum source, we may be able to flood the market and reduce the price." He paused. "If we can do that, we'll create an energy earthquake, a hydrogen shift that *will* end the era of fossil fuels."

"Why would WFFA have taken out Fraser if the technology she'd discovered was too expensive to succeed?"

"I wouldn't say it was too expensive to succeed," said

Munson, "just too expensive to overtake a large portion of the market any time soon. But one would have to assume that if Dr. Fraser had found a way using platinum, it wouldn't be long before someone else piggybacked on that research to find a less expensive solution."

"So why not do that research, instead of looking for a platinum source that might not exist?"

"Well, there's acceleration," said Munson. "A bird in the hand. And if I'm right, the platinum could make someone wealthy; why not ensure it's used for the greater good?" He paused. "But more important than any of that, because of politics."

Of course. "You're hoping to stave off an oil war."

"Absolutely. WFFA's the least of our worries. China, Russia and the U.S. want our oil reserves, and as climate change accelerates they'll want our arable land."

"You think we can turn that around?"

Munson shrugged. "For me, these discussions around man-made climate change have to consider Herto man."

Niiqway wracked her brain. "Refresh my memory."

"The oldest known modern human, who lived one hundred and sixty thousand years ago in East Africa."

"How does he tie in?"

"In Herto's time, the earth was gripped by a brutal ice age which had lasted thirty thousand years and threatened the survival of our species before ending suddenly. One hundred and twenty thousand years ago, the African continent began to warm. Global temperatures increased by six degrees and snatched our species back from the brink of extinction."

"But that's an ice age, and we're facing the opposite."

"Exactly. Over a single human lifetime, the period called Emian Warming had begun. It changed the climate. The rains returned to Africa and the continent became a paradise. The warmth that saved the species continued to increase, until it finally became a period of blistering drought. The land had now become a desert, threatening

Herto's descendants, who once again teetered on the brink of extinction."

"Which is what's happening today."

"In effect. Paleontologists have established that Herto's descendants, about 100,000 strong, were reduced to 10,000 in a few thousand years. They were huddled in narrow, barely habitable areas of their Ethiopian homeland, most of which had become a barren lifeless desert. They were in serious trouble. Then, quite suddenly, the rains returned to Africa. It was transformed back into a land full of life and vegetation."

"And all of this happened without any intervention from us."

"Right. We didn't cause it with bad science; we didn't correct it with good science. In fact, what science shows us is that we are descendants of a two-hundred-thousand-year human history that has battled violent climate change for its entire existence." Munson paused. "I am a marine geologist. I've studied ocean bottom sediment that illustrates what are called Heinrich Events. Studies of mud sediments show, for example, that icebergs drop pebbles on the seafloor when they melt. In the layers of sediment, there are periods of pebbles, then no pebbles. Many things in the sediments show that a less-intrusive climatic change kicks in over a hundred year period; it lasts one thousand years and then it goes away. These events repeat themselves. The climate has fluctuated wildly from extreme cold to blistering heat, often in the space of a human lifetime. Climate change is as old as the earth itself."

"So you believe this is predictable pattern of events."

"No; it is not always predictable. Violent weather events such as the supervolcano that formed Toba Lake in the jungle of Sumatra seventy five thousand years ago created its own cataclysmic weather event. It was a volcano thousands of times greater than those seen in our lifetime. As it exploded, over forty thousand mega-tons of sulfates spewed into the atmosphere and blocked out the sun. It is thought to have killed sixty percent of the earth's human and animal population."

"I recall reading about that." Niiqway shuddered. "What a horrible way to die."

Munson nodded. "People and animals would have suffered a painful death as its lethal cloud of pyroclastic gas, ash and rock fell to earth and filled their lungs. As the cloud spread across the globe it hid the sun and cooled the oceans. The snow that fell reflected the remaining sunlight back out into space and plunged the planet into a deep freeze that, among other things, formed the Greenland ice sheet." He waved to the east. "A scientist at the University of Toronto uncovered this with the help of scientists around the world. It has been confirmed by the Iceland ice probes."

"I guess we need to understand what happened in the past to understand what's happening now." Niiqway watched the moonlight dance across the water. "So where *do* we fit in?"

"We clean up our act," said Munson, "but we don't assume we're going to be able to control what the earth does. Our human-caused CO_2 may have played a part, but it is not the cause of our current climate troubles. There is a growing body of evidence that what we're experiencing is the result of a subtle change in the sun's intensity. We can influence such events, but as yet we have been unable to change them."

"Do what we can, but don't expect to change the world." Niiqway smiled. "Munson, play something on your flute."

"As you wish, my lady."

Reclining onto her elbows, Niiqway looked up at the stars, marveling again at how brilliantly they shone, how many more were visible in this beautiful, peaceful part of the world.

———————————————

Munson woke early and gazed out at the bleak darkness of

the ocean. Where, among the myriad of islands that made up the Arctic, had his rock-carrying iceberg come from?

During breakfast they got to work. Niiqway rolled the charts out under the lamplight, and bent over them. "The currents travel from the north through the Prince Gustav Adolf Sea into the Byram Martin Channel. From there the move through Austin channel into Viscount Melville Sound. They would have carried ice floes from the north westerly shores of Ellef Ringnes Island and Axel Heiberg Islands. It's even possible they could carry ice floes from the northerly shores of Ellesmere Island."

"So they could have come from all along here." He drew an arc from left to right along the shorelines of all three islands. ending at the most northerly tip of Canada, the Alert military base on Ellesmere Island. "Problem is, the area has sedimentary and igneous rocks so the presence of platinum is unlikely. Baffin Island or the mainland west of Hudson's Bay is far more likely to contain platinum, with its igneous and metamorphic rock formations."

Niiqway straightened and looked toward the north. "Back in 2002, a massive ice shelf broke free off the coast of Ellesmere Island, about 800 kilometers from the North Pole. It was the size of 11,000 football fields and about 30 meters thick, and spilled roughly three billion cubic meters of frozen fresh water into the Arctic Ocean."

"The Ward Hunt event?"

She nodded. "It effectively changed the Canadian map, about here."

She drew her finger along the map, tracing the northern tip of Ellesmere Island. "That ice shelf broke up into small icebergs and caused havoc with North Atlantic oil plat-forms and shipping lanes. It may have carried our dunite rock with it."

Munson nodded. "Kim Sorqaq's father Oaaqutsiak was a guide on an expedition that investigated the Ward Hunt event back in 2003. He also spent time working on Baffin Island."

She looked at him. "Why would that matter?"

"He had a rock in his possession that was pretty much identical in composition to the one we found." Munson paused. "I suppose I should have told you that sooner. At any rate, he may have found the platinum nugget at either location. Does that help point us in any direction?"

Niiqway rolled up the charts and got a cup of coffee. "My guess is that the origin of our sample could be the northernmost coastline, but it could just as easily have come from any of these inlets up through the Kane Basin, just north of here. Lots of calving happening there, too. Or the inlets up Kennedy Channel, or Roreson."

"The Ward Hunt Makes the most sense," he said. "It may explain why dunite was not seen in the area. Prior to 2002, it would have been under thirty meters of ice."

"But if it's that far north, the location could be too remote to develop a mine," warned Niiqway. "Before the acceleration, that was the very outer edge of man's ability to survive."

"Yeah," Munson frowned. "Let's hope it's not all the way the-hell-and-gone up there."

"What about fuel? Are we coming back here each day?"

Munson shook his head. "Days are too short. I've made arrangements to fuel at a couple of research stations. We'll make camp depending on the weather. It's been cooperative so far, but we can't expect it to last forever."

———————————

They had been searching for four days. Today, they leveled off flying low over Ellesmere Island and then flew across the mouth of Disraeli Fiord. To the left, the Arctic Ocean stretched toward a curved horizon and the North Pole. To the south, much of what had once been covered deep in ice was now the partly exposed windswept rock of Ellesmere Island. They were at the most northerly visible point of the Canadian landmass.

"Scientists carbon dated petrified driftwood released by

the ice melt here," said Munson. "What does that tell you about never ending climate change? We are seeing land that has not been exposed for ten thousand years."

Banking, they flew into the fiord, enthralled by the raw, untouched beauty that unfolded before them. The wind from the northwest had funneled pack ice into the fiord, where it slammed into several icebergs, grounded by the seabed and tilting at odd angles in the ocean. Sobered by the desolation, they tipped down toward open water at the end of the fiord.

Munson scanned the beach for a decent campsite. "We'll land on the bay at the end of the fiord," he decided. "It looks like there's a place to make camp across the snowy beach down there. See it?"

She nodded. "The bleakness of this is breathtaking."

He settled the plane down in the choppy water of the sheltered bay and taxied to shore, where the beach was interrupted by the vertical cliffs of the fiord. The ocean used to be at or below freezing point at this latitude. Here, one mistake could still be your last.

"Bundle up and don't fall into the water," he said.

She sent him a look before adjusting her sun goggles. "Yes, mama."

He grinned, tightening the hood of his parka.

After anchoring the Twin Otter, they carried their gear to the beach and set up camp. The Zodiac was readied for a morning inspection of the shoreline and while Niiqway made supper, Munson scouted the rock formations nearby. Nothing of interest.

They ate and then laid out sleeping bags in the plane as it rode choppy waves near the shore. Concerned that a gust of heavy wind may break the moorings and damage the pontoons, they decided to sleep in three-hour shifts with Munson taking the first watch. "This is not how I imagined our first night together," Niiqway quipped as she bedded down. "No soft music, no nothing. Although this rocking action would be great for making love."

The thought of making love to her here in her warm sleeping bag in this remote place at the very top of the world sent a pleasurable shiver though his loins.

Niiqway was watching his face, grinning. Surely she must be kidding. He better retreat from this gently. "This is not our first night together. Doesn't this beat bouncing around in a rain soaked raft, getting tossed ashore on an abandoned island? Things are improving; patience my good woman."

"Patience he says—while panning prehistoric polar permafrost for platinum and palladium with a pesky prospector." She smiled, snuggled down in her bag, and was soon asleep.

He sat in the pilot's seat, glancing back at her now and then, listening to her deep breathing. She was an intriguing woman and, he had to admit, he was more than a little attracted to her.

Switching on a small cabin light, he studied the maps again and made some notes. When three hours had passed he moved to the back, stripped down and crawled into his bag, waking her in the process. As he settled, he felt her almost-naked form crawling into his bag with him. He held her in his arms gently for a moment as the closeness of her engulfed him.

"I'll bet no human has ever made love this far north," she whispered as her lips found his.

He could feel her relax against him, and he caressed her as the Arctic Ocean's breakers held them in their undulating motion. "Yes," she whispered. "Yes. Like that…. Yes… just like that…"

CHAPTER 21

Munson awakened before six and found Niiqway was already up, out of the plane making their breakfast on their camp stove. He dressed and went out to join her. It was a beautiful morning; the ocean was calm and there was no wind.

"Good morning," he grinned. "You are up early."

"I thought of waking you," she laughed. "But then we would never have resumed our search this morning."

"You amazed me."

"I amazed myself. But life is short. Chances are, we will never recapture last night's wonderful sleepless hours on the restless Arctic Ocean."

After breakfast they hiked inland to the face of a huge ice cliff and looked up at it with awe.

"This is the ice face that broke off and floated out to sea," Niiqway said. "It has already melted back a long way from the coast and thinned from its original height."

"There is nothing of interest up here, Niiqway. We've spent days flying to the most likely areas, and drawn a complete blank. It's time to fly home." He shook his head. "We'll try again when time permits."

"I'm sorry, Munson."

"Don't be. If this had been the source, it would have been too far north to be economically viable. It's not disappointment that I feel; it is intrigue. The prize is still out here, waiting to be found."

They walked back to the plane, where he busied himself

with the pre-flight inspection and then walked down the beach. Out across the bay toward the Pole, the sky was pale blue, blending with the ocean ice so that the horizon was barely visible. As he stood for several minutes looking north, his thoughts turned to Emily.

"It's not about wealth, is it Sis?" he whispered softly. "It's about a clean fuel that is cheaper than burning petroleum. We'll find our platinum-rich ore body, Emily and the Arctic and Inuit will benefit by it. I promise. We'll do our part."

They flew straight to the Munson-Harrigan base at Smith Sound, where they found the crew in camp. Munson was surprised to see Pavel Krotov.

"Sorry, Munson," said Pavel, shaking his hand. "Irish wanted Kim to pull the plug and pack up, but for the past week or so Kim hasn't been reliable about returning calls."

Munson shook his head. "Is there still enough fuel for us to top up?"

Pavel frowned. "Hard to say. Until I find Kim and the rest of his crew, I'd rather you didn't. Can you make Grise Fiord?"

"It'll be touch and go," said Munson. "I can radio over to Pituffik, see if they can spare enough to get me to Nanisivik."

"Best spend the night," said Pavel. "Maybe by then we'll have heard from Kim."

After supper, Munson and Niiqway walked down to the beach. "Ready to go back to work?"

"No," she said, taking his arm. "This assignment will be my last. I'm going back to oceanography."

"That pleases me."

They strolled in silence for a few minutes, then stood and watched the moonlight play on the waves. "Tell me more about your sister," said Niiqway. "What was she like?"

"Emily was a high energy person, enthusiastic," said Munson. "She saw life as a world of possibilities. She loved excitement. She had a great smile and a hearty laugh." He grew silent, watching something swimming out in the sea. "She was strong and independent. She loved her field of metallurgy. In addition to our lobbying for the Inuit, she worked with the under-privileged. She was involved in financial support to the Palestinians, trying to help them find peaceful solutions to their problems with the Israelis."

"I saw Emily briefly," Niiqway said. "In London. She was very beautiful. It seems that you were closer to your sister than most brothers would have been."

"Twins are usually very close. We were no exception."

They started walking again, heading toward the plane. "Tell me about your partner, Harrigan."

"Irish is a brilliant geophysicist." Munson chuckled. "Everyone loves calling him Irish, or O'Harrigan; it's so unusual for a black man to have an Irish name and accent. He's respected in the oil and gas industry, but he and I have some challenges to work through." Suddenly he felt compelled to defend Irish. "I feel certain that Irish is not Dragonclaw."

"Seems unlikely," agreed Niiqway. "Well, I guess with employees in camp, it'll be separate tents for us."

He nodded. "Sleep well. I'll check the plane moorings before I sack out."

Munson slept little that night. Each time he drifted off, he snapped awake dreaming of the Hawk. Niiqway had arrived and killed the man only seconds before he was readying to confront the assassin. She was tough, experienced and well trained, and last night she had been... amazing.

The next morning, there was still no sign of Kim or the rest of his crew. Munson confirmed a fuel purchase at Pituffik, and set a course east for the Greenland coast.

As they neared Wolstenholme Fiord, Niiqway craned her neck to peer down at the water. "Weird," she said. "There's a heavy wake down there, but no ship."

Munson banked down for a closer look.

Digging out her camera, Niiqway focused her zoom lens on the front edge of the wake. "There you are," she said, snapping some photos. "Can you do another pass?"

"We need fuel, Niiqway," Munson reminded her.

"Oh, yeah," she grinned.

Twenty minutes later, the air base came into view. Niiqway frowned. "Hey, isn't this Thule?"

Munson nodded. "Everything in the north seems to have two names."

She rolled her eyes. "I don't know why I didn't make the connection. You need a hand?"

He shook his head. "Good time to use the washroom."

On her way back to the plane, Niiqway passed Munson. "My turn," he said. "Be right back."

Fetching her laptop, she connected her camera and downloaded the photos. Munson climbed into the cockpit. "I'm going to taxi us out of the way for a few minutes," he said. "I'm trying to connect with Irish. He must have contacted Pavel earlier; there was an urgent message waiting for me here."

"What's it about?"

Munson shrugged. "Just that I should call." He shut down the plane again and leaned over to look at her laptop. "Looks like a Russian built Sea Phantom."

She zoomed in. "But it has an Iranian flag," she said.

He nodded.

Niiqway frowned. "Why was it practically invisible?"

"They're built like the stealth ships, except larger, maybe 30 tons, and cruise at about 65 knots, give or take. The water jet's surface effect virtually lifts the craft off the water and propels it at high speed, leaving this fan shaped wake on the ocean surface."

"Hm," she said. "Wonder what it was doing here?"

"Good question." Munson frowned. "Chances are the Radarstat satellites will have missed the wake on the surface, given the cloud cover."

Niiqway squinted at the screen, then zoomed another part of the image. "Look here, on its deck," she said. "An underwater sonar unit and a remote control submersible ROV. Undersea recovery mission."

"Holy shit," Munson frowned.

She nodded. "The lost nuke."

"Damn it to hell. No one will believe—" Interrupted by a tap on the plane's door, he looked out to see a member of the ground staff miming a telephone. "Guess I better go see what Irish wants."

Niiqway was still poring over the photos when he returned. "Niiqway, we have a situation," he said, unzipping his backpack and grabbing his I.D. "Kim was found unconscious half an hour ago."

"Oh, my god," said Niiqway. "Where is he now?"

"Right here," said Munson. "He's being held at the base hospital. He's awake now, but insists he doesn't remember anything. Irish wants us to get him out of there and get him home."

Niiqway stowed her camera and laptop in her backpack, slinging it over her shoulder as she climbed out of the plane. "Where did they find him?"

"Out in the fiord," said Munson, leading her into the terminal. "He was picked up by the U.S. military crew that had gone out to investigate a report of the Phantom. He's lucky; they spotted his body in its wake as it left the area."

"My god, Munson—if he tells them—"

"Mr. Munson?" A soldier approached. "This way, sir."

At the infirmary, they saw Kim through a plate glass window. As Kim stood and approached them, another soldier barred their way. "I'm here to see Kim Sorqaq," said Munson, pointing.

"We've just received orders, sir. No visitors."

"But I'm—"

"Orders, sir."

Through the window, Niiqway watched as Kim pointed toward the door and mimed "they won't let me out."

Niiqway stepped closer to the soldier and flashed her badge.

The soldier glanced at it, stepped aside and waved her through.

Niiqway turned to Munson. "I'm sorry, you'll have to wait outside." She closed the door behind her and turned to face Kim.

———————+———————

Munson gave up trying to eavesdrop and paced outside the room. A few minutes later, Niiqway emerged. "I'll need to use a secure phone," she said, throwing Munson an apologetic glance. One of the soldiers took her into an adjoining room. "Niiqway, what the hell—"

He was speaking to a closed door.

When she emerged, she took Munson's arm. He shook her off. "What the hell is going on?"

"Please, Munson, not here."

Reluctantly he followed her, fuming, as the soldier escorted them back toward the terminal.

Their escort left them at their plane, and Niiqway placed her hand on his arm again. "Munson, I'm sorry," she said. "You were right about Kim. He had been approached by Kao, and yes, they do have the nuclear weapon. He hasn't told the U.S. military."

"So they're going to hold him until he talks?"

"Not if I can help it," she said fiercely. "I've been trying to arrange to have him released into my custody." She opened the door to the cargo hold, and began removing her belongings. "I'll stay here until that happens."

"They're U.S.," said Munson. "Why would they give Kim up to CSIS?"

Niiqway took a deep breath. "I'm not only CSIS," she said, closing the cargo door. "I'm also CIA."

Munson felt like he'd been punched in the stomach. "You're CIA."

"Yes. Only my CIA supervisor in Washington and Scott

Blake knew of my assignment. I have been working under-cover for years, trying to find the Canadian links in CSIS to Dragonclaw. It was a joint CIA-CSIS initiative."

Munson realized his jaw hurt, and struggled to regain his composure. "And one of those links is Kim?"

Niiqway shook her head. "I don't believe Kim had any idea what he was being used for. He says Ying Kao prom-ised she'd use it to blackmail the government into cleaning up the environment. He's gullible and naïve, Munson, and Kao took full advantage of his anger."

She put her hand on his arm again, and again he shook it off. "CIA," he spat. "Bloody hell—you knew how I felt, and you—"

"I couldn't tell you. Munson, I had no involvement with your Afghanistan tragedy. I have never met Hank Watson and I know nothing about his bribe or threat."

He closed his eyes, leaned his head back against the side of the plane.

"What were their names?"

He looked at her. Were those tears in *her* eyes? "Who?"

"Your platoon," she said softly. "What were their names?"

Munson closed his eyes again. He took his time, naming each of them, their rank, their home towns and a bit about each young soldier. There were ten killed, seven wounded. Eight of the dead were young Afghan recruits that he had mentored and trained. He told her their names. It took a while to talk about them all. She remained quiet, listening. His anger had waned.

"Our search for platinum, the new technology. The CIA knows—"

"No, Munson. I've kept every confidence I've ever made with you."

"I knew that you were keeping something from me," he said.

She bit her lip. "You have good instincts."

"Maybe." He shrugged. "Right now, my instincts are telling me to go home."

She nodded. "Go to Telford. Tell him about Kao. I'll email all of the photos to Blake." She reached to put her hand on his arm again but he turned, climbed into the cockpit.

"I'm so sorry, Munson."

She was still standing there, watching, as he lifted off.

CHAPTER 22

Munson was shown into the prime minister's office. "Munson, you're back. Come on in, take a seat." He got up to shake Munson's hand, then closed the door. "What the hell's been happening up north?" He settled back into his chair.

"The sub was Russian, and modern," said Munson, "and it wasn't sunk."

Telford scowled. "Better if it wasn't. We don't need that kind of international incident on our hands. China and Russia are—" He clammed up.

"Who gave the order to sink it?"

"I backed the military," said Telford, sheepishly. "I was convinced the sub had been commandeered by jihadists. It attacked your aircraft while in Canadian territory."

"Think about it," Munson urged. "Colonel Raigan told you that the sub was old. It was not. He told you that it was sunk. It was not. It was a set-up."

Telford looked puzzled. "But why—"

"They didn't carry out your order. There was no slick in the area, no debris. I caution you about Kao and Colonel Raigan. Judging from the headlines, you have China and Russia preparing to invade us for our oil, but you already have the enemy right here under your nose."

"I don't believe it," said Telford. "First of all, Ying Kao may be of Chinese descent, but she is *not* working with China. You just refuse to believe a woman like her could actually be interested in me."

174

"What?"

"And I trust Colonel Raigan. Both of these people are solid. You're thinking like a—like a paranoid American."

Munson shook off the insult. "Fine. Here's what you need to know. Niiqway and I saw a Russian Sea Phantom coming out of Wolstenholme Fiord. Kim—"

"Nate Evans told me you'd be dropping by with your latest cockamamie nonsense," said Telford.

"Evans may be WFFA," said Munson. "Hell, he may even be Dragonclaw."

"The elusive Chinese master spy, who may or may not even exist?" Telford put his head back and laughed. "Just listen to yourself, Munson. One paranoid delusion after another. Evans tells me that woman you've been hanging out with is CIA. She has been filling your head with all kinds of crap."

"Evans, Raigan and Kao have their own agenda. You're being manipulated."

"You've really become a paranoid son of a bitch, Munson. Enough!"

"I am a friend, Joe. You've always trusted me. Kao is poisoning you against me. "

"Stop. You obviously have some kind of agenda here. Maybe you are Dragonclaw, after all." He glared at Munson. "I should never have trusted you. I want you out."

"Joe, you know that I'm not—"

"I want you to leave."

Biting his tongue, Munson got up and left.

Munson hung up the phone, swearing. Telford was too busy to see him, too busy to return his voice mail. He'd already been turned away from the prime minister's office twice and was on his way to a permanent position on their list of persona non grata. The intercom buzzed, and he jumped, hoping Telford was finally getting back to him.

"Yes?"

"Your mother is on the phone from Seattle," said Addy. "It's urgent."

"Yes, Mom?"

"Curtis, it is your father."

"What's happened?"

"Heart attack," his mother choked, and Munson held his breath. "He's asking for you…"

"I'll be on the next flight," said Munson. "Is someone there with you?"

"Your Aunt Gina, and your cousin Sarah-Lynn… Oh, Curtis…the doctors say there's no…" she choked again.

"I'm on my way. I love you. Give Dad my love, too."

He buzzed Addy. "Get me on a flight to Seattle, Addy. My father is dying."

———————+———————

He made his father's bedside that evening. The old man's eyes lit up as he approached. "Curtis!" he whispered. "How are you, my boy? Glad you're here."

"I wouldn't be anywhere else, Dad."

"Where's your Mom?"

"Aunt Gina thought it best to take her home."

His father drifted off, and Munson watched him breathe for a while. He drifted off himself, awakening when a nurse came in to check his father. "Mr. Munson will sleep for a few hours," she said. "Would you like a cot?"

Munson shook his head. "Thanks," he said.

He woke again at dawn when his father squeezed his hand. "Look after your Mom, Curtis. Tell the Inuit I'm sorry… Try to help them. Promise me…"

"Dad, it wasn't your fault. I just returned from the north, and the people had such love and respect for Emily. No one holds you responsible for anything, Dad. You were just serving your country, doing your job."

"The nuke's up there boy," the dying man whispered, growing agitated. "It's going to explode and—"

"Dad, it's okay. It's over."

"I tried to have it found—"

"I know," said Munson. "You did everything you could, Dad."

"But the radiation... the Inuit..."

"It's alright, Dad. We're so fortunate you survived that B-52 crash in the first place, and so far there's no sign the nuke's causing any grief."

"It could—"

"And that's why I'll keep looking."

"Promise?"

"I promise." He patted the old man's shoulder. "Mom tells me you've found God."

"Your mother is happy," the old man whispered. "She thinks I finally got the religion." He winked and grinned. "Let her believe that... let her..."

"Sh, Dad, shh." Munson stroked his father's hand. "Dad, you've been a wonderful father. Thanks so much for teaching me the important stuff."

"Never piss..." his father chuckled, unable to continue.

"...into the wind," Munson finished for him. "Wait till it's blowing the right way and then cut 'er loose!"

His father's mouth twitched.

"You've taught me to meet life's challenges head-on. You supported my choice to stray from Mom's faith, but only when I was old enough to truly choose."

"Paleontology," his father breathed. "Earth science..."

Munson nodded. "Not to mention the controlling, bureaucratic power structure—"

"Outdated liturgies..."

"... of books written by men," Munson finished for him, nodding. This was a familiar old discussion, and somehow comforting.

His father squeezed his hand. "Don't be afraid to change your mind..."

"Never," Munson grinned. "My old man taught me to have an open mind. Are you thinking maybe you'll—"

Munson realized his father's hand had gone limp. The old man sighed, then went silent.

"Oh, Dad," said Munson.

A nurse slipped into the room, checked Mr. Munson, then put her hand on Munson's shoulder. "I'm sorry."

He nodded. "I'll go tell Mom."

CHAPTER 23

After the short prayer service, Munson tried unsuccessfully to get his mother to move to Ottawa. She preferred to be with her friends in Seattle. Flying back to Ottawa, he realized he was getting tired of living in a hotel; maybe it was time to look for a new home. Not now, he told himself. Not anytime soon. He had to get his bearings first.

The next morning, Irish Harrigan came into his office. "Sorry about your father," he said.

"Thanks," said Munson. "I hadn't realized... When he was here for Emily, I should have noticed..."

Irish shook his head. "Of course he would have looked tired and ill. How could you possibly have known?"

Munson swallowed.

"Sorry for the timing, but I want you to know that I may be leaving our partnership," Harrigan told him. "This thing with young Sorqaq—it should never have happened. I knew his anger about the north made him vulnerable, and sending him there only made it worse. When passion about a cause clouds your judgment—Well. I need to reassess my values."

"He's an adult, Irish."

Harrigan shook his head. "Barely. And too vulnerable."

Munson smiled sadly. "As I wise man just asked me: How could you possibly have known?"

Harrigan looked at him. "Aren't we a pair?"

"You have to follow your conscience Irish. What will you do?"

179

He sighed. "I made some interesting contacts at that geo-engineering conference in Paris. Some of the ideas seem crazy, but... Munson, the earth has warmed up point-eight degrees Celsius since pre-industrial times. In the past three years alone, it has matched the rise which had previously taken *over a hundred years*. Parts of the U.S., much of the China, Australia, central South America and central Africa are fast becoming uninhabitable." He shook his head. "I know, you already understand all of that. But what impressed me the most at the conference was this: The original target of scientists was to keep global warming below two degrees. Now that looks to be impossible."

"So now you're back to thinking it's all up to us, that we can somehow control what the earth's going to do?"

Irish rolled his eyes heavenward. "If I move on, what are your plans besides getting yourself killed?"

"My priorities are simple, Irish. Find out who was behind Emily's murder, protect Dr. Fraser's discovery, and find a new source of platinum. I'm hoping to use it to help shift us to hydrogen as a new energy source."

"Platinum? You mean for funding?"

"Something like that," said Munson. With a little luck, he'd be able to locate the platinum and get his ducks in a row before Irish found something else to do. He'd be the perfect person to head up a green technology that could truly make a difference.

When Irish left, Addy buzzed. "The PMO is on the line," she said. "Given how they were ignoring your calls, I was rather happy to keep them on hold for you."

He grinned. "Good for you, Addy. Thanks. Put them through."

"Munson?"

"Hi, Joe."

"I'm so sorry to hear about your father."

"Thanks, Joe. It was a shock."

"I'm also... I'm also sorry to have had you on ignore. You were right about Ying Kao."

Munson stifled the urge to snort. "What's happening?"

"I'm not sure. All I know is, she's vanished. Scott Blake came by, from CSIS? Said Ying had somehow been involved with your young protégé, Kim Sorqaq?"

"She was just using him, Joe."

"I know." Telford sighed. "She was using me, too. Anyway, she seems to have cleared out a bunch of my files, all the intel I had on some growing international conspiracies. God, Munson, the world is out to get us. I picked one hell of a time to get myself elected prime minister."

Biting off a couple of choice words about sniveling, Munson forced himself to focus on the issue at hand. "China, Russia and the U.S.?"

"It's a mess, Munson. This oil thing... if we can't find a reasonable alternative... Hell, I don't even trust my own phone lines any more. Can you meet me for lunch?"

Munson glanced at his schedule. "Yeah, I can do that. When and where?"

"Soon as you can get here. I'll get my driver to drop us somewhere," said Telford. "And Munson—thanks."

Munson buzzed Addy. "I'll be out for the afternoon," he said.

"Very good," she said. "Ms. Niiqway is here. Shall I send her in?"

Munson paused. "No. I don't have time."

"She says it's urgent."

"I'm on my way to lunch with the prime minister. Tell her she'll have to wait."

A few moments later, Addy buzzed. "She's gone. You need anything else before I go to lunch?"

"No, I'm good," he said. "Thanks, Addy."

In the parkade, he found Niiqway standing in front of his driver's side door, her arms crossed.

"I need to talk to you," she said.

"You have nothing to say that I want to hear," he said.

"You can't use your car," she told him. "Bomb squad's coming. There's a device underneath it."

"Bullshit," he said. Hearing a commotion behind him, he glanced toward the stairwell door; a man in a dark suit was refusing to allow anyone to pass.

"He's with us," she said. "I've just called in the evacuation order. No one else will be allowed in the parkade until it's clear. Where's the flash drive?"

His eyes narrowed. "Why?"

"Because unless you do something with it now, it may be too late. Walpender was killed in jail. They're closing the net, Munson."

"And I should trust you because…"

She sighed. "I know, Munson. And I've said I'm sorry. I'm just trying to keep you safe."

He snorted. His phone buzzed, and he glanced at the display. Whitey.

He swiped the screen. "Whitey? You—"

"Laddie, they've bombed my lab," he boomed. "And Tomlinson's, too. We've gotta go public, now!"

"The drive's at the bank," said Munson. He turned to Niiqway. "Whitey's been—"

"I heard him," said Niiqway. "I have a car out front. Come with me."

Even with their emergency lights and siren, it seemed to take an eternity to drive five blocks to the bank. Niiqway left the Mercedes double parked and hurried Munson inside, where she flashed her badge at the security guard. "Lock the doors," she told him. "People can leave, but no one comes in."

He nodded.

She turned to the receptionist. "Safe deposit boxes, now," she said, pushing Munson forward. "No time for paperwork—just get it."

Wide eyed, the woman nodded, leading Munson toward the back of the building.

When Munson emerged with the flash drive, the building was virtually empty. "Thank you for your cooperation," said Niiqway. "You can resume normal activities now."

Scanning the street, she hustled Munson toward her car.

"Where are we going?"

"You're taking that to headquarters, where there's better security, and using our computer system to release it to the world," said Niiqway, gesturing to get in.

"I can do that with my phone."

"Then do it," she said, activating her siren and pulling away from the curb.

He inserted the flash drive and started the download. "This will take a few moments," he said. "Shit! My battery's low." While the download was running, he accessed his email and brought up the address list. The battery light was blinking very fast; the download ended and he found the address list.

Niiqway cursed, and Munson looked up to see a transport truck swinging wide to make a left turn, blocking the intersection.

"Behind us!" Niiqway slammed on the brakes. Munson glanced back to see a white Cadillac barreling toward them.

"Holy...!"

"Hang on!" Niiqway yelled. They were skidding into a spin. From his side window he could see the truck's large dual wheels coming toward him. They were going to slam sideways straight into the damned truck.

Send the file! Where was the damned "send" icon?

Munson's side of the Mercedes crumpled, thrusting him into the punctured airbag and shattered doorpost. Glass and steel buckled. The tailgating Cadillac drove headlong into Niiqway's door, crushing it inward and pinning them inside the smoking wreckage.

Stunned, Munson recoiled as the smell of burning rubber, gasoline and smoke filled his nostrils. He struggled to free himself. "Niiqway, are you okay?" He realized her limp body was crumpled against him. "God almighty. Niiqway!"

The smoke was thick, impenetrable, turning daylight to

darkness. As he reached for Niiqway, his hand grasped hair. It was sticky. Blood. He freed his right arm, groped blindly for the door handle. There!

It was no good; the door wouldn't open.

The vehicle shuddered. Someone was shouting. He still had his phone in his left hand. The flash drive! Where was it? The wreck was burning, the flash drive would be lost, the technology lost. The world was ending. Only the flash drive—

He had to find it. Had to keep it safe. Was it still in the phone's auxiliary's port? Feeling for it, he found the port. The flash drive was still there. Should he pull it out? Had it finished sending? He had to keep it safe. He removed the flash drive and stuffed it in a shirt pocket. Had he hit the send icon? He stabbed at the phone with one finger. It was sticky—blood. His blood. Niiqway's blood.

The pain was suddenly debilitating.

A distant yell penetrated his stupor. "Back away! It's gonna blow!"

"Send," he said aloud. "Send!"

"Stay calm, I'll get you out." The voice was faint.

"Back away!" someone yelled again.

He was drifting now, the pain was intense. Through the darkness, Emily's face swirled toward him. He had to get a message to her. Send. He tried to focus.

Send. His finger traced the upper left corner of the screen, tapped it blindly. Fire crackled, and he couldn't breathe through the smoke.

His mother was right.

There was a hell, and he had descended into it.

CHAPTER 24

Munson struggled to open his eyes. Impossible. Funny, he thought, drifting off; they seemed to be taped shut.

He woke again, and it was still dark, so dark. He must be in cabin in the Rockies on a moonless night. In the morning, he'd wake Emily with bacon and eggs and coffee, and they'd go hiking up the hill, or maybe fishing. Maybe Dad and Mom would come, too…

But no, this didn't smell like the cabin. He forced himself awake. He couldn't raise his eyelids. His arms were leaden, impossible to lift. He was trapped—trapped in a burning wreck! Niiqway! He couldn't yell, couldn't breathe. Something was blocking his throat. Help! The dark somehow got blacker, and he was sinking, falling…

He woke to a soft pinging sound. It was still pitch black, and his heart began to race again. What was that smell? Hospital, he realized. A hospital. His heart slowed.

"Dr. Munson?" Her voice was kind, but businesslike.

"Yes…" his voice was only a whisper. His throat hurt dreadfully.

"You're in the hospital, Dr. Munson. No, don't try to open your eyes. We've bandaged them."

"Okay," he said. "My arms…"

"I can take off the restraints now that you're awake, but you mustn't touch the bandages on your eyes. Okay?"

"Okay."

His arms trembled as he brought his hands together, rubbing at his wrists.

"Better?"

"Yes. Thank you."

"Would you like some water?"

He nodded, and she guided his hand to a water cup. "Here's the straw," she guided his other hand. "Your throat will be sore for a while. Dr. Munson, you won't be able to see for another day or two. Your doctor is certain you will still have most of your vision, possibly all of it, but only if you allow your eyes to heal."

He swallowed and tried to return the cup to table. "Just a bit further to your right," she said. "Perfect. Now, I expect you have some questions?"

"Niiqway—Ellen Niiqway was in the car with me—"

"It's my understanding that the driver in your accident was released from hospital with some minor burns to her lower legs."

"But her head... the blood."

"The impact had re-opened a scalp wound that hadn't yet healed."

"Am I ... am I burned?"

"No, Dr. Munson."

"Just Munson, please," he said. "Our car was on fire ..."

"Yes, but the driver of the transport truck used his fire extinguisher. Your face was badly cut by shattered glass, some of which was in your eyes, and you inhaled some very nasty chemical smoke. But I can assure you, no burns." She patted his hand. "Dr. Munson, would you like to call your mother? We reached your executive assistant, and she recommended against us calling her until you could speak with her yourself."

"Addy's right," he said. "Mom's been through too much lately. I'll give her a call—" The jump drive! "Where's my cell phone?"

"Just a moment," she said, moving across the room. "I'll check the closet. Hm. Nothing's here. I'll go find out where it is. Stay in the bed, Dr. Munson. I won't be long." Her footsteps padded away.

Had he been able to send the discovery? Had he found the "send" icon in time? What had happened to his phone, and where was the flash drive? Oh, yes, he had put the flash drive in his shirt pocket. Hadn't he?

Moments later he heard footsteps again—cautious, creeping footsteps. "Who's there?"

"Hello, handsome!"

He could smell her jasmine. "Martha!" He grinned.

"About time you woke up! I've been visitin' you for two days, and our one-way conversation was getting' too damn boring. How are you feelin'?"

"I'm weak as a kitten, blind as a bat, and grumpy as a hoot owl. But I'm overjoyed that you've come!"

"That's encouragin'. You are pretty beat up, lots of bruises but no broken bones."

"What happened?"

"The police interviewed witnesses at the accident scene," she said, perching on the side of his bed. "They saw an old Cadillac leave but evidently no one got a clear look at the license tags. One person thought it was some kinda custom tag, just numbers, but the cops said there's no match for a Cadillac with a plate like that."

"Is Niiqway...?"

"Ellen Niiqway will be fine. Guess you found out what I found out: she was workin' for the CIA. Other than that, she seems to be on the up and up. Hope I haven't just cleared the way for my competition."

"Oh, stop," he said.

"Why Munson, you rogue, you're blushin'! Well, I can see I might have my work cut out for me. My vital news of interest will have to wait a moment while I get started on my action plan, otherwise you'll be much too interested in my news to pay any attention to little ol' me. Now you brace yourself for a kiss."

As her lips met his, a hospital alarm went off. He felt Martha push back a little, then heard a pop-pop-pop-pop from the doorway. Martha's full slumped down over him.

"Martha?"

Now footsteps were running—away, down the hall-way—and another alarm went off, louder than the first. "Martha!" He reached for her, felt his I.V. cords tugging his left arm; they were caught underneath her.

Footsteps again, guff voices barking orders in the hall-way. His right hand found Martha's back—wet, sticky with blood.

"Nurse!" He raised his right hand to rip the bandages from his eyes, but strong hands seized his arm.

"No, Dr. Munson, that won't help. We have her now."

People all around the bed, the sound of a gurney, "One, two, three." Martha's weight leaving him, Martha leaving him—

"Martha!"

"We have her. We'll take care of her. Have you been hit?"

"No, I—"

"Lay back down, Dr. Munson."

"Her name is Martha, she's a friend…" He lay back and listened to them working to help her. A jumble of conversations. Only one was meaningful. *She has no pulse.* They were trying to resuscitate her, wheeling her away. "Is she going to be okay?" No answer. The room had gone silent.

He lay still, feeling helpless—hoping for a miracle.

Soon after, there was a quiet voice at his bed. "Now Dr. Munson, we must re-attach these monitors."

"My friend, Martha, is she…?"

"I am very sorry. There was nothing we could do."

No, no. Dear god, no. The nurse finished attaching the monitors, then took his hand. He squeezed it. "Did anyone see the shooter?"

"No. We're checking security footage, but there were hospital scrubs near the bottom stairway. We think he wore them and blended in with the hospital staff and then left through the fire exit door to the street. Opening the fire escape exit door would have energized an alarm but…"

"Yeah, just one more alarm. Let me guess, he waited until my security had gone to the can."

His anger rose. He bit his lip and tried to ignore the tears soaking his bandages. Had Dragonclaw planned to kill Martha, or had *he* been the target? Martha had been about to tell him something she thought was of vital importance. What did she know? Or was she kidding?

"Nurse, did you find my cell phone? Or a flash drive?"

"Your possessions were picked up by someone from your company. They brought in some clean clothing for when you're ready to leave the hospital, along with your wallet and watch."

"Nothing else?"

"I'm sorry, Dr. Munson, nothing else."

"Have you heard—has there been anything on the news about a new energy discovery?"

"A new energy discovery? Hm. No, I don't think so. Although I wouldn't necessarily have noticed. Dr. Munson, would you like me to arrange for a television? I could set it to one of the news channels for you."

He shook his head. "Thanks, no." He had failed. The flash drive was gone. Thank god Niiqway had survived, but Martha—vibrant, larger than life Martha—was dead. Slumping back on his pillows, he gave in to despair.

CHAPTER 25

"Just me, Munson." It sounded like the dayshift nurse. Her footsteps approached. "It's just after 7:30 in the morning. Dr. Harris will be by to do rounds shortly. Here's your breakfast; more finger food. What shall I spread on the toast—jam, peanut butter, some honey?"

"Peanut butter's good," said Munson. "So tell me, is feeding the blind in your usual job description?"

"Keeping you safe by reducing staff contact." She guided his hand to the plate. "I'm cleared, so best I do what I can. Coffee's over here. Need anything in it?"

"Black, thanks."

"We've had a request to allow another visitor, and her clearance is even better than mine. It's Agent Niiqway. Want time to finish your breakfast, or shall I send her in?"

"Send her in," said Munson. "Thanks for your help."

He fumbled for the napkin and wiped at his face, hoping for the best.

"Wow, Munson," said Niiqway. "You look like a bad Halloween costume."

He grinned. "The mummy?"

"Mmm, crossed with some version of Frankenstein's monster." She leaned close. "Only this stitching's much tidier. Should heal okay. Go ahead and eat your breakfast. Mind if close the door and I pull up a chair?"

"Please do," he said. "So you were burned?"

"Not badly," she said. "Thank god for the trucker. Now, I'll bet you have questions. Where shall I start?"

"The file send — what happened? There was no news."

"Whitey had emailed everyone and told them to expect a file from you, but to sit on it until one of you gave the okay to release it. So far, so good, but it's only a matter of time until somebody spills it to the media."

"Tomlinson?"

"She'd just finished proving that Fraser's process does, in fact, work. Only part of her lab was destroyed, so she'll be ready to show the world in a few days. But she's waiting for word from you."

"Me? Why not Whitey?"

"I'll let him explain that. Next question?"

"Walpender?"

"He was shivved in prison. We got nothing out of him. Next?"

"Kao?"

"Vanished. She herself gave Kim the knockout punch, by the way." She lowered her voice and leaned closer. "He was photographing the bomb with his cell phone, heard her coming up behind him and regained consciousness while they were fishing him out of the water. Lucky the military found him when they did."

"What's he saying?"

"He's just sick about the whole thing. Kao told him they'd use the nuke for leverage to force the federal government to help his people. He split your geology crew up and sent them in different directions; each crew thought he was with the other when in fact he was with Kao. He took her to talk to one of the grandfathers who'd been in the area where the B-52 came down and knew something that no one else had taken into account. I'm still not clear on what that is."

"Where's Kim now?"

"In D.C. They're not too happy with him. It's going to take some talking to convince the top brass he's not a terrorist. Next question?"

"Where's the bomb?"

191

"No idea. Well, that's not entirely true. The Phantom headed south, and we found most of the bomb still onboard. Only the radioactive materials and one segment of the detonation system are missing. Our best guess is that they're planning to use it with a more modern detonation system, making the package much smaller, more maneuverable."

"Much scarier, too," said Munson. "Easier to transport, easier to hide…"

"Yup."

Munson was silent for a moment. "Anything else?"

"We have Watson."

"Watson, the CIA agent?"

"Ex-CIA. We'd cut him loose a couple of months back. WFFA had him working for them. He's spilling his guts, hoping that if he's already talked, they won't have as much reason to kill him. So far, he's admitted hiring the hit man that took out Mercier; according to Watson, the hired gun was just supposed to hold Mercier for the morning, but things got out of hand."

"Why were they holding him? Wasn't he WFFA, too?"

"Initially, but he failed to get the flash drive away from her and WFFA brass was pissed. Mercier had developed a soft spot for Dr. Fraser and refused to drug her. Watson did it himself. Got to her at coffee break, but again he says it went horribly wrong. What he used was only supposed to knock her out, but all the stress she was already under amplified the drug's effect."

"But why drug her, if not to shut her up permanently?"

"He was waiting in the wings to rush to her rescue and relieve her of the flash drive," she said. "Killing her would just attract unwanted attention, and they didn't know who else might have had copies of her research. My guess is they wanted to understand her process so they could find some way to make it impossible for her to proceed. But you got to her first."

"Oh. So that business about keeping mum on the Saudi

reserves? Was that the real reason they blew up the rental car in Toronto and killed...and killed Emily?"

"Watson claims he knew nothing about that explosion."

"So who's his boss at WFFA?"

"Walpender. So he's a dead end." She chuckled grimly. "Bad pun, huh? Oh, and Watson's prints were the other set on the stuff in Emily's chest. He has admitted involvement there, so your sister's name is cleared."

That was something. Munson reached for his coffee cup. "And Dragonclaw?"

"We're still looking."

"Well you've been busy." He found the cup and lifted it.

"Need help?"

"I'm good." He managed to get it to his mouth and set it back down without spilling.

"Munson, I'm terribly sorry about Martha."

He swallowed and said nothing.

The door swung open and Niiqway rose swiftly. Munson stiffened.

"Good morning, Dr. Munson, I'm Dr. Harris. Oh, I see you have company."

"No problem," said Niiqway. "Well, Munson, I'll leave you in the doctor's capable hands. Call me if you have any more questions."

"I will." She was gone before he remembered he had no phone.

Dr. Harris approached the bed. "Well, I'll bet you'd like to be able to see her the next time you speak with her. Let's dim the lights and we'll take a look at what's under those bandages, shall we?"

CHAPTER 26

Munson strode into the office. Addy rose from her desk. "Oh, Munson!"

He grinned. "Like my patch? Aaar, me 'arty..."

She laughed, then sobered. "Is it permanent?"

"Just for a couple more days," he said. "And the stitches will come out soon, too."

She shook her head. "You going to remove the rest of that beard?"

"Nah," said Munson. "I'm kind of liking the whole overall patchy effect. So, anything urgent here?"

"You've had a few of calls from a Dr. Whitey," she looked at him over the top of her glasses. "I'd appreciate it if you get in touch with him soon. Your new cell phone is loaded with your contacts. The mail and email is all in the usual order."

"They haven't found my old cell phone?"

"I'd be surprised if they could find anything in that wreck, Munson." She shook her head. "It was quite awful to see."

"Addy, what happened to the clothes I was wearing?"

"Akira brought them here," she said. "They were such a mess I just threw them out."

"Was there a flash drive among my things?"

Her brow wrinkled. "No, just your wallet, your CSIS badge and gun, which Scott Blake has picked up—oh, and your watch. Did the hospital—"

He pulled up his sleeve to show her.

"Was the USB drive important?"

Important. What an understatement. "Rather," he said.

"I'd be happy to make a new copy of whatever files were on it?"

"They were from someone else, Addy," he said. "I'll take care of it."

The phone rang and Addy raised her eyebrows at him.

"Go on," he said. He poked his head into Irish's office. "Aaar!"

"Lord, look at you," said Irish. "I heard you were a mess. You're lucky to be alive."

Munson slumped into a chair. "I know."

"And what's this I hear, the energy minister was murdered in your hospital room."

"Martha. She was…" Munson swallowed.

"Tell me this has nothing to do with that Dr. Fraser business."

Munson shrugged. "I'm not sure. Where's Akira?"

"She's off for a few days, says she has family in town. You need to talk to—yes Addy?"

Munson turned to the doorway. Addy was looking at him over the tops of her glasses. "Munson, Dr. Whitey is on the line again."

He nodded. "I'll take it in my office."

"Thank you," she said. "Irish, you're going to be late."

He glanced at his watch. "Gotta run. Munson, glad you're back. Catch up later."

Munson trailed Addy and then continued on into his own office, closing the door. He picked up the phone and punched the flashing line button. "Whitey!"

"Munson, laddie! I think I'm in love with your receptionist. What will it take me to woo her away from you?"

Munson chuckled. "Addy is my own executive assistant extraordinaire. Hands off."

"Ah, too bad," said Whitey. "Look, I wanted to let you know what I'm up to before I go."

"Go?"

"Astronomical adaptive optics," Whitey boomed. "The project is ready! We are going to deploy millions of tiny reflective lenses in space."

"Who's we?"

"Laddie, get up to speed. Ya told me to get in touch with John Stark, and I did."

"The researcher from the University of Alberta?"

"The very same. That project is colleague was working on, deploying wafer-thin silicon particles in direct line with the sun?"

"Yeah, the shadow-caster," said Munson.

"Shadow-caster! I like it! Let me write that down. There. Great media sound bite, laddie. As I was saying, it's ready. We're about to launch an experimental mission. First, I'll ride up to the space station where we'll load the reflective lenses. Then, after blasting off from there in a command module, I'll head out in direct line with the sun—"

"Hang on, they're sending *you?*"

"Aye, laddie! Told ya I'm ex-NASA; trained as an astronaut for years."

"But—"

"But nothing. Let me finish. I'll be way the hell out there. So far that NASA has no way of deployin' the reflective lenses with commands from earth. An astronaut must fine tune the deployment and send the final launch data back via a remote capsule. And I landed the job!"

"But that sounds like a suicide mission!"

"It may be, laddie. If it works, they'll be able to use the data from the remote capsule to send up unmanned launches."

"But you can't—"

"Ah, but I can. This is my exit strategy. I'm heading into the final stages of prostate cancer."

Munson was stunned into silence.

"I got a plan I'll share in strict confidence. The capsule will be in a flat-line non-orbit. That's the beauty of it. There would be a lot of pain and sufferin' in my last days down here. I'd be doped up on pain killers. It'd be a bitch. Up there I can go out in style."

"What do you mean?"

"When I've done the deployment, I'll drink a jug of scotch, set a course for home, and blow the damned hatch!"

Munson shook his head. "You sure about this?"

"I'm as certain about this as anything I've ever done in this life, laddie."

"You're sure the shadow-caster will work?"

"I know the project inside and out," said Whitey. "The deployment and magnetic control set up has to be done just right, so the angle of the reflective canopy can be adjusted from the space station with laser commands. You know: warmer, warm, cool, cooler, coolest," he laughed heartily. "How's that for a partin' gift to humanity?"

Munson had to chuckle at Whitey's enthusiasm. "I'll miss you, Whitey," he managed. "I'm going to get a bottle of the best scotch I can find, and toast your success."

"Now you're talkin'," Whitey smiled happily. "Say, I need a home for Winston Churchill and Eleanor Roosevelt. You don't suppose?"

"Sure, Whitey, I'll look after your huskies."

"Good lad. There's a parcel coming for you by courier. It's the patents and the ownership of the discovery. I'm leaving them to you."

Addy buzzed. "Acting CSIS Director Scott Blake is here to see you, Munson. Shall I send him in?"

"Warn him," said Munson.

She chuckled. "I already did."

"Wow," said Blake. "You are quite a mess."

"Yeah, but I'm alive," said Munson. "Have a seat."

"Terrible about Martha Ambrose," said Blake, setting his briefcase on the floor. "Security footage hasn't been any help; the assassin was gowned and masked. Gloves too."

"Was she the target, or was—" Munson swallowed.

"Probably both of you. She'd been digging stuff up, digging deep enough to trigger our security systems. She was scouring intelligence websites about Russia and China, and my guess is she'd come across something that got her killed. Dragonclaw is behind all this." He shook his head. "We must find Dragonclaw."

"Addy introduced you as CSIS director—did she inadvertently promote you, or has something happened?"

Blake grinned, nodding. "Evans is gone. Ying Kao's disappearance implicated him, along with Colonel Raigan. All three were removed from office pending further investigation. Telford gave the order, but not before all three had disappeared. What are you thinking? Is Telford in on it?"

Munson shook his head. "Highly unlikely. Telford's always been easy to lead, but he's not clever enough to be behind any of it." Kao, Evans and Raigan. Evans could be Dragonclaw, but Raigan was a clumsy liar. Munson's money was on Kao. "No idea where the three of them are now?"

"Kim was the last one to see Kao, and the others vanished a couple of days ago when the CIA started turning up the heat."

"What do they figure Kao's up to with the nuke?"

Blake shrugged. "We don't really know. The American president is in the loop; the U.S. has ordered every agency into action. We've contacted all police forces and intelligence agencies. The President has asked that we not brief the press to avoid panic in our cities. They've raised their terror alert to red. Right now, our only objective is to find the bomb."

"Any luck so far?

"We have intelligence that they're targeting Seattle. Our people searched Kao's and Raigan's residences found solid leads. Because it's on the western coastline and very near the Canadian border, detonating a nuclear weapon there would thoroughly devastate both countries at once, and the prevailing winds would carry the fallout east."

"My god," said Munson.

"Additionally there was an unauthorized military flight from Ellesmere Island to an unused airstrip on Vancouver Island. We're pretty certain that it carried the bomb. An ocean-going tug was leased in Vancouver; that tug has disappeared. Looks like they plan to bring the bomb down the coast and into the Seattle harbor."

Munson frowned. "No wonder Telford thinks Canada's under imminent threat. But have you told him about the Seattle link? He's so paranoid about the U.S. that the last time we spoke, he suggested they're pulling a fast one, focusing us on the various off-shore threats while they invade up the middle."

"I suppose it's possible." Blake grinned. "Even paranoid people do have enemies. My money's on the Chinese." He leaned back. Let's hope we do a better job of it this time around."

Munson frowned. "This time?"

"During the Korean War, American marines battled three hundred thousand Chinese troops who were defending North Korean territory near the Chosin Reservoir."

"Were we involved?"

"Kind of. We had five hundred Canadians over there fighting in the American army. It was in the bitterly cold winter when they effectively drove us out of North Korea."

"Ah, yes." Munson nodded. "I've read the history of the break-out at Chosin. MacArthur, right?"

"The Chinese gathered overwhelming forces, surrounded his army. An American platoon leader of Chinese descent named Lee led five hundred American marines in to break out the trapped army. As I recall, som six hundred marines died and four thousand were wounded."

"But MacArthur's army escaped?"

"That's right," Blake said. "Lee returned from Korea a hero, but our retreat left North and South Korea divided. And we learned not to underestimate the Chinese."

"I suppose a war with China could place some of our

citizens of Chinese ancestry in a quandary," Munson mused.

"Like Lee, our citizens of Chinese descent would end up fighting their own brothers. But China is not to be messed with when it comes to Korea. This could blow up again."

"So this isn't just about oil?"

Blake sighed. "Oil's just part of the picture. Arable land, fresh water...it all comes down to power."

Munson wondered if he should tell Blake about Whitey's shadow-caster project. Was it secret? It hadn't occurred to him to ask.

Blake opened his briefcase. "I came to give you these." He placed the CSIS badge and holstered gun on Munson's desk. "You understand that we can't trust our own organization. Niiqway's still counting on you for backup."

"I thought she was through?"

"Mission's not over," said Blake. "There's a lot at stake. Can we count on you?"

Munson stared at the gun. "I'm—"

"Munson, she couldn't tell you she was CIA," said Blake. "That was eating her up. I understand if you can't get past that, but please believe me when I tell you that she always had your back. Can she count on you?"

Munson nodded slowly.

"Thanks," said Blake. "She called earlier today and told me she's on to something. I'll let her know you're in. She'll be in touch."

CHAPTER 27

Munson opened the package Telford had couriered over. He shook his head. The file was clearly marked *For the Prime Minister's eyes only,* yet here it was, on his desk. He sighed. He lifted the sticky note that said *Just read the cover page & call me—J.T.* and began reading.

The primary cause of the global temperature acceleration has been confirmed. It establishes that the escalation began thirty months ago, when global temperature graphs curved sharply upward, spurring a world-wide search for the cause. At our Brussels meeting this week, the cause has been established as a growing level of solar heat from sun flares, very difficult to measure, originating from the sun itself. It is melting methane hydrates, until now frozen as white crystalline solids on the Arctic sea beds and sub-Arctic permafrost.

As the sun's heat intensifies, billions of tons of methane—a greenhouse gas over a thousand times more damaging than carbon dioxide—are being released from the depths of the Barents Sea and Arctic Ocean. Atmospheric carbon and large high pressure cloudless areas over the Arctic have enabled the sun's intensifying heat to penetrate the dark iceless oceans and melt these crystalline solids on the sea floor.

Because methane gas, when released from its crystalline solid form, has a volume 150 times greater than when bonded, it has resulted in a massive and continuing discharge of methane into the atmosphere. This, coupled with carbon from fossil fuels and other greenhouse gasses, is causing a rapid acceleration of global temperatures. In short, unless the sun flares diminish, the planet may reach a tipping point beyond which recovery is no longer possible.

To further intensify the problem Antarctic ice has begun a slow alarming collapse into the sea. Scientists warn that if this continues, it will eventually raise the sea levels by twelve feet. This is in addition to the rising sea levels from the Greenland ice sheet's slow and erratic collapse.

The current spiraling temperatures account for the increasing human population migrations from the central latitudes toward the cooler Poles, in search of land for food production and water.

Scientists are searching for solutions, but fearing panic do not wish to release this devastating information until world leaders are fully briefed.

No wonder the shadow-casting mission was a go. Munson dialed Telford's number and waited patiently to be put through.

"Well?" Telford sounded terribly anxious. "Does it mean what I think it means?"

"I'm afraid so."

Telford sighed. "Your scientist friends were right about the seriousness of the global heat thing. It's worse than having Russia and China and the U. S. all ready to overrun our borders."

"Yup. Suddenly everything pales by comparison," said Munson. "We are facing catastrophe, Joe."

"So the sky really *is* falling this time," said Telford. "Keep this to yourself until you see it in the news."

"Of course."

"We have just a few days until the summit meeting." Telford's voice was weak with fear. "Pray for a miracle."

Munson hung up and took the file to the shredder, deep in thought. Canada was on the brink of becoming a wasteland, a battlefield, or both. Did Telford know about the shadow-caster project? If successful, that might stave off the biggest problem.

He had a vision of foreign troops massing into an ever-drier Canada, young men and women fighting for oil with their dying breath. He had to reach Pavel, keep him and his crew in the north.

———————+———————

Munson checked his email; still no answer from Akira. He buzzed Addy. "Do we have Akria's cell or home number?"

"Just a moment," she said. "Got a pen?"

He jotted it down, thanked her and called Akira.

It went straight to voicemail. "Akira? Munson. Sorry to interrupt your time off. Just wondering if anything was in that bundle of clothing you picked up. I'm missing a flash drive. Could you please call me? If you do have it, I'd like to come and pick it up as soon as possible. Thanks."

He hung up and tried Niiqway. Hers was still going to voicemail. Damn, where *was* everyone. He buzzed Addy again. "You heard from Pavel?"

"Not a word, Munson," she said. "I'm sure they're just in the midst of pulling up camp. Not to worry."

He sighed. "Yeah, you're probably right."

"Are you going home tonight?"

He looked at the time. "Might as well. I'm surprised you're still here."

"Just finishing payroll," she said. "Everyone else is long gone. You go on. I'll lock up."

He shrugged into his jacket, collected his car keys and cell phone, and headed for the elevator. "Night, Addy."

"Good night, Munson." She looked over her glasses at him. "Go straight to bed."

He grinned. "Yes, ma'am."

As he stepped out of the elevator, his phone buzzed; text message from Niiqway.

Peace Tower observ deck a.s.a.p.

He frowned. What was this about? Nodding to the security guard, he headed for his car. His phone buzzed again, and he recognized Blake's number. "Blake?"

"Munson, can you pass your phone to Niiqway? Hers isn't—"

"She's not here, Blake. She just texted me to meet her at the Peace Tower."

"Well, where the hell are you? You were supposed to be her backup!"

"What?" Munson started the engine.

"God almighty!" Blake's voice rose several notches. "Didn't you get her messages?"

"I just got her text. I'm on my way." Dropping the phone on the passenger seat, he drove out of the parkade as quickly as he dared and headed toward the Parliament Buildings. Navigating with one eye still felt odd, but the early evening traffic was light, and he made good time. On Wellington Street he pulled up on the sidewalk. A pedestrian hollered "Hey! You can't park there!"

Munson flashed his CSIS badge and headed for the Peace Tower. The security guard stepped forward. "Visiting hours are—"

He flashed his badge again. "I need access. Get me some back-up, fast!" The guard stepped aside, pushing the button on his radio. Inside the building, Munson ran up the stairs to the third floor elevator, prepared to flash his badge again but surprised to see no guard. The foyer and elevator were both empty. He pressed the button for the 9th floor and the elevator began to move, its glass walls gliding slowly upward past the clockworks.

Munson clutched the handrail and closed his good eye.

The doors slid open, and Munson stepped shakily out onto the observation deck, head reeling. Fighting vertigo, cursing the patch that limited his vision, he forced himself to look at anything but the windows. There was the glass display case that held the original clock works, and over there the diagram of the tower... Where was Niiqway? Steeling himself, he edged further into the room. Was that blood on the floor, there? The floor-level window looked out over the lights of the city, far below. Panicked, he dropped to his knees.

"Let me do this!" Was the tower actually swaying? No,

of course not. Just the vertigo. Crawl forward, look only at the floor… the blood smear continued up the frame of the window and—shit. Damn those floor-level windows! Suddenly helpless, gripped by a mindless fear, he waited for the room to stop spinning.

Who's blood was that, Niiqway's? Shakily, he reached for his gun. Crawling along the floor, forcing himself to focus, he followed the trail to the stairwell door. Pulling himself upright, he eased it open. Something was blocking it from opening completely—a leg, he realized.

Niiqway's?

No, that was a man's shoe. Pushing harder, he forced the door open. It was the security guard.

As Munson bent to check for a pulse, the man's radio crackled to life. "Forster, come in!"

The man was breathing. Munson reached for the microphone and pressed the button. "Floor nine stairwell," he said. "Man down. Send—"

A shot rang out above him. "Shots fired!" He released the microphone and raised his gun. Heart racing, he crept up the stairs, gun at the ready. Two flights up he found another body: Evans was slumped against the wall at the base of a ladder. Blood oozed from a small hole in his brow. Munson's foot bumped something, and he glanced down. A gun. He picked it up and set the safety, then tucked it into his waistband.

He looked up, realizing he'd have to stow his own gun, and steeled himself to climb. It's just a ladder, he thought. Niiqway needs you.

He heard the distant whup-whup of a helicopter, and realized he was well above the tower's clock face, inside the steep metal-roofed peak where a series of stairs and ladders would take him to the tiny platform that accessed the flagpole, more than 300 feet above the ground.

His head spun. *Dear god.* Reeling, he clung to the ladder.

Another shot rang above, and Munson forced himself to focus on climbing. There, there was the top. He poked his head through the opening, trying to block out the city view, trying to imagine he was on solid ground.

The roof is flat. You can walk on a flat surface without falling. You will not fall. He forced his good eye open.

Niiqway.

Her body was slumped over the guard rail, dangling perilously; a stiff wind would push her over. The chopper hovered overhead, but a change in the noise of its engine made him react instinctively: he dove for Niiqway. A bullet whistled past his ear as he grabbed her ankle and the bird took flight, its rope ladder trailing.

"I've got you, Niiqway!" Rising to his knees, he pulled her body from the railing and onto the platform.

"Munson?" She crouched beside him and glared at the receding helicopter, the spotlights on the roof casting weird shadows over her face and onto the flag high above them. "Thanks for showing up."

"You're okay?"

"Totally. Kao's a lousy shot, but she did manage to get me to drop my gun. I was playing possum so she'd— Munson, you okay? You're white as a ghost."

"Heights," he said.

"There's no time for that," she said, prodding him. "The bomb's here, in the tower."

"Here?"

From beneath them, the clock chimes rang. "That was the half hour," she said, pulling out her cell phone. "Blake? It's here in the building. Yes, the bomb. Detonator's rigged to the clapper for the biggest bell, so it'll go off on the hour. We have less than thirty minutes." She stuffed her phone into her pocket. "For god's sake, Munson, get moving!"

Munson forced his shaking knees into action and began retreating downward. At the bottom of the first ladder, Niiqway scurried around him and rushed on ahead. "Floor six," she yelled. "Don't use the elevator, it's too slow."

By the time he caught up, Blake and two uniformed police officers had arrived. Niiqway turned to Munson. "The guy from the raft, the Homeland Security fellow—"

He sank to the floor. "Anderson?"

"Yeah. He in your phone contacts?"

Munson handed her his phone. "Aaron Anderson..." She was already dialing. Munson looked up at Blake. "Bomb squad?"

He shook his head. "No time." He pointed to the clapper inside the bell. "There's the detonator."

"Aaron Anderson? Agent Niiqway, CIA. Remember me from the raft? ... Yeah. He's here, too. We have a situation. Detonator wired to a bell clapper. It'll move in about 25 minutes. If I send you photos, can you tell us how to disarm it?" She listened a moment. "Clearing the area's absolutely impossible. This is a nuclear emergency. ... Good. Send to this phone? ... A live camera, good idea." She looked down at the phone and touched the screen. "Here. Now you're on speaker phone, too. Tell me where to point it."

"Little to the left," said Anderson's voice. "Can you get some more light on it?"

One of the police officers stepped forward with a flashlight.

"That's better. Bit more to the left, Agent. Yeah, I recognize it. That's a crude system. Remote, but it doesn't have a lot of range. Where are you?"

"Inside the Peace Tower," said Niiqway.

"Stone building? Thick walls?"

Niiqway glanced at the officer, eyebrows raised.

"Three to six feet thick," said the officer, "although we're in the shuttered belfry area."

"Right," said Anderson. "I've pulled up a diagram on a website. Given the angles I'm betting your bomb's onsite. Niiqway, tilt the camera a bit to the right. Bit more."

Munson got to his feet and turned to Blake. "Can't we just turn off the chimes?"

Blake shook his head. "There's another detonator—"

"Hold it," said Anderson. "Another detonator?"

"Yeah," said Blake. "Chime control room."

"Christ," said Anderson. "Get someone over there with another camera, get some photos. We'll need to do this in sequence."

Blake nodded to the second officer, who hurried down the stairs."

"And find the bomb," continued Anderson. "You said nuclear. What—"

"Plutonium and uranium," said Munson. "Cold war era."

"Mother of god. Find—" Anderson was silenced by the chimes began to declare the three-quarter hour, deafening them all for a moment. "Find it, Munson! It'll be big and heavy as hell. And it can't be too far away. Now, does anyone have a pocket knife?"

Munson tried to clear his head. The bomb could be above him, or below. Heavy, and the elevator was old and unpredictable. More likely below.

Knees still shaking, Munson made his way down through the tower, passing the officer on his way back up. "Anything down there besides the detonator?"

The officer was taking the stairs two at a time. "Nothing obvious," he called back.

That left the Memorial Chamber. It made sense, thought Munson; to get it in there, they wouldn't have needed to use the elevator at all.

As he arrived in the foyer, clattering boots announced the arrival of the bomb squad. "I think it's in here," he said, trying to open the door. "Shit! It's locked."

"I'll get that!" A building security guard pushed his way around the heavily-uniformed men, key in hand.

One of the squad men stepped back to let him through. "Where's Blake?"

"They're disarming two detonation systems in the large belfry and the chime control room," said Munson. "We don't know if there's another—"

"McMillan, Crawley—your teams, upstairs!" He brushed

past Munson and into the Memorial Chamber. There, on the stone altar, sat the bomb.

"Oh, my god." The building guard's face was reddening in fury. "Monstrous!"

"Dragonclaw's doing," Munson muttered.

The police officer pushed his way into the room, holding a cell phone out to Munson. "Anderson wants to know what we've found," he said.

"It's here," said Munson. "Is the camera—yeah. Here."

"Good," said Anderson. "Move it along the left side there—yeah, pan the whole thing. Whoever set this up knew exactly what they were doing. The bomb squad's there, right? Put 'em on."

Munson was glad to hand the phone over and get the hell out of the way.

He was outside on the front steps when Niiqway sank down beside him. "We need to clear the area," she said, handing him his phone.

He looked up at the clock, his head swimming at the thought of being up there. In less than two minutes, it would be over; they'd be dead, and the world as he knew it would cease to exist.

"What's the point?"

She put her hand on the shoulder. "Munson, it's over."

He nodded. "I know. Sorry I was so bullheaded, Niiqway."

"No hard feelings." She grinned. "Hey, Munson, don't look so blue. We won."

In spite of himself, he looked up at the clock again.

The hands hadn't moved.

"It's over," she said again. "They've disarmed it. There's still a risk while they dismantle and move it, so they're clearing the area—Munson, are you okay?"

Good question. He couldn't tell whether he was laughing or crying. "Yeah, Niiqway, I'm okay."

"Let me take you home."

CHAPTER 28

Munson woke up in her guest bedroom, ravenous. The door to her room was closed, so he checked the fridge and the pantry and started making breakfast. She emerged a few minutes later, fully dressed with her hair wound in a towel.

He looked at her, and was suddenly very tired. His knees were weak and his hands shook.

"Let me finish up," she said. "You rest. That was brave of you, coming to my rescue with your fear of heights."

"Kao could have killed you."

"Nah, she's a lousy shot." Niiqway grinned. "Good thing she's bad at something."

She set a plate of bacon and eggs in front of him and poured a cup of coffee.

"What took you so long to show up yesterday?"

"I came as soon as I got your text."

"I'd left three voice messages," she said.

He pulled his cell phone from his pocket, frowning.

Niiqway's cell buzzed, and she chuckled. "Hi, Blake," she said. "Yeah, he's here with me." She looked at Munson. "Blake's been trying to—what? Yeah, I'll switch to speakerphone. There, you're on. What's up?"

"Good morning, Munson," said Blake.

"Morning," said Munson.

"Some news. A bit anticlimactic after last night's events. Thank you both for your hard work."

"You find my gun?"

"Yup. It slid down the roof and got caught on one of those weird gargoyle things that hangs off the tower. The dragon one. I'm going to take that as a sign: Kao must have been Dragonclaw after all."

"Been?" Munson looked at Niiqway.

"She and Raigan were surrounded when the chopper set down. Raigan refused to take the chopper back up, so she shot him and tried to take it up herself. When she could see that wasn't going to work, she killed herself."

"So we might never know," said Niiqway.

"We'll figure it out," said Blake.

"How'd they get the chopper?"

"Raigan and Evans still had loyal people on the inside. Some of our people were convinced I was pushing Evans out so I could get to the top. Even that guard at the Peace Tower believed him when he said he and Kao were there to stop terrorists; he cleared the helicopter's use of protected airspace."

"Raigan wasn't as good at it," said Munson.

"No, but he had Evans for credibility, and Kao was a master manipulator." Blake coughed. "Sorry, lungs didn't like being up all night."

"You should get to bed," said Niiqway.

"CSIS never sleeps," said Blake. "Something else: They've also recovered enough of the wreckage from the AC-990 to know there was a bomb on board, probably detonated prematurely by the lightning. Same kind of explosives that were used on your rental car in Toronto, Munson."

He shook his head. If Kao wasn't already dead, he'd kill her himself.

"Niiqway, we've got Munson's car released from impound. It's at his office."

"I'll drop him there on my way in," said Niiqway. "See you shortly."

She yawned. "Oh, my, saving the world takes it out of a person. Munson, finish your breakfast."

Niiqway dropped him in front of the building. As Munson walked past the spot where Addy usually parked her ancient BMW, his hair stood on end. A white Cadillac, brand new. He glanced down at the familiar, distinctive plate he'd gotten her years ago.

NVMB3RS.

Cursing, he dialed Niiqway's cell, cursing more when it went straight to voicemail. "Come right away. Park out front. Bring backup."

He took the stairs two at a time.

Addy's desk was bare; even her computer tower was gone. He found her at his desk. "Why, Munson, I wasn't expecting you so early," she said. "Just sorting your email."

"Where's your computer, Addy?"

"Out for servicing," she said. "Seems to have a virus."

He closed the door, leaning against it.

"Munson?" She stood.

He realized this was the first time he'd seen Addy look uncertain about anything, and he smiled. "Dragonclaw."

Her smile faltered. "What's this about, Dr. Munson?"

"You've been with me for years, first as my secretary with Galaxy-21 and then here. You've been hacking into our energy strategies and technologies for the Chinese all this time, even during my Arctic exploration days."

She stared at him, her diminutive body rigid, her expression hardening as her right hand slipped into her bag.

"You murdered Emily, Addy. She used my credit card to rent that car. You had it bombed, thinking that you were killing me. Your Chinese bosses wanted you to keep me from revealing the Saudi oil shortfall. Damn you to hell Addy. You killed my sister!"

She laughed. "Seems I misunderstood Emily's call; I thought you were with her. I booked seats on that first flight for both of you."

Pulling out a Berretta with a silencer, she smiled sourly at him and cocked the weapon.

"You helped to kill hundreds of innocent people on the AC-990. Why?"

Addy aimed the Berretta. "All those sniveling delegates, insisting we must give up everything we enjoy to save a planet that is only going to destroy itself. Besides, I was about to lose huge investments once they figured out Centwenti screwed over the engineering on their fancy new plane." Her eyes narrowed. "Bloody incompetent fools. How ironic that the lightning took Walpender's fat ass down before he could get off in Toronto. Too bad he survived, with *you*, of all people, on that damned raft in the Atlantic."

"So you sent Bolavar's goons after us. "

"Bolavar had to get hold of Fraser's discovery. Find some way to kill it before it got off the ground."

"You kept throwing suspicion on me. You made my life a living hell."

She grinned. "Aw, poor you." She stared at him, her eyes cold. "Guess it's time to put you out of your misery."

"You fire bombed my house. You tried to have us killed in France. You sent Karim after me. You tried to kill us with your Cadillac in Toronto. And you killed Martha in my hospital room. Why was she on your hit list?"

"She was blocking the west coast pipeline and China's oil deal, and she'd figured out Bolavar was heading up WFFA. I needed her gone before he could implicate me."

"Martha didn't deserve to die. Neither did Emily, or any of those people on the AC-990. Damn you, Addy!"

She smiled. "You really liked Ambrose, didn't you?"

"And you would have blown up the Canadian capital. Killed thousands, hundreds of thousands…"

As she raised the gun, there was a commotion in the foyer behind Munson. He swung the door open. "It's over, Dragonclaw."

Addy glanced at the doorway, where Niiqway was

backed up by a police tactical team. With a look of resigna-
tion, she turned and fired at the plate glass window,
shattering the glass, then ran headlong through it. She
made not a sound as she sailed out into space and fell
headlong, six stories to the street below.

The leader of the police tactical team stepped over to the
window and looked down. "Jesus," he said, crossing himself. "The way Agent Niiqway described who we were
after, I was expecting someone larger than life, Satan himself. She was a wee mite of a person!"

After a long moment Munson said, "She was a monster."

Irish Harrigan strode into the office. "I just passed your
friend Niiqway on the stairs. What the hell—"

"Addy," said Munson. "She was behind everything."

Harrigan's mouth hung open for a long moment. "Well,
that explains why you haven't been returning our calls."

Munson frowned. "What's up?"

"Pavel's been leaving voicemail for you all night. We've
struck pay dirt," he said. "They were checking a glacier on
Baffin on their way home, and found exactly what you
thought they would find. He reached Addy here this
morning, and she promised to file the paperwork."

Ignoring the yawning gap in the window, Munson went
to his computer. "That's exactly what she was up to," he
said, bending to peer at the screen. "Shit. She was filing
them for a numbered company, not ours."

"Where's her computer?"

"My bet is it's far, far from here," said Munson, typing
overtop of Addy's entry. "If she'd had her way, Ottawa
would have ceased to exist overnight. That didn't work, so
she hustled back here to tie up loose ends that could lead
us to her."

Irish went to the window and looked down. "God.
Addy?" He shook his head. "Who would have thought?
The world truly is going to hell in a handbasket."

"Irish, I have a proposition for you," said Munson. "A
whole new career in saving the world."

At the camp on Baffin Island, Munson watched the news-feed of Telford's media conference. Irish and Dr. Tomlinson had addressed the summit meeting, explaining the enormous potential of Dr. Fraser's discovery. There was every possibility the technology would create a viable energy alternative before the Saudi reserves failed, and the key players had all agreed to an uneasy peace.

It remained to be seen what unintended consequences the market would suffer, with the price of platinum bottoming out. Although Irish assured the world that he would do everything within his power to ensure that the new supply of platinum would be used only in fuel applications, no doubt they were in for a rough ride.

Reporters asking if the discovery was linked to the recent arrests of Galaxy-21 president Max Bolavar or the rumored assassination of a spy code named Dragonclaw were quickly brushed off. The press conference ended with beaming world leaders all shaking hands, and Munson was about to close the screen when more breaking news came on:

NASA announced today that, regardless strong calls for delay of the project by several prominent climate scientists and well-known environmental icons, the first deployment of Astronomical Adaptive Optics has begun. Within a few hours, we should be able to tell you whether or not the experiment, nicknamed the Shadow Caster, is successful. First indications are promising—"

Munson laughed. "Good for Whitey. Perhaps it will work. Let's hope that we've learned enough to know what we're doing."

The two huskies at his feet lifted their heads, and Munson heard a helicopter approaching. "Come," he said. "Let's go welcome Niiqway."

The dogs danced with excitement as Niiqway climbed out of the helicopter. "Welcome," he said. "Meet our two newest team members, Eleanor Roosevelt and Winston

Churchill. You've already met our young geologists, Akira Tanaka and Pavel Krotov."

She exchanged hellos, then he took her arm. "Come and look, Niiqway. See the scouring, the scraping marks along the rock face? They were caused by thousands of years of ice movement down the glacier bed. That's dunite, rich in trace elements of platinum and palladium—miles of it, until last year hidden by ice. It is the holy grail of hydrogen fuel cells."

Placing several small rocks in her hand, he closed her fingers around them and held them closed.

"Feel those? We've done it. In your hand lie the exotic metals that make possible what Dr. Fraser called the Seafire Shift; the move away from our costly, declining petroleum supply to cheap, clean, unlimited hydrogen. It offers hope to our increasingly tense and ailing civilization."

He released her hand, and she examined the four little rocks ground smooth by years of glacial and ocean movement. "Something so small," she said.

"Imagine that," he grinned. "This all started when you dragged me down to the iceberg. It's here, Niiqway. It's right here, and it's massive! It's been hidden deep below the ice for thousands of years."

"Can you get it out without destroying the land, bringing more harm to my people?"

"That's our plan." He turned serious." We'll apply to purchase the land from the Crown for a town site and deep sea port facility to be owned by your people." He paused. "The port will be navigable for most of the year. We'll lay out an airstrip to the south. The mining engineers will design enclosed equipment that will be reliable even in extreme winter temperatures. The future commerce that flows from this discovery will help secure the economic future of the Inuit in the region." He stopped. "Does this sound like a good thing?"

"It certainly does," she agreed, watching as nearby, a weasel scrambled in to the rocks, stared at the dogs and then scurried for cover. "The north might save the world. Let's hope the superpowers will back off and accept your plan."

"They must," he said. "The world depends upon it."

"I think Kim Sorqaq will be pleased."

"I hear he's out on bail?"

She nodded. "His actions could have cost us dearly, but he really did little more than fall under the spell of a beautiful and manipulative woman. He is embarrassed about it, and he has been very depressed. I hope you're not still angry with him."

"I'm not," said Munson. "Emily once told me that each of us has three lives. The first life is for learning, the second is for living and learning, and the third is for living and remembering." He sighed. "Time for him to move forward, into his second life."

"Move forward," she said. "Standing still is almost impossible, isn't it? It's funny how major events start. Have you ever heard of the butterfly effect?"

"Chaos theory?"

"Yes. Change one small thing, and you change everything. For example, the lookout crew of the Titanic forgot one small thing—to bring along their binoculars—so they didn't see the iceberg."

"Mmm, that was one theory," he nodded.

"Think back, Munson when did all this start? What was the one small thing that you did, that changed everything?"

"That I did? Well, let's see," he thought a moment. "It was in London when I had an impulse to help Dr. Fraser. She entrusted me with her discovery. If not for that, none of this would have happened." He smiled. "I think, however, that there was more than blind luck and chaos theory at work in our intense few weeks of struggle."

She smiled. "You mean God may have guided and protected us from time to time?"

Munson nodded. "It's possible, but..."

"But?"

"I have a guardian angel. She's tall, auburn-haired and very, very tough."

Niiqway was quiet for a moment. "I wish things could have worked out differently for us," she said.

"Me too," said Munson.

"Maybe with time…"

"No," said Munson. "Don't wait. Move forward. I have a hard time trusting, and there's no point pretending otherwise. Trust is essential in a relationship. Don't wait, hoping that I might change."

Niiqway looked out over the shore. "You might want to call this new townsite Port Emily," she said.

"Port Emily," he said. "I like that."

Munson hugged Niiqway, then watched her duck under the rotor and climb back into the helicopter. He waved, one hand shading his eyes, until the helicopter became a tiny speck and vanished into the horizon. Then he called to the dogs and returned to his tent.

The newsfeed for the Shadow Caster was positive; the deployment had been successful. "All's right with the universe," he told the dogs. Everything was unfolding as it should. Fetching a bottle of scotch and his flute, he walked down to the shoreline, dogs at his heels.

"Well done, Whitey!" He raised a toast. "Now, blow the damned hatch!"

From G.D.Matheson's

THE NAPLES PREDICTION

Kristin Stefsdotir lay on the cabin roof, gazing out at the lights of Naples twinkling in the darkness. The June night was hot and humid, but a slight breeze through the *Challenger's* rigging made it easier to sleep up here than in the yacht's stateroom below. Across the water, Vesuvius's towering hulk rose like a sentinel against a pale night sky, providing a sobering backdrop to the sleeping city while surrounding the huge volcano's base, a band of shimmering city lights coiled like a snake around its prey.

But here, the prey was by far the greater threat: Vesuvius and its big daddy Campi Flegrei, the supervolcano that lurked beneath the Gulf of Pozzuoli, made this one of the most dangerous places on Earth.

Today, though, it had become a little safer. Kristin and her colleague, Dr. Reginald Pyper, had just finished installing their newly developed volcano monitoring software, VolcanoWatch. As of this afternoon, both volcanoes were being heavily scrutinized by the most advanced system in existence. Replacing a time-consuming hands-on analysis method, VolcanoWatch would speed summarized information to scientists by instantly and simultaneously interpreting data from dozens of instruments spread throughout the volcanic danger area.

The full moon reappeared from behind the clouds. Kristin glanced down at her son, asleep on the mat next to hers. Heph had turned nine today. Yes, she thought with satisfaction, it had been a very good day. The anxiety that was keeping her awake was a holdover from that strange argument with Hilda Marsh and Antonio Camponolo the previous evening.

The meeting with the two Naples scientists, here on the yacht, had been cordial yet tense. Kristin and Reg shouldn't have had to defend their expectation to continue as consultants, visiting regularly to oversee operation of the new system. It was standard procedure. VolcanoWatch was already successfully monitoring Popocatéptl in Mexico, Pavlov in Alaska and the Taupo caldera in New Zealand. But Hilda and Antonio had vigorously resisted signing the consulting support contract.

Why had they been so difficult?

Kristin had been particularly surprised that her old colleague Hilda insisted she and Reg should back down. Maybe Hilda felt she had to agree with the other scientist. After all, Camponolo was not only influential and politically connected, he was also her boss. But what was *his* problem? It could not be a budget matter; ample funds were available. Why was he so insistent? At one point, Hilda almost seemed—afraid. What was it she'd said? "Kristin, it would be in your best interest to cooperate. You and Dr. Pyper don't know what..."

A look from Camponolo had silenced her.

Well, she'd soon be working with Hilda again in the African Congo. That would provide an opportunity to find out what was going on.

Still musing, Kristin drifted off.

She woke and instinctively glanced over at Heph, who was still sleeping. A muffled thud below deck brought her fully awake. Reg was sleeping in the stateroom; he had probably just used the bathroom. She sensed movement and watched his half-naked figure come on deck and walk across to the rail. Was he preparing to dive over? The clouds parted and the moon lit up the deck, and she gasped. It wasn't Reg.

Blood seeped down the side of his face. He was sheathing a knife, and his hand against his pale torso glowed crimson.

"Mom?" Heph sat up.

The man at the rail looked back at her and teetered, trying to abort the dive, but he lost his balance and went overboard with a splash.

Kristin placed a finger over her young son's mouth. "We're in terrible danger," she whispered. "Be quiet and follow me." Pulling him with her, she descended a ladder to the opposite deck. They hurried aft, climbed over the side and slipped into the dark water of the bay. There, she whispered in his ear, "Let's play dolphins. Ready?"

He nodded.

Swimming under water, she kept the boy close, every few yards bobbing up for air. When they were fifty yards out she treaded water and spoke softly to him. "Okay, now let's race to that buoy over there—" All the lights of the *Challenger* came on. "Down!" The yacht's searchlight panned over the water above them, then moved on.

They came up for air. "Dolphins again," Kristin said.

Finally reaching the buoy, they hung on and rested. "Good thing you are a water-baby," she told him as the searchlight continued to scan the water. "For a nine-year-old, you're an excellent swimmer."

"What's happening, Mom?"

"A very bad man is after us, Heph. Think you can swim all the way to the shore?"

The boy looked at the lights of a distant wharf. "I can make it easy, Mom."

"Rest here for a bit," she said, watching the yacht.

"Is Uncle Reg okay?"

Kristin pulled him close. "I don't think so," she said.

"Did the bad man hurt him?"

Kristin nodded.

"But why?"

She kissed the top of his head. "I don't know." Was this just a random act of violence, theft? If so, why was the man back on the yacht, looking for them? Remembering Camponolo's sudden brusque capitulation last night, and Hilda's fear, Kristin shuddered.

"Heph, when the bad man leaves the yacht, I'll have to go back and get our passports. We can't leave Italy without them."

"Why don't we just have Uncle Reg take us to Spain on his yacht?"

She looked at the boy. "Because, dear, I think Uncle Reg is dead."

She could sense him trying to comprehend. "Dead?"

"Yes. I think the bad man murdered him."

The boy was silent, thinking. "Then you could drive the yacht."

She shook her head. "I can't. I don't know how."

They waited. Finally, the yacht's lights turned off. Moments later, clouds obscured the moon. Kristin put her watch on the boy's wrist. "It is 2:20. If I am not back by 2:40, swim for that wharf, find a policeman and tell him what happened. Okay?"

"Okay. But be careful, Mom."

Swimming in the warm water of the bay was easy, yet she was experiencing cold shivers. The adrenalin rush was gone. Only a sickening fear for her child remained. In this part of Italy, Mafia were rumored to have murdered thousands. She must get out of the country with her son, and do it quickly.

She struck out fast, watching for movement on deck, and reached the yacht before the moon peeked out from behind the clouds. Waiting a moment, treading water, she listened for any sound up there—nothing. Hauling herself up, she crouched on the deck and watched.

All clear. Climbing the ladder to the roof of the cabin she found her flashlight. She crawled down and, holding the flashlight like a club, entered the salon. Was he waiting for her? Hurrying to the galley she stuffed two seal-tight plastic bags in her pocket and grabbed a butcher knife.

Stifling her fear and holding the knife at ready, she crept down a passageway and descended the stairway. She entered her stateroom, placed her wallet, her journal and the passports in sealed plastic bags, then selected light clothing for herself and for Heph and stuffed everything in her shoulder bag. Back out in the hallway she hesitated; the door to Dr. Pyper's room was half-open. Steeling herself, she pushed it open and shone a light on his bed.

It was crimson. Reg lay sprawled across the mattress sideways in a pool of blood, lifeless eyes staring up, the shattered bedside lamp still clutched in his hand.

Kristin backed away, heading for the deck. Then, with her shoulder bag around her neck, she dove in.

When she got to the buoy, Heph was not there. Had she been gone more than twenty minutes? She wasn't sure.

Dear God. Had the assassin found him? She looked toward the wharf and couldn't see a swimmer. If the killer had… There was only one option. She began swimming for the wharf. The moon was out again, silhouetting the wharves with their ship loading gantry cranes, their lighted booms aiming upward every which-way, fingers pointing toward the different constellations in the night sky.

She scanned the water. Still no sign of Heph. The moon dipped behind the clouds again, making it impossible to see whether her son was ahead. Surely her powerful breaststroke should have overtaken him by now. She stopped and called out softly. "Heph! Heph can you hear me?" Nothing—not a sound other than a siren somewhere in the city. Really anxious now, she treaded water, peering into the darkness.

A whisper. "Mom—I'm here."

She turned, felt him touch her shoulder. "Heph!"

"I followed you," he whispered. "I was near the buoy when you swam up, but so was he. He was following us."

"Keep close. We'll swim at right-angles to the shore." Swimming on more slowly so he could keep up, all she could think of was the bloody knife. How could she defend them? What if the moon came out and he could see them? There were breakers now, difficult to swim against. Perhaps they should turn and head in to shore.

She must save her child. If he attacked, so would she. To back off would be fatal. The knife scabbard was on his right side, so he was right-handed. He wasn't a large man but armed with a knife his attack would be—

It was sudden and vicious. Fortunately his first thrust missed, and his knife snagged in the leather bag strapped diagonally across her torso. She turned and kicked at him with all her strength, feeling her heel sink deep into his flesh. Grabbing to drag him under she struggled to grasp his right arm. Where was the knife? As he kicked at her she realized she was now hanging on to his ankle.

Advantage! Twisting and turning, swimming deeper, she kept pulling, rotating his ankle as she imagined him trying to slash at her. Deeper—deeper—his kicking was less violent, and now she'd caught his wrist. She could feel him tense for one last thrust. Air! She needed air! Twist his wrist! Kick him! Drag him down!

Finally the kicking stopped and his body went limp. As she let go and tried to swim upward her arms were like stone. Air! Damn it! Where was the surface?

Lungs bursting, she kicked and pulled. Suddenly she was out. She looked for Heph. Holy Mother! Had he got Heph before he attacked her? "Heph!"

"Right here, Mom. Are you okay? Did you drown him?"

"Thank God." She was amazed to discover her leather carry-bag, its contents secure, was still strapped across her torso. She could feel a deep gash in the leather where the knife went in.

"Okay, Heph—let's swim to shore."

And then what? Exhausted, trying to think clearly, she guided her son through the breakers, toward whatever lay ahead.

About the Author

G. D. Matheson began writing after his retirement from management in the North American forest industry. He lives in British Columbia's Okanagan Valley.